SPIRITOF
FIRE

BOOKS BY MADELINE DYER

THE UNTAMED SERIES
Untamed
Fragmented
Divided
Destroyed

THE DANGEROUS ONES SERIES
(Set in the Untamed world)
A Dangerous Game
This Vicious Way
The Threat of the Hunt

STANDALONE NOVELS
The Curse of the Winged Wight
Inside the Night (in the *Unbound* anthology)

MEMOIR-IN-POETRY
Captive: A Poetry Collection on OCD, Psychosis, and Brain Inflammation

WRITING AS ELIN DYER

THE SPIRIT OF FIRE SERIES
Spirit of Fire
Blood of the Phoenix

THE ACCIDENTAL ANGEL BOOKS
Angel, Falling
Angel, Rising

WRITING AS ELIN ANNALISE

ACES IN LOVE SERIES
In My Dreams
My Heart to Find
It's Always Been You
The Rhythm of My Soul

SPIRIT OF FIRE

ELIN DYER

INEJA PRESS

INEJA PRESS

First published in Great Britain in July 2021 by Ineja Press

SPIRIT OF FIRE

Paperback ISBN: 978-1-912369-19-5
eBook ISBN: 978-1-912369-18-8

Cover Design by Broken Candle Book Designs
Interior Design and Formatting by Sarah Anderson Designs
Edited by Emily Colin

First Paperback Edition, July 2021

In memory of Rachel Caine,
whose books encouraged seventeen-year-old me to write a
YA urban fantasy story.

This is that book, nine years later.

ONE
Jade

"YOU KNOW, I COULD QUITE EASILY KILL YOU."
Elliot Pollizzi stares at me, his dark eyes full of shadows. "No
one would know." His voice is husky and deep as he grins
slightly. He takes a step closer to me, lifting the blade in his
hand.

Oh, hell no. Get away. Get out now. This is too—

I breathe deeply, force myself to stand up straighter. I
need to appear confident, despite the screaming in my head.
Because he *is* right—no one knows my brother and I are
here, in a garage with a deranged man from the Greylakes
Gang. A deranged gang member who's armed. And Jack—
where is he now? I can't even see my brother, but his scream
is still echoing in my head. Guttural and loud, as Elliot
stabbed him. Actually *stabbed* him. When was it? Seconds
ago? Minutes? I don't know. My head's spinning, and I can't
make sense of time now. There's too much stuff pounding.
My blood. My pulse. The storm outside.

"You want me to do that?" Elliot whispers. His words are only just audible over the pounding rain on the tin roof. "Kill you?"

"N-n-no." My voice is barely a squeak. I curse myself. Need to sound strong. Like I'm not scared, like—

Sweet, hot pain erupts across the base of my neck. I scream, and Elliot laughs.

"Not so brave now, are you?" He snorts, and something warm and wet slides down my chest. "Huh. The blade barely even nicked you."

The warm, wet stuff is growing—more and more of it. *Blood.* My vision darkens, and things seem to swirl. I clench my hands together—can't faint. Not here. Not...

Oh, God. Get out. Get out now, Jade!

My breath comes in short, sharp bursts—so loud in my ears. Louder than the raging storm outside. I clap a hand to my throat, my fingers sliding in the warm, sticky mess, as I lift my head as high as I can.

Don't think about the blood. Or Jack's scream and how silent he is now.

But I don't know if Jack's still conscious or...alive.

Dead? No! My heart pounds.

Come on! Think. You've got to get out of here.

I meet Elliot's eyes. A quick flick of his silver knife brings my gaze straight to the stained blade. I gulp. But it's not by my neck now. It's six inches away. Can I grab it and—

"Get away from her." Jack's voice—low, dim. He sounds weak, broken.

"Jack? Jack?" I twist my head, sending more pain around the base of my neck, as I try to see past Elliot. "Jack, are you okay?" My heart pounds faster as I search and search and—*there*. In the dim light, I can just about see my brother's muscular shape on the floor as he tries to get up. His labored breathing is loud suddenly—and it's all I can hear now. His breaths. Strained and coarse. "Jack?"

"Don't try anything," Elliot snarls. His hand flies out, and he shoves me backward.

I hit the wall. Rough bricks. The texture snags against the back of my hoodie and before I can move, before I can think, Elliot puts his heavily-tattooed arms on either side of my shoulders, trapping me in the cage of his body. I look to the left, see a glimpse of the knife. It's still in his hand, sticking up at an angle, too close to my shoulder.

Elliot makes a noise deep in his throat, like a growl. The musky scent of smoke clings to his clothing, and the ragged cut on the side of his head is still dripping. The cut from where Jack hit him earlier—with the baseball bat. Because Jack's cut out for this, and I'm not. I'm pathetic, freezing up, and—and I'm bleeding. My hand's still at my throat, and my head's feeling too heavy and—

Elliot leans in closer to me, his body still trapping me. I shudder as I look into his grotesque face. What the hell did Lily ever see in him?

"I said get away from her." Jack's shout is louder this time, and his words penetrate the pounding in my ears. I think he's scrabbling about on the ground. Something *clinks*.

Elliot's weapon-free hand closes around my right shoulder. His fingers are rigid and strong. I swallow hard, trying not to breathe in the lurking cigarette smoke. His hand moves down toward my elbow, and I flinch as his fingers bruise my skin. I try to form words—but I can't. They get stuck in my throat and I just make a strangled sound.

"Do you understand?" Elliot mutters. The half-light filtering through the small window streaks across his face, emphasizing the sharp lines of his jaw and cheekbones with long, jagged shadows. His skin looks gray and pasty. His nose-ring glints, and he smiles, revealing a perfect set of teeth. His breath stinks. "Because my mates would *love* to help me make sure you understand."

His mates—the rest of the gang. The Greylakes are notorious around here. The deadliest gang in decades. I gulp. Even the Devils, the other gang in this area, are terrified of them. By default the Devils and Greylakes are rivals, both inhabiting Northwood, but everyone knows the Devils do all they can to avoid the Greylakes. Avoiding confrontation with the Greylakes is safer for them than actual confrontation.

"You bastard," Jack shouts, and then he's yelling something else, but I can't make out his words. Instead, I am painfully aware of Elliot so close to me. The smells radiating off him, the menace in his eyes, the threats—and the fear he instigates in me and how pathetic I am. I don't know what to do. I'm not a fighter. Not like this.

And the smells—it's not aftershave, more just sweat and fuel. But there's a tang of something else that's making me even more nervous. I have Mast Cell Activation Syndrome. My allergic reactions vary in severity from nausea and fatigue to severe diarrhea and anaphylaxis, and none of those are things I want to happen right here in this garage. Usually, it's perfumes and high-histamine foods that trigger these reactions, as well as heightened emotions, but I've had random episodes too where I couldn't identify a trigger.

Just stay calm, I tell myself. *You're fine.*

Outside the garage, thunder roars. The storm that was starting as Jack and I walked here must still be going strong—and I concentrate on it. Think about how we're going to get drenched going back, me and Jack—because thinking ahead to when we'll be safe calms me. It's something I always do when I'm in a tricky situation—even if those situations are normally to do with me not doing my homework and being told off by teachers. But it works here too, because this terror, being here, can't last forever. Jack and I will be out there, soaked, in the heart of the storm, but that'll be fine because we won't be *here*.

That's if Jack can make it back with his leg.

And if we can get out of here.

"You think you're so clever, don't you?" Elliot mutters. He pulls his right hand back—the one with the knife—and points the blade at my neck again.

"Please," I whisper, and I take a deep breath that makes me gulp. "Please. This is not going to help." My breathing is ragged, and every word seems to be using much more energy than it should. But I need to appeal to him. I have to. For Lily. And for our lives. "Please, just let us go. We won't do anything. We…" As I speak, hardly even aware of my words, I press my fingers against my jeans pocket. Good. It's there. My phone, along with my spare antihistamines. My EpiPen is in Jack's pocket because it wouldn't fit in mine.

I try to look over Elliot's shoulder, but it is dark in here, and the light from the window's gone. Faintly, I can smell petrol amid the cigarette smoke. I don't think the petrol is enough to set me off, not when I take prescribed antihistamines every day as a preventative.

"I think this will *definitely* help," Elliot snarls. The blade gets closer, again. "Girl's got to learn."

"Jade, get out now!" Jack pants, and the voice in my head is screaming the same thing. *Get out, get out, get out.*

But I can't. I can't move. I remain where I am, frozen. I wonder if this is how Lily felt every time she saw Elliot. Even now, I can imagine my sister's scared expression. I can see the fear in her green eyes. Thank God she finally told us what he'd been doing—the abusive jerk. And we are supposed to be protecting her, me and Jack. How the hell didn't we realize what he'd been doing? Those bruises on her arms, the way she'd become so timid, how she'd lost interest in everything, made excuses not to do anything with us, how we rarely saw her with her friends anymore...

All the signs were there, yet we didn't realize. It was only when she came to me in tears earlier today that I put all the pieces together. Some sister I am.

Elliot shakes his head slowly. His mouth twists as he grins again. "Do you see?" His voice is barely a whisper. His accent is strong—predominantly heavy West Country but it also has tangs of something else—and it twists with the maliciousness in his tone. "Do you get it? Hmm? You get it? You get it now?" He whips the blade toward me.

I scream. My head catches the wall—pain flits through me. I am distantly aware of Jack's movement on the floor, but then there's shouting. Elliot's voice, and I can't focus on the words.

Hell, we should never have come here. What were we thinking—that we could get revenge on Elliot alone? That he wouldn't hurt us? That we could make him listen?

My breaths come in short, sharp bursts. It takes me a second to realize I'm on the floor.

I scramble up, turning, but my body just slides down again. Shit. And where'd Elliot go? And Jack?

But I can't see. It's too dark and—and suddenly, I can *hear*. Sound erupts around me—angry shouts—like the volume's just been turned up.

"You are *never* going to be able to stop me—"

"You fucking—"

"And you can't stop Lily either—"

"I'm going to kill you!" Jack shouts.

"We love each other, so you're going to stop interfering. Got it? Else I'll sort you and your sister out properly."

Jack yells something, and I pull myself up again, feel stronger this time—but I'm leaning against the wall. Dizziness tugs at me, and the blood—am I losing too much? I touch my neck, but my hands are just wet and warm, and I can't tell if it's still bleeding or—

Elliot looms in front of me, and then a small object hurtles toward us. I duck, my lungs screaming, and I try to go under Elliot's arm. He crushes me to his side and then swears loudly. My ribs bruise. His fingers grip the already-tender skin of my upper arm as he spins me around. I kick out. My foot connects with his thigh. Hard.

Elliot grunts. Good.

Rain pounds on the tin roof of the garage, drowning out all sound as Jack appears behind Elliot, his skin bathed in a sheen of sweat. He strikes the guy fast. Elliot flinches and turns. I kick him and I run. My feet skid on the stone floor and I grab at Jack but only get a hold on his coat. Still, it's enough and I pull him out of the path of Elliot's knife just in time.

Jack shoves me behind him, just as Elliot turns toward us. The blade glistens.

"Do you get it?" Elliot roars. The knife edges closer. "Lily is *mine*." He punctuates each word with a jabbing of the blade into the ever-decreasing space between us.

I edge closer to my brother, as if just by being closer I can siphon off some of his confidence—because that's the thing about Jack, he's *always* confident. Always ready for a fight. Always knows what he wants. Whereas me? Well, I feel like I'm floating, half the time. And I feel scared, and I feel like I'm constantly in my brother's shadow. Always the shyer twin, no matter how brave I try to be. Nika and Macey are always telling me to get over my inferiority complex.

"You don't own our sister," Jack shouts. He's trying to hold me back, away from Elliot, with his arm, but his hand is shaking and his fingers glisten like clammy wet wax.

Frantically, I look around the garage. A weapon. Need a weapon. Under the window, tools sit on a makeshift desk. I lunge for them and—

Dark shapes fall toward me. Jack shouts. Something flies past me. My fingers close around a screwdriver.

"Get out, Jade… *Jade*!"

I spin toward Elliot and ram the screwdriver into his shoulder. I lose my balance, and my foot flies out—and somehow it kicks the knife from his hand. The blade flies a few feet over to the left, and, seconds later, I hear the clatter as it lands on the stone floor. I kicked the knife? But there's no time for me to smile or feel proud or think about how kickass that must've looked. No time for anything, because Elliot's focusing solely on me now. He's right here, his nostrils flaring.

My free hand reaches behind me for another tool. My fingers grapple with empty space. Elliot spits in my face. One of his hands catches hold of me, and I try to twist around, away from him. My hip catches the side of the table, and I gasp, feeling like I've been shot.

"You will *never* separate Lily from me," Elliot growls. "You want to know what happens to people who try, do you? Because this—" He gestures around the garage. "*This* is nothing."

I let out a small squeak—I don't know what the sound is trying to convey. Agreement? I don't know. I can't concentrate because, out of the corner of my eye, I'm watching Jack. He's advancing on us, his breathing heavy. I think he has Elliot's knife now, but I'm not sure. It's like I see everything as a series of snapshots, not a smooth video. Some half-light from the window catches him in one of the snapshots, and I cringe as I take in his injuries. His forehead, his arm, his leg—and the blood! Too much, too—

"Let Jade go. *Now.*" Yes, Jack does have the knife. He's waving it, but his arm is shaking. His hoody is in tatters, and sweat laces his brow.

Elliot steps away from me, muttering something.

Kick him now! He's not paying attention to you!

And I do. I kick him between his legs, then shove past him. Jack grabs me, nearly throwing me across the garage, toward the metal door.

"Get out," he yells. "I'll be there in a minute."

"No!" My heart pounds. "I'm not leaving you—"

"Just go!" Jack's eyes are on fire. "Just get out. Leave the door for me."

I look at Elliot. Thanks to my kick, he has collapsed on the floor in a fetal position, muttering and hissing. He is big, very big. Oddly, I hadn't realized just how big he was before. Suddenly, I picture him leaning over Lily, backing her against a wall, blocking her exit with his thick, muscular arms.

I look at Jack and I feel small. "If you're not outside within thirty seconds, I'm coming back for you."

He nods.

Now, go! For God's sake!

I take a deep breath and run to the door, my hand against my neck again. Behind me, I hear Jack's and Elliot's shouts again, but it's all just *sound*. A wall of it. Something must be wrong with my brain—did I bang my head?—because sometimes I can hear words, make them out, and other times it's just *loud and nothing*.

I free the metal door and slip outside. The strong Atlantic breeze and arrows of cold frozen rain buffet me. My skin stings as I run. It's dark and deserted. Elliot's garage is in the middle of nowhere, away from the town. Just a run-down road with cracked tarmac and potholes.

Water seeps through my clothing, dripping down my back. My hoody clings to me. My hair flies everywhere, before being slammed back toward my face. I push my hood up. My fingers feel like ice.

I pull my phone out my pocket, nearly dropping it, and a blister pack of Fexofenadine comes out too, falls in a puddle.

I grab it—only three tablets left in it now—and try and shake the water off before shoving it back in my pocket. Then I focus on my phone and try to shelter the screen from the worst of the weather. No signal. I curse. But we need help. Jack's leg is bad, and me? I press my spare hand to my throat again. Am I still bleeding? I can't tell. It's all just wet. The blood and the rain. I can't feel the pain now—but am I in shock? That happens to people, doesn't it? Maybe that's how I'm still functioning. Then again, it can't have been a deep cut because I am still alive. No amount of adrenaline and shock would keep me upright if a major vein or artery or whatever it is that's there had been sliced open.

I shove my phone back into my pocket and turn, look at the garage. The door is still wide open, waiting… But there's no sound nor sight of my brother. It's just dark inside—and I can't hear them. I squint, listening hard. Is it actually quiet there or is the roaring wind out here blocking the sound?

I shift my weight from foot to foot. Shit. What do I do? Go back in there or—

Jack's yell pierces my eardrums, and then Elliot's screaming too. Their sounds burst into the night, joining the roaring gale. My heart pounds, and I step nearer the open doorway. What is going on in there? The wind howls. I look back down the road—the way to freedom, to get away from this all—then back at the door to Elliot's garage again. I drum my fingers against my damp jeans and attempt to shake the water from my eyes. My teeth chatter. It's cold. So cold.

Moments later, my brother appears, staggering out of the garage. With incredible speed, he slams the door shut while shouting something at me.

"What?" I yell. I can't make out his words.

He lunges toward me, reaching out for me, and grabs my hand.

"Is he alive?" I shout.

"Don't know," Jack pants.

"You don't know?" My chest tightens. "How can you not know?" But my heart's pounding, and suddenly I see Jack being arrested. Arrested for murder.

Murder.

I nearly throw up.

"We've got to go," Jack pants, and then we're running.

Mud sprays up from our feet, and the rain gets heavier. So cold. My muscles are numb and—

"You all right?" Jack's voice is raspy.

I nod, even though I'm freaking out because my brother may have just killed a man—and how can he not know—but before I can even start processing that, my feet skid on the wet tarmac. I hurtle forward and my foot hits a rough patch. I grip Jack's hand tighter and somehow don't fall over. "Yeah." The word is a squeak. "I'm okay. You?"

"Just about." His grip on my arm tightens, almost painfully, reminding me of Elliot. Elliot who may be *dead*.

And, oh God. If we've killed a Greylake. And not just any Greylake—because Elliot's high up in their ranks. And they're going to want revenge. They'll kill us. We're dead meat.

"Jade, what's the quickest way back?"

I look around, shoving sopping hair from my eyes. We're on the outskirts of Northwood now. The dodgiest part. A flickering streetlight. Dustbins by the dark walls covered in graffiti. We are late already for curfew, very late—Jamelson, the headmaster, who hates us, will probably give us another week's worth of detentions for breaking the rules again. That's if we get back. Because we've all heard the stories. Ordinary people get mugged at knife-point here. People are kidnapped. People are stabbed. And though this isn't the Greylakes' territory, there are rumors about Greylakes guarding this area and hurting anyone who might be a Devil. Greylakes are always looking to expand. They're here—and if Elliot's alive, he'll have told them.

They're going to grab us any second.

Or if he's dead, they'll grab us at school. They'll know it's us—I just know it. There's no way Jamelson's security will keep them out.

We're murderers.

No. Stop. You don't know Elliot's dead. Don't freak out. Just stop it. Concentrate on getting back to the school.

"That way." I steer my brother toward a minor road. I think it's right. I turn, half expecting to see Elliot's grotesque figure—or another Greylake—looming up behind us. "Come on."

"You sure?" Jack grunts, his voice labored. "Looks lonely."

Lonely is something it definitely looks. It's a dark and narrow street that is doing its best to resemble an old alleyway. "It's quicker, I think. A shortcut." And that's what we need.

Jack mutters, "Okay."

I don't like how pale he's going. Or how much he is limping. Anger bursts through my veins as I remember Elliot's knife plunging into Jack's leg, the squelching sound it made, and the tearing, and my brother's screams. And the blood. So much blood. But it can't be that bad, can it? Jack's moving.

The rain lashes down even heavier as I pull him toward the small road. It's nearly dark, and dark, angry clouds rapidly diminish the moon's light. I look around, analyzing our surroundings. I can't detect any life at all. And that's good. That's good. That's good.

We splash our way through the gushing water, Jack leaning heavily on me. He's a few inches taller than me, at five foot eleven, and his muscular frame only adds to his weight. I bring his arm up around my neck, trying to support him more, and he groans loudly.

"Come on," I plead, slowing down further still. I look behind us. The wind whips into my eyes and I narrow them, trying to see into the storm.

The muscles in my arms are screaming. My brother grunts. We trudge through the backstreet. Every sound has me looking for danger, for Greylakes. The rain might be easing off a little, but I can't really tell. In the distance, I hear sirens.

Danger.

Everywhere I look, there is danger.

"If he's alive, he'd better not go near her again," Jack says a few minutes later, his voice low. I help him over a lump of concrete that is blocking the way, praying he'll make it back to the school. But he's getting slower, and the little moonlight shows how sallow his skin now is.

"He better not," I echo, trying to pull him along quicker. But the muscles in my neck are seizing up. I'm too cold. And tired. "He won't, not if he's got any sense."

If he's even alive.

A few minutes later we reach the end of the little road. The next one is brighter—streetlamps line one side of it. I scan the road and—

I freeze. There's a man. He's on the other side of the road, standing still under a streetlight. And he's looking right at us. A lump forms in my throat, and I feel sick.

"What?" Jack squints.

"Greylake," I hiss, jerking my head toward the man.

He looks a little older than Elliot. Maybe early twenties. White skin. Blond, spiky hair. I can't see his Greylake tattoo, but I know it's one of them. And he's staring at us.

"Oh, God." My voice is a whimper.

"It's all right," Jack says.

The blond Greylake gets out his phone, peers at the screen while intermittently looking at me and Jack. Has he just received a text from Elliot? A warning to be on the lookout for us?

"We've got to go," I say, and my words are strangled because my throat's closing. Everything's closing in. I tighten my grip on Jack and hurry him along. My heart pounds.

When I look back, the man is walking away. I breathe a sigh of relief. Not a Greylake then? Or if he is, he hasn't got a message from Elliot? Because Elliot's dead? And we'll either go to prison or get murdered. Or both.

Jack starts to slow. "Is this the right way?" His voice is strained.

"Think so," I mutter.

Sirens. I can hear the sirens again—and I can't tell if they're back now or if they were going all the time. But they're loud now, and the rain is fierce. I glance at Jack, then quickly look away. He is shaking, and I wonder how much longer he can keep going. I try to hold onto him tighter, try to protect him.

"I think there's a field just across there." I flick my head to the right. "I'm pretty sure it meets up with the road the nightclub's on. Another shortcut."

Jack grunts, allowing me to lead him over. I am right. The field is straight ahead of us. I look around—we'll be completely out in the open if we cross it. Anyone could see us. Are there more Greylakes out here? But it *is* quicker to go across the field.

"Come on," I say. I have to get him back.

The grass is waterlogged and mud slides under our feet. I feel Jack tense up as we are halfway across it, and for one sickening moment, I think he is going to faint. I get ready to try and take all his weight.

"I'm all right," he says finally, but I've never heard his voice so weak. I look at his injured leg. I can't see much now, because of the rain, but what I *can* see isn't pretty.

"We need an ambulance." And is there one nearby? The sirens?

I freeze. It could be for Elliot. He could've called it for himself and—

Jack groans.

"Hey, it's all right." I haul more of his weight onto me. He inhales sharply, and I pause. What if there is major damage? But no, there can't be—right? He wouldn't still be walking if that was the case, surely?

"No… Need to get back." He swears under his breath as he tries to walk faster. "Is anyone behind us?"

I crane my neck, narrowing my eyes against the rain. "Can't see anything."

"Good."

Just keep calm. You've got to stay calm. You've got to look after Jack. You've—

The landscape flashes before us. Lightning. And thunder—so loud, deafening, shaking everything.

"Jade, I…" Jack pitches forward, falling and—

And…and everything stops as the world explodes.

TWO
Jade

FIRE AND HEAT AND ANGER, IN FRONT OF US, around us, a monster engulfing us. Too much heat and—

A fire—there's a fire *here*. In front of us. What the—

"Jade!" Jack screams, and I am screaming too. Screaming and—and *the fire*.

That was the explosion? An actual explosion? My heart pounds, beating so fast I feel sick, lightheaded. Sweat pours down me. My mouth dries, and the sudden pulse of heat and smoke stings my eyes. Heat rushes out in waves, the torrents of rain hissing and sizzling, steam flying everywhere.

We're on the ground. Both of us. I taste blood and ash and earth in my mouth. I grab Jack's hand. His eyes are alight and he's saying something, but there's too much blood rushing in my ears.

I look up at the fire. It's huge—so suddenly here. And it's raining, still. The rain tries to fight the flames, but to no avail. The fire *isn't* going out. It's getting stronger, bigger. What the hell?

"Fuck's sake, Jade!" Jack's trying to stand. "Come on!" His fingers pull at my hoody. "We need to get farther back. I don't know what started that—a bomb? If there's another and…"

Another bomb? Was it a bomb?

I'm numb and I can't be taking this all in, not processing it properly. Can hardly focus on anything. But then we're moving. The two of us cling to each other, and we're moving backward and we're shaking and shouting.

And the fire is growing, getting taller and taller. Not wider though. Just going up. A column of flames.

"What the hell is it?" Jack grunts.

"I don't *bloody* know!" Tears stream down my face. I try to wipe them away, but they are coming fast. "Police," I mutter. This is just too much. "We need the police." We need someone.

I pull out my phone. Still no signal. I curse and—

And I see it all in slow motion as lightning strikes the top of the fire column.

Flames and embers and sparks leap. They run across the sky, like tiny people escaping. And the world's lit up. Lit up white and bright and—

My eyes—burning. Too bright!

I scream, cowering against Jack, yet trying to hold him upright at the same time.

"There's another one here!"

The shout comes from behind me. I flinch. Jack and I turn in unison. Men and women—police officers, I think—are sprinting towards us. It's like they just materialize here. Relief floods me, even if we're going to be arrested for

Elliot's murder, because they're here. And this isn't normal, this fire. I mean, what the hell?

Behind the officers, I see a fire engine. It's driving full-pelt toward us.

Jack holds me closer, trying to stand properly. The heat of the fire slaps the back of my neck. The fire engine stops, brakes squealing, and one of the officers on foot approaches us. He's dressed in protective gear. His eyes scan us, brows furrowed.

"Get over there," he shouts, pointing to his left. "My colleagues will see to you."

I follow the direction with my eyes, see police vans at the side of the road a few hundred feet away. When did they arrive? But that doesn't matter—because there are adults here now and it's not up to two seventeen-year-olds to sort this out.

I move, pulling Jack along with me. And…and the field is buzzing with officers, so quickly. Have I lost time? How did they get here so quickly? And more and more people just keep arriving.

"Have you got any more DC-10?" someone shouts.

DC-what? I blink.

"It's one of 'em, innit?"

"Any life been detecting from it?"

"Only them. Two teenagers." A gruff voice. "The boy's been hurt by it. But they're us."

More shouts fill the air, and the shouts are loud, and I don't know where to look. Everyone seems to know what to do. Except me. Feeling dangerously—and stupidly—close to more tears, I turn back to Jack. We should've just stayed at school. I shouldn't have told Jack what Lily had told me. Because of course he'd go straight out here, to sort out Elliot.

I rub my eyes against the smarting heat. Still, we're alive. And Lily's safe. Nika, my best friend, said she'd look after her while we were out. I'd briefly updated her before we'd left. She's probably in the basement now, listening to music with Lily. Or maybe they're in Lily's room. I can picture my sister, curled up in a chair, like a cat; she'll look small and fragile. Her glossy black hair—the same as mine—will be in its usual loose waves around her shoulders. I hope Nika isn't pressing her for too many details. Lily will guess I've told her some of what she told me, and I hope she isn't too angry at me.

"We need another vat of DC-10, soon as possible," a burly policeman shouts as he runs past us. His voice jerks me back to the present, the now. My eyes zoom in on the gun strapped into his belt. It is huge. "This one's not as big as the last, but it's fueling itself."

"There's only a small canister of it left," a low voice replies.

"Okay, try water on it, first. Just in case—"

"Even though the rain's doing nothing?"

"—then move onto the canister. And we'll need another round-up squad. There's got to be some of them here, with the size of this. I want them caught."

The Greylakes? The police think the gang did this?

No, they didn't say the gang's name. But who else could they be talking about?

A woman runs up to us. She is lithely built and has an air of authority about her. I watch as the expression on her face changes when her eyes brush over Jack's injuries.

"Come on." Her voice is brisk. "Let's get you two to the van."

She calls for help and two paramedics appear and then everything just seems to happen around us, until we're at the area by a van. It's brightly lit here, streetlights.

"Is there anyone else with you?" the woman asks. She looks older now, now that we're under the artificial lights. Forties, maybe fifties.

I shake my head, dazed. She nods and shouts something to the paramedic who is helping Jack into the van. I follow, turning once to look back at the fire. It is still going strong, sending out sparks. Three hose-pipes are now centered on it, dowsing it, but the flames keep growing. Still in that column shape.

One of the officers shouts a command, and then a red van drives a little closer to it. Another hose-pipe is focused onto the fire. More adjustments are made, and someone gets a net out. I see it billowing in the strong wind. I frown, because none of this makes sense, and my head's just pounding.

"Come on," a voice says. "Come in here."

I step into the van. Jack is lying on the bed and the two paramedics are examining his leg. It looks gruesome.

"You all right?" One of the paramedics looks at me.

I nod.

The paramedics turn back to Jack.

"We need to get him to the hospital. What's your name, lad?"

Jack mumbles.

My hand reaches out for the back of a chair, and I steady myself. The men start bandaging his leg, but the blood is seeping through, like a tiny snake, desperate to escape. The whole time he protests about going to the hospital.

"We can't see any major damage," one of them is saying—into a radio? I'm not sure. "But an MRI scan would confirm that and give us a better idea as to what tissue damage he has sustained... Yes, code 12. It's odd that they'd attack a boy like this—"

"Who?" My fingers grip the chair tighter, and I see my knuckles lighten.

The man looks up at me. He is old with a long, drawn-out face and sockets too big for his eyes. He looks like he should be in a horror movie. He frowns at me. "Have you had that cut seen to? On your forehead?"

"What cut?" I frown and touch my head. Am I hurt there too? The skin is knobbly and gelatinous, but if there is any blood it must've congealed by now. Gingerly, I touch the base of my neck. The texture is the same. I shudder, trying not to think about Elliot.

"Miss, uh..." The man looks at me blankly.

"Jade," I say.

"Okay, Jade. If you just go out to the other van—it's just parked about three spaces away from here—you can report what you've seen. You'll need to sign stuff too. We'll see your friend here—"

"Brother," I cut in.

"We'll see he does it too, when he's in a fit state."

I look at Jack. His eyes are shut now, and his lips are firmly pressed together. His skin looks clammy, and I want nothing more than to run over to his side and never leave him among these strangers. Awkwardly, I swallow, feeling nauseous, but nod.

I step out of the van, catching onto the side for support, and look across the field. Some sort of neon-blue liquid is being sprayed onto the fire. As I watch, the liquid turns orange, and then back to blue. I frown. What sort of liquid does that? This is… This is all too weird. Too strange. Like I'm dreaming or something.

I have to be dreaming. Real life isn't like this. Everything's moving too quickly, like someone's fast-forwarding everything.

Come on. The van.

Right.

I turn and look. It isn't far away. About a thirty-second walk. The rain has stopped. So has the wind. It is eerily still—and why I didn't I notice this before? I gulp and glance back to where Jack is receiving medical treatment.

All around me, everyone knows what to do. People are shouting and running for stuff. Others have strange electrical objects out and appear to be scanning the fire.

The *van*. Right. That is where I am going. The van. I blink. My head feels foggy.

Wrapping my hands in the over-long sleeves of my hoody, I start forward. There's a streetlight right next to the van, and as I get closer, I see a figure is on the ground next to it. An old lady. She's slumped against the streetlight base, leaning on it as though it is her last life source, her last hope. Her skin is gray in the artificial light, and she looks tired, exhausted even, as she raises her weary eyes to meet mine. She is old, very old, and her gray hair is brittle with age and conflict. A scar edges its way down the left side of her face—a graceful arc from her temple reaching the corner of her dry, cracked lips. Darker blotches cover her skin like patchwork, and she shudders in time to the flickers of the light above her.

"Do you need help?" I step closer and jump when her whole body shakes violently. A few seconds later, she pulls herself up and stands, leaning heavily on the metal stem of the light.

I freeze. My throat feels too thick.

"Daughter!" she croons softly, her lips twisting.

Daughter? I nearly laugh. Only she's serious. Because she's still saying it. *Daughter. Daughter. Daughter.*

"My daughter—help me at last!" She raises one hand, a shriveled-up thing, reaching out toward me.

I take a step back. And another, and another. Something rushes up against my legs, and I fall backward, crying out. Pain shoots through my wrist, and I scream.

And then, with inhuman speed, she is here, leaning over me. I shriek as her grotesque face is illuminated in the eerie light.

"What the—"

Her cold, cold skin touches my hand.

"Get off!" I kick and try to push her away, but her grip only gets *stronger*. Her eyes are haunting as she stares into mine. I try to look away, but find I can't. I can only look at her. What the actual hell?

"Help!" I scream, my voice rapidly going hoarse. "Help me!"

"Daughter, please. I've chosen you to—Daughter, *please*."

She has a strange look in her left eye, like her eye isn't real. Like it's glass and it's going to shatter under pressure. Her grip becomes even stronger. Her fingers are pressed firmly against my wrist, as though she is trying to pass on a telepathic message through a physical medium. Her eyes light up, and as I push and kick, her face contorts. She grabs hold of my other hand, enclosing more long, clammy fingers around my limbs. My wrists sear with pain.

"Get off me! Help! Anyone?"

She is getting stronger, and something is happening to me—what, I am not sure. My *head*... My head is...

Dizziness pulls at me.

And then the pain begins. It is a sharp, stabbing pain. A knife? Maybe it is like Elliot's, with a silver hilt and a blade so deadly that you only have to look at it to feel pain.

But the pain? It is different. It is beautiful; like a thin, sweet snake it meanders across my skin, creating its own network. The venom is spreading, the serpent is getting away, and the pain is pulsing through my body, *burning* my flesh.

THREE
Jade

FOR SECONDS, I AM PARALYZED. HELPLESS. THE old woman's face contorts as though *she* is the one in pain. Her lips are pale rubber, and her jowls sway as she rocks back and forth, murmuring something. She is staring into my eyes. I look away, but then she is there. Her face, floating. Everywhere, she is there.

I try to pry her clammy fingers away from my searing skin. But I can't. I scream, looking around. "Help me!"

A figure appears to my left, and I fall against the person as he crouches beside me and—

A gunshot breaks the air.

I fall into blackness, crying. Can only see the column of fire and—

And then it is *gone*.

The raging fire has gone.

I turn to my left. The woman has gone.

"Miss? Are you okay?"

Strong hands seize me. I lean in to whoever it is, feeling faint and like my head is about to explode. I nod, just as bile rises in my throat. I expel it, not gracefully.

On my hands and knees, I try to steady my head. The strong stench of my own vomit clings to me. The hands grip my shoulders again, this time pulling me into an upright position.

"What's happened?" Another man appears. He's dressed in a policeman's uniform, but every time I try to focus on him, my vision just gets blurry.

The man holding me speaks. His voice is right next to my ear. "An old lady grabbed this girl and—"

"Was she—"

"The sensors haven't detected any. Not at all."

The policeman frowns as he looks down his beaky nose at me. "Is she okay? Calm her down in there." He indicates the van. I don't like how he's talking to everyone but me, but I can't speak. Can't do anything.

"I'll bring some paperwork through," he continues. "And there's another teenager with the medics? Right, I'll see some is passed to him as well."

Abruptly, I am led into a van. Its décor is white and clean. I sit on a hard metal seat and stare at my hands and wrists. The sleeves of my hoody have been pushed up—by the woman, I presume—and dark imprints of her fingers are stained onto my skin. Streaks of gray, like stamps. Aghast, I touch the discolored patches. It tingles. The pain—although lessened significantly—is still there.

"What's your name?" A middle-aged lady, with hair so bright red that it has to be dyed, is sitting in front of me. She has a clipboard and holds a pen.

"Jade Taylor." I feel strange. I rub my eyes, but then I just end up with something gritty in them. They sting, and tears fall.

"And your age and address?"

"Seventeen," I say. I look around the van again. Something is wrong, strange, unnatural. Every surface in here is…shimmering. What the hell?

"Your address, dear?"

I give it to her, and she raises her eyebrows.

"You're a long way from home."

"I go to Northwood College. I board there." My breath is coming out in short bursts and I don't know why I gave my home address and not the school's. I never even think of my parents' house as *home*. I haven't been there in years. Even during the holidays, Jack, Lily, and I stay at school. It's one of the reasons my parents chose to send us to Northwood, as they offer 365-day boarding. That and, with the school being in the southwest of England, we're pretty far away from Liverpool, where our parents reside.

"Ah." She nods. "Now, this fire that you saw. Tell me about it."

I stare at her. Surely, she saw it too? And doesn't she want to know about that old woman? My eyes narrow a little. She smiles brightly at me, and I wonder if she's been trained to do that. I frown again. Maybe this is some kind of test?

"It just started," I say. I bring a hand up to my chest. My heart is beating furiously. The shock. It must be the shock. "Really suddenly. My brother and I were walking across the field."

She scribbles something down. "Your brother? Is he the one who's receiving medical treatment? How old is he?"

"Seventeen. We're twins."

She nods again. I don't like the way she nods. It seems too…mechanical. "Okay, now, did you notice anything strange about this fire?"

I rub my eyes. "Uh, yeah. It was a perfect column. And it appeared out of nowhere. And the rain… The rain wasn't putting it out."

My words appear to be the right answer because the woman smiles that fake grin again. I look away. Her neon-pink hair is making me feel sick. I swallow it down.

I rub my head. Is this even real? Maybe this whole thing is a nightmare? Maybe…maybe I'm dead. Maybe Elliot killed me and this is some kind of purgatory I'm stuck in?

"Now," the woman says. "In order for this to be investigated thoroughly, we are trying to keep public interest to a minimum. This will reduce the fear levels accordingly. I can assure you that the County Council officials are following the necessary procedures outlined by the North Devon Police Department, in accordance with the safety bodies. We ask that you don't publicly talk about this fire to anyone, record any notes about it—either privately or publicly—or raise any interest in topics that may bring this occurrence up. I'll need you to sign here, and here, agreeing to these rules."

"What?" I stare at her.

She hands me a piece of paper with print on. "Please sign."

I frown and try to focus on the small type. But the words are too small, and my vision is still wobbling about.

"It says exactly what I've just told you," she says. "Please just sign it quickly and then we can get you back to your school."

She stares at me, and that's when I know this can't be real. This has to be a nightmare or something. Because the police don't act like this—and fires don't behave like that one did. I just need to wake up. If I get to the end of the dream, I'll wake up.

The woman gives me a pen, and I sign the document.

"Good," she says. "Thank you."

She leaves the van, and I stay where I am. The metal seat is hard beneath my thighs. Cold too.

I rub my eyes. My eyelids feel heavy—so heavy. I blink several times, like I'm trying to stay awake—only I must be trying to wake up.

Yes, that's it…

My eyes close. A floaty feeling fills me, and then I must fall asleep—if that's what you call it—because the next thing I know, someone is shaking me and telling me to "wake up this instant" in a very stern voice. Groggily, I stir. Pain shoots around my wrists, like tiny serpents. I am on the floor of the van now, a blanket over me. Still this nightmare? What the hell?

The man shaking me looks vaguely familiar with his police uniform. "Right, I'm dropping you and your brother back at Northwood College. Come on."

Rubbing my head, I get up and follow him out, staggering a little. The air is cold, and the rain is a fine mist that dances across my skin. And it feels real, all this. The rain on my skin. The cold weather. But I'll wake up soon. I have to.

His car isn't far away, and groggily I wonder if I should really be getting into a car with someone I don't know—you know, in case this is real. But this man *is* a policeman. And Jack is already in the car. I can see him. I get in. There's an odd smell in here. Musty. I wrinkle my nose. At least there's not a car air-freshener in here. Those are awful for my MCAS.

"Jade." Jack smiles weakly at me.

I lean into the soft leather seat and look across at him. He looks better than I feel—I think. Hell, I don't even know how I feel, really. This is all...

"How's your leg?" I ask. And my voice sounds like me.

Jack taps it, then winces. It is heavily bandaged, and a good proportion of his trouser leg has been cut away. "Better. No major damage or nothing—they said I don't need an MRI after all. Had, like, this small portable scanner in the van. The gel for that was bloody cold though." He leans closer to me as the policeman gets in the front and turns the ignition on. "Are you okay? I heard some woman hurt you?"

"Uh, yeah." I speak slowly, frowning. "She was... I stare at the back of the passenger seat in front of me. "It's all really weird. She hurt my wrists." I show him the bruising and discoloration. "But, I think they...shot her?" No. I shake my head. That doesn't sound right. But she disappeared... She'd just gone. And no one asked where she went.

My head spins.

It doesn't take long for the policeman to drive us back to school.

"I'll explain your late arrival to the principal myself," he says as he turns into the drive. His eyes fix on me in his rear-view mirror. There is a sort of hardness about them. "There's no need for either of you to explain anything. I'll sort it all out."

Jack and I nod. I am having a tough time just keeping my eyes open. Like I've been drugged or something? Is that what's happened? I rub my face with my hand and—

What the hell? My skin feels *old*. Wrinkled. Like the woman—and suddenly I picture her face again, in front of me. I let out a small squeak and Jack looks at me, concern in his eyes. I just nod, but I don't know what to do.

A few minutes later, the policeman walks us to the main office and signs us both in. He speaks to a teacher—but I can't recognize her. Yet I know I should.

I touch my forehead, the cut I didn't know I had. Did I bang my head? Am I concussed?

"I suggest you both go to bed. You look bad." There's an almost melodic quality to the policeman's voice.

I rub my eyes again, trying to relieve the stinging, and nod at Jack. In a daze, I walk to the girls' dormitory building. It's on the eastern side of the main buildings and rises into the sky like a haunted house. There is no teacher at the bottom desk to chastise me for my curfew-breaking, and I make it to the second floor—and the room I share with Nika—without meeting a soul.

I knock at the door, unsure of where my key is—it almost doesn't occur to me to look through my pockets for it. I'm just…floating.

Nika, my best friend, opens it in a second. She looks worried, and her pale skin has the barest traces of tears. She throws herself at me, her arms wrapping tightly around me, her red hair going everywhere.

"Jade, oh my God. I was so, so worried. What happened? Oh God, Mace and I knew we should've gone with you. Is Jack okay?" She gasps. "Is that a cut? Jade, what the hell happened?"

I stumble past her into the room and sink onto my bed. It feels beautiful. I've never fully appreciated just how comfortable it was before. I stare up at the ceiling. Everything spins around me.

"How's Lily?" I ask finally and glance across at Nika. She is cross-legged on her own bed now, brushing her red hair. I frown—when did she sit down and stop fussing over me? "Nika?"

She shrugs. "Okay, I think." She looks at me sternly. "Were you two really okay, with Elliot?"

Elliot… Elliot dead. Murdered. By my brother.

I groan. Oh, God.

"Because Mace and I were *so* worried," Nika says. "You have no idea. And when you weren't back by curfew… Jade, you were gone for *five* hours!"

Five hours? I stare at her. We can't have been gone that long.

She bites her lip. "Are you sure you are all right?"

I yawn and rub my forehead. "We were fine," I say at last. The visit to Elliot's garage feels like years ago. "He had a knife." Gingerly, I touch the base of my neck. There's a scab there now.

Nika's eyes widen. "You shouldn't have gone on your own. Is Jack all right, too?"

"Elliot stabbed him in the leg. But he seems to be okay. Got it bandaged."

"You went to the hospital?"

I shake my head and explain groggily about the events that followed, remembering only after I've spoken that I am not supposed to tell anyone. I shrug it off. I mean, none of this feels right, anyway. Everything is foggy. It's probably all a dream anyway. A nightmare.

Nika frowns. "They actually got you to sign to say you weren't gonna talk about it? Why'd they need to hide a fire?"

"It *was* a weird fire. They… I think they put it out with this blue-and-orange chemical, too."

"That's weird." She gets up and stretches her arms out, yawning. Her eyes smart like I've seen them do a thousand times when she's overtired. "I'd like to see this field, some time… Maybe the fire was caused by electrical disturbance or something? Especially if there was lightning…"

"Maybe…"

I have a shower shortly after our conversation—barely having the energy to stand—then go to bed.

But I toss and turn as I try to get into a comfortable position. My wrists are still painful, and I just feel *strange*. I get up at 3 a.m. and open the curtains, look outside. Darkness, but the moon's there too.

Nika's asleep, breathing softly from her bed. I leave the curtains ajar and a small channel of moonlight spills into our room. It looks heavenly—and for some reason, I can't stop thinking about it. About how beautiful light is. The thoughts won't leave me. And this has to be it, right? Proof that I'm either going crazy or that something weird has happened.

FOUR
Ariel

"HOW COULD YOU BE SO STUPID?" MY FATHER roars, his face going an impressing beet-shade. "Do you actually want us to be caught too?"

I pour every ounce of my energy into keeping my expression neutral. Mustn't roll my eyes. Mustn't answer back. Mustn't do anything. Can't even apologize until he's got to the end of his speech.

"We've got enough on our plates at the moment with the recent captures, and yet you're trying to reveal our existence? And not just through telling people, but no—you have to do some big display." He shakes his head. His hair is the same white-blond as mine, but whereas mine is short and spiky, his is sleek and tied up in a long ponytail. I always think he looks a bit like Lucius Malfoy in the Harry Potter films—but he didn't like me saying so when I told him. "We're lucky that it's just the police who know about us—because they're working to keep us *unknown*. You remember what happened four hundred years ago, don't you?"

I nod. Huh. As if I could forget. As if any of us could forget.

We're a different type of human. A type that has elemental control over fire. And when the public discovered we existed, four hundred years ago in London, they hunted us down. Killed us. And *of course* they outnumbered us. We're only really found in Europe, with our highest numbers being in the United Kingdom. It's the same distribution pattern that the Xphenorie have. A few of our people have moved farther afield before, on the lookout for Fenners in other continents, but they're never there. And there's no point us being in places where the Fenners aren't because we're here to protect the humans from them.

"You want that to happen again, do you?" My father's voice has an edge so sharp to it I almost feel like his words are slashing my skin. "Because there's only so much the police can do to keep our existence out of the public eye."

Keep our existence out of the public eye? I want to snort. The police *imprison* any of us who they find. They don't want our species becoming public knowledge as then there'll be mass fear among the ordinaries.

"But if you keep doing this," my father says, "if you keep setting our fires on their lands, making huge displays, the police aren't going to be able to keep us a secret anymore. Not that they're even on our side. All the police care about is themselves and maintaining their illusion of control."

I nod.

"Ariel, you have to stop this. Else the police are going to take you away too—you want to join your mother in their cellars? Is that what this is about?"

I shake my head.

"Good. Because I won't be able to rescue you if that happens. I can't even get Evelyn out, or the others they've got."

I nod. We can't set their buildings alight without killing humans too—and if that happens, the treaty with the Xphenorie is broken. There'd be outright war, outright killings of more humans, and then neither of our species would survive. All because the humans don't realize we're helping them. They just see us as a threat.

"I have to protect this warehouse, do you understand?" my father continues. "But if you keep doing these stupid fire stunts, Northwood police are going to know there's still a huge colony nearby, rather than just the odd or two of us. They've only got to do thorough searches of all the land, or pay more attention to electricity usage, and we'll all be found. And then all of us will be in their cellars, living half-dead. Or worse—dead thanks to the gangs. You want that?"

I stare at him. Can't believe he's asking me that question. He knows what I saw, how I found the bodies two years ago. Two Calerians believed to be killed by gangs. We don't know if those gang members knew what we were—before, when gangs have discovered us, it's resulted in a vast number of killings—or if it was just incidental. But it took months before I could shut my eyes without seeing their mutilated bodies, without seeing the horror etched on their faces, without imagining their voices following me.

And my father thinks I want that?

But I just shake my head. I know better than to try to stand up against him.

After ten more minutes of this spiel, my father runs out of steam and tells me to get out of his office. I retreat quickly.

Lucy is waiting for me outside. Her fingers find mine as we walk away, our steps quick. We pass several others—mainly dispatchers who are off-duty now—and they give me evil looks.

"Thanks," Lucy says, when we reach her room. She pulls me closer to her and brushes a kiss against my lips. "I owe you."

"That's the last time," I say, and it has to be. "You need to get yourself sorted."

"I'm fine."

"No, you're an arsonist."

She snorts, opening the door to her bedroom. I follow her in, just as I have done so many times before—but this time's different. This time, I'm not desperate to get her clothes off.

"Is it even possible that we can be arsonists, given we can do this?" She pulls fire into her palm. "We're *supposed* to do this."

"We're not supposed to draw attention to ourselves," I say. "And if any humans had been hurt or killed, you know what that would mean for the treaty with the Xphenorie."

Lucy rolls her eyes. "It wouldn't have been *my* fault if some humans were stupid enough to get caught up in the flames."

"It would be when you're creating massive fires in human territory. That was the park, for God's sake."

"It was evening." Lucy shrugs. "Practically night-time. They should've been tucked up in bed. That's what good little ordinaries do, when it gets dark."

"You've got to sort yourself out," I say. "Get help."

"Yeah, really going to walk into a therapist's office, aren't I? *Oh, hello. My name is Lucy, and I am a Calerian. Yes, we've been living among you for thousands of years. Yes, the police and the governments know of us, they just hide us.*" She rolls her eyes.

"You could talk to Wes," I say. "I mean it. And you really can't keep doing this. My father thinks I—"

"You don't *have* to cover for me." She narrows her eyes. "I never asked you to."

"But you knew I would," I say. And I had no choice. My father's the leader of our group, and so that gives me a level of protection. Whereas I just get a slap on the wrist for this, Lucy would've been expelled from our group the first time it happened. Let alone the third time. And I don't want that. I don't want to lose her—she's the only person who really gets me. "You *have* to stop this."

She shrugs. "I'll think about it."

I pull away from her. "You're going to do more than think about it. You have to. Else we're over."

FIVE
Jade

BY MORNING, OUR ROOM IS LIT WITH A golden glow that reflects off the mirror on the dressing table, fracturing the color spectrum across the creamy walls.

The room sways slightly as I get out of bed.

"You got a lesson now?"

Nika's voice makes me jump.

I nod. "Uh, yeah, psychology… Is it all right if I take the first shower?" I rub at my wrists. They're stinging where that old woman grabbed me. Maybe the water will help soothe them.

Nika nods, still apparently half-asleep, and I spring into the en suite bathroom.

I have just over half an hour before first lesson starts, and I have to shower, get ready, gather up my homework, *and* eat breakfast in that time. Plus, I'd hoped to catch Lily at some point too. This morning is going to be a marathon. I pray I can stay awake for it. Especially after last night. All that…stuff.

But at least I don't feel weird like that now. This feels real, in the way that real life should feel. Maybe…maybe some of that was a dream?

The beat of the warm water against my bare skin as I shower feels good, and it *does* relieve some of the pain around my wrists. Not all of it though. Under the running water, I peer at my skin. At the blemishes.

Weird.

I quickly lather up my hair, my eyes falling on Nika's shaving kit lying at the side of the room. It's next to a rather large rubber duck. We found that duck several years ago at an abandoned house we used to visit and hang out in. It became our den, and one day this duck was just there. Nika had grabbed it, and it's been in the corner of our bathroom ever since.

Two minutes later, I towel myself dry and get dressed. The sound of Nika's radio drifts through the door and my favorite song is playing. I grab a hair-band from the little shelf and tie my sopping hair into a high bun and then try to wipe some of the condensation off the small mirror. I apply a thin layer of mascara to my eyelashes, squinting at my smeary reflection.

"You go on down," Nika says as I open the en suite's door. "I've not got a lesson 'til second, and I want to style my hair properly. I'll get breakfast later."

I nod and leave, trying to calculate exactly how much time I can afford to spend eating.

The breakfast hall isn't far away from the dormitory block, but as usual when you're in a hurry, you get held up. First, it is by a gaggle of Year 7 girls—who knows why they were wandering about the sixth-formers' dorms? And the second time is by Dom Levaney: the great hunk of a guy is standing in the narrowest part of the first-floor corridor.

When it becomes apparent he isn't going to move out of my way, I come to an abrupt stop right in front of him and give him my best glare. He has a clean-shaven head, white skin, and his tank top—which is definitely against the school's dress code—reveals just how muscular he is. My eyes are drawn to his tattoo: the neon blue snake meanders its way from his left temple and down to his ear. It's a recent addition that he is technically too young to have. I still can't believe the teachers let him get away with it. But, then again, not many people stand up to Dom Levaney—he is one of those people you just don't argue with, not unless you want a broken nose. His stepbrother, Macey—one of my best friends—has proof of that. Plus, the Levaneys are always donating to the school. They practically funded the new sports facilities single-handedly.

"Move?" It's more of a question than a command.

Dom doesn't move. His eyes—a clear blue—are locked on me.

"For God's sake, Dom?"

Still, nothing. Is he high or something?

"What the hell are you even doing in the *girls'* dorms?" I fold my arms. Even a Levaney would get detention for that. They're strict here on those rules—no mixing in others' dorms, especially those of the opposite gender.

Dom gives me an odd look and fixes his eyes on me, while his chunky body seems to completely block my way even more. He isn't fat exactly, just *big*. Sunlight from the window shines directly onto the inky serpent, and then it actually *moves*—the head of the blue snake twitches.

I jump back. My mouth dries. *What the hell?* I look at the snake again. It is still. Perfectly still, like all tattoos are.

I am going crazy.

Dom watches me carefully.

"Uh, hello?" I say, trying to push past him—but he really is big, and the corridor's small. "I'm late. You can't just stop here."

His eyes narrow and it feels like he's scanning me. Which only makes him look creepy. That, and besides, he is in a girls'-only dorm. But, apparently, according to the girls in the years below us, he is 'blushingly fit.' Nika has even gone out with him a couple of times, but she broke up with him when his drug-using habits spiraled out of control, mid-last year.

"Jade, isn't it?" Finally, he speaks. But his voice is low and muffled—it doesn't sound like him, and he actually sounds confused.

"Yes," I say, my voice level. He knows my name; we are in the same English class. If this is some crazy chat-up line, then it is not going to work. "I'm late and I'm hungry. Move!"

At long last, he steps to the side of the corridor. I sidle past him, my nose wrinkling as the aroma of cigarette smoke wafts over me. It reminds me of Elliot, and I fight the urge to gag. Is Elliot dead? I gulp, trying to put that thought out of my mind. But how soon before Greylakes turn up on school grounds?

I turn slightly as I walk, checking that no one has suddenly crept up on me. But, nope, there's only Dom and he is still standing where I left him, staring after me, a look of utter confusion on his face. Could he be a Greylake?

I walk quicker.

I FIND LILY THE MOMENT I ENTER THE canteen. She is sitting on her own at an empty table, toying with her cereal as it floats in liters of milk.

"Hey," I say, sliding into the seat next to her. "Are you all right?"

She turns toward me, her brow furrowed. Her hair is dull and tied back in a loose ponytail. "You didn't hurt him, did you?"

According to a lot of people, Lily and I look incredibly alike. We both have pale skin, black hair, and wide green eyes set in almost-heart shaped faces. Annoyingly, Lily is the same height as me, despite my two-year advance on her, and I'm sure she's skinnier than I am.

Choosing not to answer that particular question, I ask if she's seen Jack. She shakes her head, and immediately worries start pulsing through mine.

Lily narrows her eyes. "Why? What did he do?"

"He got a little hurt, yesterday," I say carefully. "Elliot didn't want to listen to us. But it's okay."

Or at least it is until the cops come and arrest Jack and me for murder…if Elliot's dead.

Lily turns angry eyes on me. "You *promised* you wouldn't hurt him! You *said* you wouldn't. I shouldn't have let you go around there. I shouldn't have even told you. Oh God. He's going to hate me." She crumples into tears.

I look around quickly. We haven't drawn any attention to ourselves. The hall is pretty packed; most of my year are sitting on the other side. "Lily." I pat her awkwardly on the back. "It doesn't matter what he thinks—"

"Yes, it does!" she cries. "I love him!"

I scowl. There it is again: the lie. The twisted lie that he's pummeled into her. "Lily, what Elliot's doing to you, that isn't love. Hurting you like that. It's really *not* love." My words are fast, nervous. I picture Elliot lying dead in the garage.

"Oh my God. Can you just give it a rest?" she cries. "Instead of lecturing me on and on about it all." She sighs. "Look, there's one of your friends over there. Go talk to him."

My gaze follows hers and I see Craig O'Donahue sitting at a table nearby. He has what I suspect is last-minute homework spread out before him and is staring at it, clearly puzzled. Strictly speaking, Craig is one of Jack's friends, but with us being twins our friendship groups kind of blur together.

Craig sees me and waves. He has a dazed sort of look about him. I wave back. He has pale sandy-brown hair, just a few shades darker than his olive skin, but most of his 'boyband haircut'—as it's known around here—is now obscured by an Aston Villa cap that's become a permanent accessory for him since he got it after some match. The teachers are always asking him to take it off, but lately, they seem not to care as much. They even let Kelley-Anne—a girl I don't particularly know that well—get away with her bright-purple hair.

"You're not going to get rid of me that easily," I warn Lily in a low voice. "What lesson have you got first?"

My sister, not being in the sixth form, doesn't have the privileges Jack and I have, and she has a full-time table. Something she isn't pleased about. She is always subtly commenting on how unfair it is that Jack and I can go into town whenever we feel like it. I've given up pointing out to her that our free lessons are for studying, given I rarely use them for such. Don't even know how I've managed to wing it this far really.

"Math." Lily doesn't sound happy. "And it's a double."

"Okay, well, do you want to meet at break?"

"Jade," she says, her eyes narrowing even more. "I can look after myself."

The bell rings and before I can stop her, she's up and across the canteen. Lily is never on time to lessons—she's always late. But now she's hurrying off. All because of what Jack and I did—or didn't do—to Elliot?

Lily looks back at me once before she disappears through the door. And I know that look on my sister's face—she's scared. She's pretending she's not, and pretending she's annoyed at me and Jack, but she's scared.

"You coming?" Craig calls out. "To Psych?"

"Yeah." I stand up. "I am."

I'll talk to Lily later. I'll find out what else is going on.

MY PSYCHOLOGY LESSON PASSES QUICKLY enough, and soon I am heading back up to the common room for my free lesson. My mind's still on Lily, and I try to sort out what I need to talk to her about. I mean, she showed me her bruises yesterday. But is that the extent of the damage? I've read novels about women being abused, and when there's physical abuse there's nearly always some emotional abuse too. That'll be why she's defending Elliot.

And Elliot—well, I don't know if he's alive. And I need to. I'm jumping out of my skin at the slightest thing, such as when the psychology teacher called my name to answer a question. I need to know if Elliot's alive. Still, either way, there are going to be Greylakes after me and Jack. Maybe Lily too?

I take a deep breath and focus on my sister. She needs to talk to someone professional. Can I get her that help? Or is she not ready yet? The last thing I want to do is do something that will have her thinking she can't confide in me.

"Hey, Jade!" Macey waves at me from a few feet away as he balances three folders in one arm and tries to shut his locker with the other. One of his folders slides to the ground.

I pick it up.

Macey has been friends with Jack and me since we started at Northwood, a couple of years ago. He's always been studious, and it's something we tease him about—well, Jack more than me.

"Do you want me to take anything else?" I offer, holding onto the blue folder.

He shakes his head, his dark hair flopping forward, over his warm, brown skin. Judging from his slight stubble, he hasn't shaved for a few days, and the shadow somehow enhances his face, heightening the sharpness of his cheekbones and jawline. I'm always kind of fascinated by his face—but it's not really in a sexual attractiveness sort of way. I mean, I've never looked at anyone and thought *Oh, I want to have sex.* Nika says that makes me weird, and sometimes I wonder if Macey's face—which I like—should make me want to rip his clothes off.

"Nah. I'm okay," he says. "But can you help me with filming again later?" He smiles brightly.

"Yeah," I say. Filming. Right.

"Thanks." His dark eyes scan me. "You are okay, aren't you? Jack said—"

"I'm fine. How is he?"

"Okay." He nods. "Not saying much. Other than the usual annoying stuff he thinks is witty. Well, see you later." He rushes off down the corridor, leaving his locker open. I shut it for him and watch as the combination lock springs into place, revealing the code. Well, I know the code anyway; Macey has forgotten it so many times that he decided it was better if Jack, Nika, and I know it too. Not that my brother ever remembers it.

Shaking my head, I adjust the numbers so it won't just open, and then I carry on down the corridor. I take the stairs up two floors and pass the little science store rooms and—

"—and that's exactly *why.* Yes, I said her name is Jade. Jade Taylor," a deep voice says.

I whirl around.

There is no one else in the corridor. But the door to my left is slightly ajar, and I step toward it. Yes—the voice is coming from in there. I push the door open as quietly as I can. Then I take a step inside.

"Yes, yes, that's her," a man says.

I stop where I am. The storeroom is L-shaped, and whoever it is, is around the corner. His voice is sort of familiar, but I can't quite place it. And he's talking about me?

What the hell?

I creep forward and see his shadow. Not that it tells me much. Need to get closer.

Just as I'm about to move, he mutters, "No, it's not *just* me. Yeah, yeah, I know we have trust issues and all, but Tris felt it too. Yeah, this morning. She was quite late as well…"

I listen harder, my eyes falling on the various bottles of chemicals in here—it's the chemistry store cupboard. Oh God. I shouldn't be in here. No with my MCAS. But everything is bottled and sealed here—and I can't smell anything that could set off a reaction.

I try to quieten my breathing, but adrenaline pumps through my veins and I am sure that anyone in a ten-mile radius can hear my heart. What's going on?

"What?" the man exclaims. His voice is pretty loud. "You don't want to come over and—"

The sound of tinkling glass cuts him off. He swears and I freeze, try not to breathe. Did he knock test tubes off a shelf? I take a step backward, hovering on the threshold. My heart hammers. If I were Jack, I'd march straight in and demand answers—but something's holding me back, and I don't know what. Or why.

"No." The man's voice is firm and sends goosebumps down my spine. "She's *different* now… What? Just watch her?"

Watch *me*? What the actual—

"Fine… Yes…" His voice is strong and powerful. He sounds thoroughly pissed off.

"Fine, Jameilia. But you'll tell them, won't you? Right, I've got to go."

The sound of the man's footsteps is enough to have me stepping back into the corridor, walking fast. Turning slightly, I see I've left the door open wider than I found it. I pause. If I go back, I could bump into the man. I'll get a look at him, but he'd also see me, and maybe know that I heard. No, I decide. Too risky to go back.

I keep walking, trying to maintain a normal speed.

What had he been talking about? I focus on the end of the corridor, trying to walk quickly and with purpose. But, that conversation; what did it mean? He said my name. My whole name. There are lots of Jades at this school, but I *know* I am the only Jade Taylor. And who was he? I curse under my breath that I didn't get a clear look at him. Just the shadow— but that doesn't tell me much.

I hear the door close farther down the corridor, and I try not to startle as I hear the unmistakable sounds of footsteps gaining on me. Faster, faster, faster. It's *him*.

Act normally, I tell myself. *Breathe!* But the voice in my head is telling me to turn, to get a look at him, to see who I'm up against.

Only…only I can't. I keep walking—like I'm not in charge of my body.

And I sense him right behind me. I tense.

Stay calm.

His footsteps close in on me, faster, faster, faster.

Then he grabs me.

SIX
Jade

HANDS GRIP MY SHOULDERS. I SCREAM, TURN, and—

"What the hell?" I shout, just as Jack shouts, "Woah, calm down!"

I yank myself away from him, breathing hard. "What the hell are you doing? I nearly had a heart attack."

He laughs. "It was supposed to be a joke, but I had no idea you were going to react like that!"

"You can't just creep up on people," I hiss.

"Jade—it was hardly creeping up. I've been calling after you, ever since the lockers—though why you went into the chem storeroom I don't know."

"You were following me since the lockers?" I stare at him, my mouth open. "No—you weren't." I was on my own. I know I was.

Jack just laughs. "Maybe you need your hearing tested."

I touch my ears. They feel too hot. But everything does. I'm sweating, and my heart's pounding. My head spins as I look around. It's just the two of us. The man who was talking about me must still be in the store cupboard.

"Okay," I say, keeping my voice low. "Jack, *something* is going on."

"You mean other than us nearly killing that scum?"

God, Elliot. I take a deep breath. *Nearly killing*. "He is alive then?"

"He tweeted," Jack says.

"He *tweeted*?" I frown. "You follow him on Twitter? Wait—that doesn't matter." I look back at the cupboard. We need to get away from here. I grab Jack's arm. "Come on."

"And my leg where I got *stabbed* is fine—thanks for asking," Jack says as we walk. "Well, not fine—but you know. I'll live. Want to see the scar that the stitches made? They used these dissolvable ones. Really cool." He stops and starts to roll his trouser leg up. "Here, have a look, I can take the bandage off—"

"No!" I shake my head and I try to pull him along again. We've got to get away—we have to. There's a man in that storeroom who's going to be watching me. And I know I should be telling Jack all that now, and he'd go and confront whoever it is, but something inside me is telling me that would be a bad idea. A very bad idea. I just have to get away.

"It's in the shape of a dinosaur, the stitches." Jack laughs and we reach the stairwell. "Anyway, I must be going. Don't want to be late for Miss Madley again, do I? She'll have my head on a platter if I'm not careful." He pauses, grinning.

"Anyway, what are you doing in the science block? Haven't you got History?"

Have I? I blink.

"Catch you later, sis," Jack says, then he's flying down the stairs.

I stare after him for a long time, my feet rooted to the spot. I glance back down the corridor. The storeroom door is now shut. I shudder and my scalp tingles. When did the man shut it? Did he leave? Does he know I heard? Did he see me at all? And who is he?

Or maybe I'm just being paranoid. Hallucinating...

I turn and walk straight into something—someone.

"Oh, Jade." Mrs. Lambley—a rather stout middle-aged woman—frowns a little as she looks down her long nose at me. "There you are. Mr. Wilson is looking for you." She flicks one end of her silk scarf over the shoulder of her flowing dress.

"What? *Now?*"

Mr. Wilson is my tutor and we do not get on. And, besides, I've already had my tutorial for this week. It was two days ago. What could he want with me now?

Mrs. Lambley nods. "I think what he needs to say is pretty important."

After a long pause—in which I try to think of an excuse and fail—I tell her I'll go straight away. Even if it means missing the start of History.

I scurry toward Mr. Wilson's office, just focusing on breathing and getting there and trying not to think about the tangled mess of things in my brain. I knock on the office door. There is a gritty silence, then his unmistakable voice barks for me to enter.

I enter and the pungent aroma of chemicals engulfs me. I recoil, halting by the doorway.

"I can't come in here," I say. "Because of my mast cell disorder." Can't risk anaphylaxis. It's one of the reasons the school previously took me out of GCSE chemistry lessons—well, they only did that after I went into anaphylaxis. "But you wanted to see me?"

Mr. Wilson is hunched over his desk—his chin tucked into his oversized suit—at the back of the room, mixing a concoction of ingredients together in a test-tube over a Bunsen burner. He looks up at me and rolls his eyes. Then he tilts his head upward and surveys me in his scientist's manner. Against the harsh light falling through the window behind him, his face seems even longer and pointier than usual; the resemblance to a goblin, as well as a dachshund, is uncanny. He could win prizes for that achievement.

"Oh, yes." He nods as he bubbles another chemical through some dark-navy liquid. "Miss Taylor. Please take a seat. I'll be done in just a minute."

"Um, I can't," I say. Already I'm getting a headache. I blink several times. Am I getting dizzy too? I don't react to every scent, but it's unpredictable. One day I can react to one thing and the next day I'll be absolutely fine with the same thing.

"Well, stand out there until I'm finished and we'll go to a different office," he says. "I'll only be a minute, like I said."

The single minute turns into fifteen.

"Now, Miss Taylor." Mr. Wilson nods toward me as he peels his gloves off. They make a slow squelching noise, then suddenly snap. He leaves his office and gestures for me to go into the next room off the corridor. It's a scent-free room, thankfully, and he sits in the leather chair behind the desk and looks down his beaky nose at me. "Sit." His tone is abrupt, and I sit. "We'll be quick about this, shall we?"

"Uh, yeah?" I shift my weight a little.

"So, you were off the school's campus past the curfew last night." He clasps his hands together and narrows his eyes. His nose is a ruddy color, standing out from his otherwise pale face.

I nod. "But the policeman explained why to Mr. Jamelson," I say, reverently hoping that I won't be asked for those reasons—because, well, I don't know how to explain it. But my mind is foggy. Everything's just sort of floating around, and nothing feels real. Hell, since last night everything has been strange.

"And you're aware of the rules, Miss Taylor?"

Again, I nod. Something *whirs* behind me, and I flinch and turn. A small fan moves feebly.

"So, it will come as no surprise to hear that you have a week's worth of detentions?" Mr. Wilson says.

"But it wasn't my fault—you know it wasn't!" Only, only I can't think what happened. Why the police were talking to the principal. Because of me and Jack nearly killing Elliot? Elliot who's still alive… I sort through the blurry images in my mind. Elliot and Jack and I in his garage. And then…then Jack and I in the policeman's car. But the space in between is just a huge gap.

I rub my forehead.

Mr. Wilson sits up straighter. "Sometimes, Miss Taylor, I feel you'll never learn." He holds his head up higher, probably in an attempt to come across as more superior.

"Every day at six-thirty, I expect to see you in here, my office. You can help do my photocopying and then measure out the hydrochloric acid and copper that the younger students will be using next week. Oh yes." He smiles. "And we'll need someone to write up the new inventory. That's always fun."

"I can't do the acid," I say. Does he genuinely just not think of my illness or is it deliberate? I'm sure half the teachers don't believe that MCAS actually exists. Enough of them made a protest of the no-scent rule the school introduced shortly after my first anaphylaxis.

"Fine. Do the photocopying and inventory then."

"Uh…okay." I look around the office, but the walls seem heavier than usual. And the space is smaller, like the walls are closing in.

"Can I go now?" The words burst from me. "I am supposed to be in History."

"Make sure you go straight there." Mr. Wilson smiles. "And don't forget detention tonight."

I swear under my breath as soon as I am out of the office. The walls with various posters on seem to shimmer. Like they're not real. Like none of this is real.

I touch the bottom of my neck, feel the scar from Elliot's knife. That's real. My broken skin is real.

And that's when I realize it—no one has asked me about it. Not Nika or Lily or Macey. Not Mrs. Lambley. Not Mr. Wilson. Have they just not noticed?

"Proof," I whisper, inhaling deeply. And it is proof, it has to be. Proof of something. Something that is very wrong at the moment.

And I need to find out what the hell is going on.

SEVEN
Elliot

"I DON'T TRUST THEM." I SHAKE MY HEAD AND look at Max. He's my second, but we both answer to Robbie. Robbie owns Northwood, and he's the biggest and smartest of all the Greylakes.

Max nods slightly. Always agrees with me, he does. "That's what I told Spencer," he says. Spencer keeps an eye on the newer recruits, the ones who do the drug runs. "But he says these new'uns are trustworthy."

"No." I shake my head again, then stand up and look around the garage. It's dark, but I like the dark. "They're with the Devils."

"They ain't marked."

"They're Devils though," I say, picking up a spanner. The movement hurts my shoulder—where that fucking bastard stabbed me—but it wasn't a deep cut. Spencer's girl looked at it, said it's okay. Cleaned out the wound.

I set the spanner back down. Though CK's Autos is just a front, we have all the tools here. Robbie even organizes a high turnover of vehicles through here, pretending we do actually fix them. Huh. I don't know the first thing about mechanics.

I focus back on Max and think about the three young men who are trying to initiate themselves into the Greylakes. "Annabelle's seen them on the Devils' turf too many times. They're Devils, through and through. Tell Spencer it's a no."

Max breathes deeply and then rifles through his pockets. "But Spencer wants you to ask Robbie." He pulls out a pack of cigarettes and a lighter. "He—"

"No. We ain't bothering Robbie with this. Are you fucking stupid?" I shake my head. "We ain't having Devils in with us. No way. You tell Spencer that I said no. I know what Robbie would say."

Max shrugs and flicks the lighter, casting a slight orange glow onto his pale skin as he lights his cigarette.

"Did you get rid of all the gear from yesterday?"

He nods. "The runners have got it. Meeting 'em later for the handover. They better have got full price for it all this time."

"Good," I say. I turn back to the desk where my phone is and pick it up. Still nothing from Lily. Anger unfurls through me. Why the fuck isn't she replying? She always replies. No. This is something to do with that brother and sister. Jack and Jade. Thinking they own her. I snort. Lily is mine. The sooner those twins realize that, the better. And I know exactly what to do next.

"You okay to watch the fort?" I ask Max.

He nods. "Where you going?"

"Nowhere important," I say, pulling my hood up. "Nowhere important at all."

EIGHT
Jade

HE GAVE YOU A DETENTION FOR *THAT*?" JACK looks ready to explode.

I nod.

"But the policeman sorted it all out," he says.

"You *were* off campus way after the curfew though," Macey points out, waving his pen at me, before writing down some complicated equation in the back of his physics book—which takes him all of four seconds to do. He puts the book down and pulls his MacBook onto his lap.

"Whose side are you on?" Jack demands.

Macey doesn't say anything.

"And I didn't get detention."

"That's because your tutor actually likes you. Anyway, where's Nika?" I ask. I haven't actually seen her since this morning.

Jack shrugs, stretching his bandaged leg out on the sofa. "She was in chemistry last lesson… Think she went off with Dom."

"Dom Levaney?" Macey raises an eyebrow, something I wish I could do. "As in my stepbrother?"

"Yes, Mace." Jack yawns. "How many other Doms are there in this school?" He glances across at me, frowning slightly. "You don't think that they are still, uh…?"

I shake my head, but the image of Dom blocking the corridor this morning comes flooding back. As does the moving tattoo—no, the tattoo that I *thought* moved. Because it can't have. Tattoos don't move.

"Nika would've said something," I say—but weird things *are* happening. "But, uh, he was in the girls' dorms this morning. It's probably nothing," I add as Jack looks like he is ready to go and crush Dom's knuckles this very second. See, that's my brother's answer to everything—violence.

"Hmm." Jack doesn't sound convinced. He looks across at Macey. "Is he still dealing the…you know?"

Macey looks outraged, and in his indignation nearly flings his laptop onto the floor. "How would I know?"

"You're related." Jack crosses his arms.

"No, we're not."

"He's your stepbrother."

"Exactly, they're not blood-related," I cut in quickly. "Jack, Macey doesn't know, okay? They're hardly joined at the hip. And anyway, you're just as bad." Heat pours through me. I need to be asking Jack if he remembers last night after we left Elliot's garage and before the police car. But I don't want to do it in front of Macey.

Jack narrows his eyes at me. "I'm not. I don't deal drugs."

"Alcohol's just the same," Macey mutters, his eyes now glued to his laptop screen.

"Yeah, well," Jack says. "You've got to have some fun every now and again. Nothing fun's gonna happen if you just eat cheese sandwiches every day."

"No," Macey says, "but you'll just be more at risk of getting CHD, what with all the fat that cheese contains. But, then again, drinking raises your blood pressure. So, if cheese sandwiches and that cheap vodka makes up your diet, you're doomed." He nods triumphantly. Sometimes, I can't understand how Macey and Jack ever became friends. "Salads, on the other hand—"

"All right. Health freak."

I shake my head. It's always like this with these two. Always me waiting to get a word in—and I should just barge my way into the conversation, I know that. It's what Jack always does. But I'm not like that. I'm—

"Jade!"

I look up to see Nika entering the common room, followed by Aisha and Jen. Aisha, I am fine about—she is one of my friends—but that also means that we are friends (by default) with her roommate, Jen, and she's the most pessimistic girl I've ever met. She also doesn't like me and keeps making digs at me about whatever she thinks will get me. She even started an 'expel Jade' campaign a few years ago, after my MCAS diagnosis and the school's subsequent no-scent rule meant she couldn't douse herself in perfume. A surprising number of students signed that petition. Jen has hated me ever since, is always looking for new digs she can get in at me, and there's no way I'm asking Jack about his memories of last night with her here.

Nika dumps two heavy folders and a math textbook on the table, then throws herself down onto the plush chair next to me. Her red hair is awry—it doesn't even look like she's styled it, which is odd as that's why she stayed in the room, and she normally takes great care with her hair. She's a natural redhead—and I know she loves her hair. One of the first things she said to me when we met as eleven-year-olds was how rare her hair color is, given she's Japanese, and how she thinks it's the coolest thing. But now she looks tired.

Aisha takes the seat next to her. Her dark skin is as flawless as ever and her black curls splay out over the back of the chair. Jen looks as though she is chewing her permanent lemon as she stands behind Aisha, looking down on all of us, yet surveying the common room in the eagle-style of hers at the same time.

"Where've you been?" Jack's tone is sharp as he turns toward Nika.

"Nice to see you and all," she says cheerfully. "Mace. Jade." She nods at each of us, and I snort when she leaves Jack out. "Urgh. My nails are horrible. Look at this." She holds up one hand for my inspection and then shows it to Aisha. "I only painted them yesterday. And it's *already* chipped." She sighs and leans back into the chair.

"First-world problems," I mutter.

"Oh, but it *is* a massive problem," she says. "And—"

"Are you sleeping with Dom?" Jack asks, looking at Nika.

Aisha's eyes widen, and Jen momentarily looks excited as she pushes her greasy dark hair away from her face. She rarely washes her hair, and I know that sometimes I can't do mine—if my MCAS is playing up, sometimes even the fragrance-free shampoo is enough to set it off—but I always try to cover up my unwashed hair if it's in a bad state. Talc works great as dry shampoo, or I just wear a head-scarf or hat.

Nika laughs and crosses her legs, showing off her red heels in the process. I frown—are they new? I don't recognize them. "No. As if." She snorts. "That ship sailed long ago, mate."

Jack slides his injured leg off the sofa and maneuvers himself into a more upright position. His face conveys only one emotion: jealousy. Oh, God. Great. So, while I'm worrying about actually important stuff—like why the hell everything seems off now, and what happened last night, my brother's only got one thing on his mind.

"You are, aren't you?" He gives Nika an accusatory look.

"Jack!" I hiss.

Nika's dark eyes flit from Jack, to me, then Macey. She frowns. "You know I broke up with him ages ago. Not that it is any of your business." Her tone is sharp, almost defying him to accuse her again—because then she'd really go off on one. Nika is like a whirlwind when she gets going about something. Stormy and cold and full of energy, destroying anything in her path.

It's not a secret my brother likes her, but she's not interested. Told him he'd have to just get used to it.

Jack takes his lighter from his pocket and flicks it on and off three times as he glares at it. Nika laughs and I swear she pushes her chest out more. Yeah—she's definitely trying to get a reaction from him. And if she wasn't my best friend, I'd probably feel annoyed at her on my brother's behalf. But, really, Jack kind of deserves this, what with how jealous he got of Dom last year when he was going out with Nika.

Jack mumbles something.

"What was that?" Nika raises her eyebrows.

"Just that you could do so much better than him," Jack says.

"Seriously?" Nika snorts. "You're actually doing this?"

"Jack, stop." I rub my temples. My head's feeling achy now.

But of course Jack doesn't stop. He starts arguing with Nika—which is what she wants, because Nika is good at arguments. She's confident and she's clever. She always wins and Jack always ends up looking stupid. Not to mention it's embarrassing as they always end up getting the whole common room listening after a few moments. Jack just doesn't know when to stop.

"Right, well, I'm going to go and get my coursework," Aisha says, standing. She turns her back on Jack and Nika—who are still arguing about Dom—and leaves. Jen follows her, like always.

Macey looks like he is about to say something too, but then changes his mind, looking back at his MacBook's immaculate screen.

"And you think you're all it?" Nika snorts. "For God's sake, Jack—"

"Can you just *stop*?" My voice cracks and I stare at them. "Look, my head is pounding, and I can't concentrate on this essay—and probably neither can anyone else in this room." I look around—indeed, the whole common room is watching us. "And I need to get this done before detention."

Jack and Nika nod, and I try to focus back on my essay, the one I was drafting when Jack arrived earlier. But I'm too keyed up now. And Jack keeps giving Nika the occasional suspicious glance as she reads *Quadratic Equations: The Fun You Need.* She doesn't look at him once.

Macey clicks his way through some web page that seems to be of the utmost importance, if his expression is anything to go by. I watch his eyes as they drift from left to right, and then back again, and make note of the tiny changes in his expression as he reads. At some points—maybe when he gets to a particularly exciting bit—his lips twitch, like he just has to share it with us. I even catch him glancing up at Jack a few times, as if he is going to say something. But then he looks at me, and it's like he's scared to speak. Which is weird. Because my outburst was nothing.

Jack, on the other hand, is staring moodily into the distance. After a moment, he grabs his earphones and plugs them into his phone. He plays something with a heavy bass and metal pulse—loud enough for us all to hear through his earphones too. I am just about to warn him about permanent hearing-loss—more because I'm annoyed right now, than to save his hearing—when Macey squawks.

And when I say *squawks*, I mean *squawks*, as in the sound that a parrot would make upon being ambushed by a very ferocious tiger.

Nika jumps and *Quadratic Equations: The Fun You Need* ends up face down on the floor. A few pages fall out as the spine splits. Several people around us turn in their seats.

And we're all staring at Macey. He's staring at his laptop screen, his eyes wide, and he doesn't look at any of us. Like he's oblivious to all the attention on him.

"Macey?" I prompt.

He looks up at me and pushes his dark hair out of his eyes. "This…" His eyebrows twitch. "Read this." He hands his MacBook to me. It is surprisingly heavy.

"What? The article?" I frown, rubbing my head. The screen's super bright.

"What else?" Macey rolls his eyes, but his expression is anything but sarcastic. In fact, he looks like he could hardly contain himself. Just the way his eyes dance with excitement makes me want to laugh.

"He looks like he's just graduated or something," Jack mutters, taking an earphone out.

I look at the article on the laptop screen. It's on BBC News, and the headline makes me frown. I read it out loud: "'Found: First New Human Species for A Million Years.'" I stifle the urge to laugh.

"Strictly speaking," Macey says, "that's not true. But carry on reading."

I look back at the screen.

Witness, Dr. Joe Sera, received confirmation earlier this morning, on March 18th, that the woman's body found in the Dunsland Fire is not that of a modern human.

"A number of things were different," Dr. Sera☐ a Human Evolutionary Specialist at Durham University, told our spokesman, "such as the composition of the blood. There were far more red blood cells to every liter, when compared to that of a typical person. And this woman☐ who we are calling Shelley☐ also had several extra layers of skin cells around all of her fingertips."

But, indeed, perhaps the most remarkable thing about this whole situation is the evolutionary advantage that this woman had, which Dr.

Sera described as a 'miracle.' What's perhaps more astonishing, he later went on to say, is that "the woman's body⬚ although charred from the flames⬚ obtained very few severe burns compared to her colleagues, despite being closer to the heart of the fire. And research already being conducted by the UK's top scientists has already suggested that this woman was fire-resistant, especially on her hands."

Further DNA studies and typing have proven valuable to the scientists' work, in securing more evidence that this woman is not the average person. Indeed, Shelley's DNA only appears to be 99% similar to ours, with the base 'guanine' having been entirely replaced by another⬚ as of now⬚ unknown base. Further studies and investigations are ongoing with this 'Fire-Woman.' Other results that have already been obtained are being kept exclusively within the scientists' circle, until further confirmation that this is a new species is given.

I glance back up at Macey, unsure what to say. "Is this really true?"

Macey looks like Christmas has come early. "Imagine if it is! The advance in technology that this could mean! And we could've been living with an entirely new human species for the last four hundred thousand years!"

I bite my lip. It does sound a bit mad. As in crazy-mad. And anyway, if it *is* true and that, we'd find out soon enough. "A discovery like this would be all over the news though, if it's true. Not just online. Like, it would be breaking news, right?"

"I wonder if there are any live ones out there," Macey muses. "I mean, there must be really. If there's a dead one, there's going to be a live one too. More, probably."

A dead one. I don't like how clinical and cold Macey is sounding now—because this is a woman's body we're talking about, and she had a life. She was a person.

"Just think of all the possibilities," Macey says.

Nika rolls her eyes. "Wait, what is this?"

I hand her the laptop, and she reads fast. "That doesn't sound even possible," she says a few minutes later. She raises one eyebrow and nods. "It just sounds to me like some poor guy's claim to fame. And I bet this Dr. Joe's on meth or something."

"But supposing it *is* real." Macey's practically breathless. He brushes a hand through his dark hair, then pulls his MacBook toward him.

"Look," Nika says. "If there really has been another human race for the last millennium, or whatever, we'd have known about it. There'd have been clues. We're not stupid. And they've said there's *one* person like this. One body. And she's dead—so it's not like anyone can talk to her."

"But the DNA," Macey says, but Nika cuts him off.

"It's all fake, made up. I mean, even that stuff about them keeping the results exclusive to themselves—that just says they're trying to hide it from us because they know it's not true. Because it's not real."

Hide it from us…

Like the police hiding that fire from the public… My eyes widen—yes, that's what I'd forgotten. The fire. The column fire.

It's back now—the memory. The feel of the heat and the smell of the smoke…

I look down at my essay plan and then turn it over and write *fire* at the top of the page. I add more notes—in case I forget again. Because something tells me I could. That I will. And something else tells me it's also important that I remember.

Could they be linked, these two things? The fire and this fire-woman?

"Can you keep your voices down, please?" Jack says, and it takes me a moment to realize that Macey and Nika are arguing about the plausibility of a new human species. "I've got a headache."

"Not surprising with the volume of that music," I say, still focused on my notes. I add, *The fire didn't go out with water. And there was some chemical the police were talking about.*

Jack huffs, then gets up—apparently with great difficulty—and limps out of the room. I frown. Because of his stab wound? He wasn't limping like that earlier. I bet he's not been taking it easy, trying to do too much and has made it worse.

"Oh, he's gonna be in a lovely mood for rugby practice later," Macey says.

"What? He can't play rugby with his leg like that!"

Macey nods. "Exactly what I said this morning. But does he listen? No."

I wave my hand. "Anyway—Macey, Nika." I hand Macey my paper with the notes on and lower my voice. "Did Jack tell you about the fire we saw last night?"

"He was mumbling something about a fire," Macey says. "But I thought he was high."

"Right—but it was real. I saw it too—and then I forgot, and they don't want us telling anyone. And what if that's related to this fire-woman?" I can hardly get my words out quickly enough. "Like, there could be live ones then."

Macey glances at Nika. "What do you think? This article and what they saw?"

She pulls an I-don't-know face. "I wasn't there. But," she adds, "this thing about them being a new species is utterly ridiculous. Absolute…" She trails off, her gaze falling behind me.

I turn. Lily has just entered the room. A couple of guys who Craig is friends with jeer at her, shouting for her to get out of our common room. I leap up, reading the worried expression on her face.

"Come on," I say, leading her outside.

I touch her arm gently. She is shaking.

"What's happened?" I ask the moment we are out in the foyer. There aren't many other people here, just a teacher pinning up a notice to the board, and a cleaner muttering about the amount of mess we make.

Lily's lip trembles. I hug her to me. She seems so vulnerable and fragile and I want nothing more than to whisk her away to a safe place where Elliot can never touch her again.

Then she begins to cry.

"Is it Elliot?"

Lily whimpers and wipes her nose on her sleeve—a disgusting habit, but I don't think now is the time to mention it. She looks up at me with her big green eyes.

"Has he hurt you? He hasn't got into the school, has he? Lily?" All the possibilities are running through my mind at an alarming rate. Because he's going to be angry. Jack hurt him, but would he hurt Lily in revenge? "Come on, you can tell me."

She takes a deep breath, and my mind's spinning with the quickest way to get hold of Jack and a couple of the other, more heavily-built, guys when she says the words that make me freeze.

"I'm pregnant."

Oh, God.

For a few seconds, I don't say anything, and Lily completely dissolves into tears. I exhale loudly, gritting my teeth. Am I supposed to act angry, or comfort her? Well, our parents are going to kill her. They hate us enough as it is.

The last time I saw my mother and father, it was a disaster. The school had had to close over Christmas due to problems with the heating. Whereas before, Jack, Lily, and I would stay there for the holidays, we no longer could. We were shipped back to our parents' estate. They left us home alone once— deeming Jack and I old enough at fourteen—while they went out to cocktail parties with their friends. We'd been trying to make chippie-style chips and the pan had caught fire. Mum was furious when I'd phoned her because the fire brigade came. After that, the three of us had to go out with them to all their events: sessions at the races, museum tours, more cocktail parties. We were expected to sit silently and not be heard.

Mum pinched Lily's arm when she started whining about being tired on what was probably the fourth night. Left an angry red mark. Lily hissed that she'd report her for child abuse. Dad laughed at her.

Jack and I didn't laugh. We just vowed that we'd always protect Lily. And we have done—until recently. When we didn't see the signs.

And now *this*…

"Why didn't you tell me yesterday? Before we went round there?"

She bites her lip, trying to wipe away the tears. "I was scared…and Jack was there… Please, you can't tell him."

"Lily! He'll find out!" I want to shake her, but I restrain myself.

She shakes her head. "Not yet, he can't find out yet. He'll go after him."

I stare at her for a long time. "You'll need to tell the teachers."

She looks at me, all the angles of her face seeming to sharpen. "Stop trying to control me!"

"Lily? I wasn't!"

Her eyes spark. "Look, I'm dealing with it."

I shake my head. She looks so young, and no way near old enough to have a baby. Or maybe that's just me being judgmental.

"Come on," I say, and—

The whole world turns into a slow-motion movie as I see *it*.

I grab a handful of Lily's coat and pull her over to the left, wrenching my arm. She screams as a silver knife misses her ear by half an inch.

NINE
Jade

ELLIOT—WHERE'S ELLIOT? IT'S HIM, IT'S—

I spin, pushing Lily behind me, and bash my hand on the wall. Pain snakes through me, but I barely notice it. My breaths pound in my ears, and it's too hot in here, so hot, as I look around. I can't see Elliot. Where is he?

"Jade?" Lily edges closer to me, then looks down.

I turn again, trying to see him—see anyone. But there's no one here. The cleaner and teacher have both gone too. It's just me and Lily. Whoever threw the knife at us has gone.

The silver knife is on the floor. It looks expensive; the huge silver hilt is ornately engraved and a red stone—maybe a garnet—sits in the middle of the handle. On the linoleum, it appears as innocent as a prop.

"Jade?"

"Get back in there," I say, pointing at the common room. "And tell Nika and Macey to come out here." I'm breathing hard, and I keep my back to the common room door.

Lily does as I ask, and seconds later, the door opens again. "Jade?" Nika sounds concerned.

"Okay, stay in the doorway," I say. "Both of you. Someone's just thrown a knife at me and Lily. I can't see anyone else here—but I don't know who it was. Or where they are now. I need one of you to get teachers or someone, but not going down this corridor." I point ahead of me. "That's the only way the knife-thrower could've gone, and they could be just around the corner." And they could be hearing all of this too.

"I can climb through the window," Nika says.

I nod. She's had practice at that. Jack dared her once that she couldn't do it in a tight skirt, but she proved him wrong—and flashed everyone with her neon-pink underwear.

"Go now," I say. "And don't say a word to anyone—if there's panic and chaos, whoever threw the knife could use that to escape undetected or whatever. And Macey, can you check Lily's okay?"

"Okay, well, are you coming back in here then?" Macey asks. "I—I think you should."

I shake my head. "The knife's expensive. Whoever threw it could come back for it. See? Look at its design. I want to know who did it and—" And then what? Confront them? But that's more what Jack does—not me. And realizing that makes me start to shake. My hands tremble and I clasp them together and—

Kelley-Anne bursts through the door, crashing into Macey. "Is it true?" Her purple hair shimmers. She's one of those girls who doesn't really have many friends but says she doesn't need them. She's got her family, and she always goes on about how family is most important. She's a Galloway, which makes her filthy rich and she's not afraid to be mean. Not many people here like her.

I shoot her a look. Did Nika tell her? Or Lily—shit, I didn't tell Lily not to tell anyone, and I look past Kelley-Anne and see my sister crying with several girls from my year crowded around her. there's no sign of Nika—she's already gone?

Craig and several boys from my year head to the doorway. Macey and Kelley-Anne are pushed aside, and then Craig's at my side, asking if I'm okay. And this is exactly what I wanted to avoid happening. I wince.

"Woah, what's going on here?"

I turn and look down the corridor—the way the knife-thrower must've gone—to see Mr. Wilson striding toward us. My eyes narrow. Was it him who threw the knife?

"No congregating in corridors," he says. "Come on, you all know this. We've got to be able to get past." Then he looks down, and I can tell he sees the knife by the way he stops and clutches his stomach. His face pales.

And he *laughs*, actually laughs. "Didn't realize you were all so good at drama."

I stare at him, my brow furrowed. "It's a *real* knife."

"Someone just threw it at Jade and her sister," Macey says.

Mr. Wilson's eyes narrow.

"It's true," Kelley-Anne says. "Lily Taylor's in there in bits." She jerks her thumb back at the common room.

"Right, uh, okay!" he shouts, throwing one arm forward. "Everyone in the common room now. And I'll sort out this—" He bends to pick up the weapon.

"Don't touch it!" I stare at him. Hasn't he got any sense at all? "You don't want to get your fingerprints on it too—we need the police."

"Don't contaminate the crime scene," Macey says.

Mr. Wilson, frowning, gets a most-definitely-*used* tissue out of his pocket, and picks up the knife with it. He peers through his round glasses, frowning. "I best take this to the office. I'm sure it's just, uh, someone playing a trick." And with that, he walks off, his shuffling steps getting faster and faster.

I stare after him. That was odd.

"How on earth did he get a job?" Macey mutters. He glances at me. "Are you okay?"

I nod. Too much weird and dangerous stuff has been happening lately. "I'm fine. It didn't hit either of us. But I don't like it."

"It's okay," he says. "We'll find out who did that. And then I'm sure Jack will make them pay."

"HELLO, STUDENTS OF NORTHWOOD COLLEGE." The intercom booms. The speakers in the common room aren't great, and there's a lot of static, especially where I'm standing—by the door. "This is your headmaster, Mr. Jamelson speaking."

Behind me, Nika snorts. "Who does he think he is? Sounds like an airline announcement."

"For the safety of all students, we're currently asking you to stay in the rooms you're in."

Huh. Not like we have a choice. Within seconds of Mr. Wilson leaving with the knife wrapped in his grotty tissue, another teacher appeared and ushered all of us who were in the corridor back into the common room. Then he locked us in.

"This is just for a safety check," Mr. Jamelson continues. "And it's nothing to worry about. But of course we have these measures in place to keep all our students safe."

"Safety check my arse," mutters Craig. He's a little way away, lounging on one of the leather sofas with others who are in the rugby team. "Someone tried to kill us."

"Well, it was thrown at Lily," Kelley-Anne says. "And Jade." Her dark eyes cross over to me.

Huh. Like that makes me feel any better. I try to tune out the chatter around me, because it's practically descending into gossip now. And I can't believe how someone trying to stab Lily or me is now a source of entertainment. They're all talking all bright-eyed and with quick, hushed voices. No one looks scared.

"Who do you think it was?"

"Do you think he'll come back?"

"Have the police even be called?"

Nika touches my arm. "Do you think we're the only ones who know what's going on?" Her eyes are sharp. "Like, in this room? Jamelson didn't give any details.

I shrug. "That teacher came pretty quick and locked us in here. So, all teachers must? Or most? They're gonna wonder why everyone's had to be locked in the rooms."

"And I've already texted Jack," Lily says. She's sitting on the loveseat next to my sofa.

"So the whole school will know pretty soon," I say.

It's weird waiting. Waiting to see what happens next. I took the sofa in the corner for me and Nika, and directed Lily over here too, to the love seat next to it. I've got a direct view of the doorway—I'll know if anyone's coming—but we're not the nearest people sitting to it. We're also by the window—which is what I always aim for in case I need fresh air if someone comes in here with perfume. But perfume is the least of my worries now.

If the knife-wielder comes back, there are people between me and them. People who could get injured instead of me and Lily, if injury is what the person is planning on. And I know that makes me a horrible person, positioning me and my sister over here—as this is probably the safest corner of the room—but it's just self-preservation. I tell myself that. It's what anyone would do. We're all going to protect ourselves and our loved ones over other people. And the knife was aimed at Lily and I to start with.

I look up at the wooden paneling of the common room ceiling. It's smooth, well-polished, and I can't help but wonder why the ceiling in here is so nice when the sofas and carpet are ratty, at best. The gnarls of the wood are even darker still, like obsidian, and they take on weird shapes of their own once my eyes have become too accustomed to them. I watch them now, swallowing down my fear—because my heart is still pounding too hard, too fast. And I shouldn't be looking at the ceiling now, now when I should be on full alert. Because no one else here is. Nika's looking bored, examining her nails now, Macey's pouring over some textbook, Lily's staring at her lap, and everyone else is just chatting. I listen in to some of their conversations, and discover most are about me and Lily and what some are calling 'our close call with death.'

"I can't believe we're being kept in here," one of the rugby boys says. "For hours, too."

"Yeah," Kelley-Anne agrees, her voice bubble-gum sticky. "It's against our human rights, keeping us locked up."

"It's hardly locking us up," Aisha says. "This is for our safety." She looks across at me and Lily. "I bet it was really scary for you."

I nod. And it was scary—but something tells me I haven't processed it all yet. I mean, too much stuff is going on. And that dead fire-woman that the BBC have written about? I frown and look around again. No one is talking about her. I do a quick Google search for more articles on her—but there aren't any. There's only the BBC one that Macey showed me. I frown. Does that confirm that it was just lies then? Because if there really was a body of a fire-resistant person, someone of a different human species, wouldn't everyone be talking about that?

My phone pings. It's Jack. *I'm coming to the common room.*

Door's locked, I reply. I don't even bother asking how he's getting out of whichever lesson he's in right now. Or should be in. Because this is Jack. If my brother wants to do something, he just does it.

I show Nika and Lily the text and they both nod. Another appears on the screen from Jack. The window it is then.

And, sure enough, exactly four minutes later, Jack appears on the other side of the window. He taps on it, making Kelley-Anne scream and shout how she's just nearly had a heart attack and how her new boyfriend won't be happy about guys scaring her.

Keeping one eye on the door, I move toward Jack and the window. Craig and others from the rugby team are near it now, and several of them give Jack toothy grins as they open the window for him.

"Come on, boys, haul me through."

Whereas Nika can get through the window quite quickly and with minimal effort, Jack can't. He's muscular and sturdy, and it takes several of the boys to pull him through.

"But he could be the killer," Kelley-Anne hisses.

"The killer?" I stare at her. "Seriously? No one's dead."

"But you could've been." Her gaze crosses over to Lily.

My sister hasn't moved, she's still just curled up on the love seat.

"Just shut the window," someone hisses, and then it's slammed shut.

Jack makes his way straight to me and Lily and Nika. Macey finally puts down his textbook.

"So you're okay?" Jack asks, his eyes raking over me before he moves to Lily. We both tell him we're fine, but he doesn't look convinced. In a low voice, he says to me, "You think this was him?"

Elliot. I nod.

"Just what we need. Greylakes on our backs," Jack mutters under his breath.

"Greylakes?" Lily sits up straighter. "What've you done to Elliot?"

"Nothing," I say.

"Anyway, the school will sort this out," Macey says. "They're going to be doing thorough searches."

"Relying on this school to do anything is not a good plan," I say. "Especially if it's our only plan." I let out a long breath. "They're not going to find him, are they?"

"They will," Macey says.

"Nah," I say. "He'll be long gone." And that doesn't make me feel any better. Because this knife was a warning. A warning to me and Jack to back off Elliot.

But I can't do that. I won't do that. Lily's my sister, and I'll do anything to protect her.

TEN
Jade

MR. JAMELSON ANNOUNCES OVER THE intercom system, two hours later, that the school is safe. He calls it a false alarm, and I don't think I've ever been so angry. False alarm? There was literally a Greylake on campus and he threw a knife at me and Lily. Well, it must've just been aimed at me. Elliot wouldn't want Lily harmed.

"This school is such a joke," Nika mutters, just as a teacher unlocks the door. A gaggle of annoyed Year 12s and 13s floods out, leaving only a few of us behind: me, Nika, Jack, Macey, and Lily.

"They're not even getting the police involved," I say.

"They wouldn't though. Not if it's Greylakes," Jack points out. "We know what happens to grasses."

A few years ago, when Jack and I were in Year 8 or 9, a woman went to the police about the Greylakes. She got two of them locked up within weeks. Three days after that, her body was found. One report said she'd been drowned, another said she'd been strangled. The thing that both reports agreed on was that it was a revenge killing by the Greylakes. A warning. She'd had their tattoo branded on her forehead, and then someone had gouged out two angry red lines there, one crossing the other so it made a cross.

For months, her death—her murder—was all anyone would talk about.

I remember how scared even the teachers were then. So of course no teacher here is going to get the police involved when it was a Greylake. But that means the teachers also have to know it is the Greylakes here and not someone random who did this. Someone must've seen them.

"Again, I apologize for this disruption and lessons will resume as normal, along with any clubs or detentions taking place tonight." The intercom clicks off.

Detention. I glance at the clock. Oh, God. "I've got my first detention in two minutes."

"Good luck," Nika says.

"We're probably going to the study room next," Jack says. "See you back there?"

I nod and leave the room, cursing to myself. If there is one teacher that you don't want to ever be late for, it's Mr. Wilson.

The corridors are heaving, thanks to us all being locked up for most of the afternoon, and people are being silly, shouting and shoving each other playfully. I get a sharp elbow in my stomach as I jostle my way through a crowd of fifteen-year-old boys, and then I end up running the last few corridors to Mr. Wilson's door. I make it there just about a second before half six, and my tummy grumbles loudly.

Mr. Wilson shouts for me to come in and looks at me in a scrutinizing way as I enter the office. It is hot inside, and the air smells stale, off. I wonder if he was trapped in here for the lockdown. I tug at my hoody sleeves and am about to take it off—after all, hoodies aren't technically allowed as part of the dress code, and I've got a jumper on underneath—but then I stop. The sleeves of my jumper are short, and they'd show those weird gray marks on my wrists from where that crazy old woman grabbed me. Something tells me to keep the hoody on, to keep the marks covered.

"Sit down, Miss Taylor. Nice of you to be so punctual." He rises and walks over to the bookcase, then pulls a volume out of it. Dust billows out with it and he coughs before turning back to me.

"What happened to the knife, sir?" I ask.

"The knife?" He says it like it's a question—only it's not. He knows which one I'm talking about, the one I last saw in his used tissue.

"Yes. Did you find who did it or…"

His eyes glaze over for a second. "It was a prank."

"A prank?" I almost laugh. "It was *not*. You can't actually believe that."

"Miss Taylor, I know you want everything in your life to be exciting, but sometimes you have to accept that the truth is not exciting."

"I don't want it to be exciting! I want this to be taken seriously—because an actual knife was thrown."

The glint in his eye gets more severe and he sighs loudly. "Shall we start?" He returns to his desk. "Take a seat, Miss

Taylor. Ah, you have not brought a pen, I see. So disorganized." He tuts. "When *will* you learn?"

"Sorry," I mutter, and I take the same seat I occupied this morning. All signs of his previous experiment have vanished from his desk and have been replaced with a cage. "Is that a rat?" I stare at it in horror.

Mr. Wilson regards me for a few seconds. I can't work out what he's thinking—there's no emotion on his face. It's just…blank.

"Yes," he says at last. "This is Percy."

I eye Percy carefully. He pretty much looks like a city rat, and for all I know my tutor could've captured him from the drains only minutes ago. Percy does not look happy. I push my chair back a few inches. Rats are dangerous. Just like knives. And Mr. Wilson—this isn't normal behavior. It can't be. I think of all the weird stuff that's been happening. And still is happening—only now it's getting more dangerous.

"Well, you'll have to borrow my pen," Mr. Wilson says. "Now, you're going to carry out a little experiment for me. See, I'm very interested in animal behavior. Particularly that of wild animals who've had no previous encounter with humans in a proper way."

I gulp and try to ease the chair farther backwards. The legs squeak slightly on the floor and then stop as one of them hits an object. I have to get out of here.

"Jade, you're not afraid of my new little pet, are you?"

I shake my head. The rat jumps up a little, turning toward me. It has dark, beady eyes that just seem *wrong*.

Mr. Wilson walks around to my side of the desk. "Good, because I am. And that makes it a whole lot easier to do this experiment if I have a willing participant who isn't afraid to hold my dear little friend." He nods firmly. "Now, for the next hour, I want you to record every single thing that Percy does—I know you study psychology, and have somewhat decent grades in it, so you should know all about the different types of behavior—and I want you to record them all precisely in this." He hands me a notebook. It is heavy. "No, actually, I don't want you to do it in pen, do it in pencil. Yes. And every fifteen minutes, I'd like you to pick this rat up and see how he responds."

I stare at him, my mouth slightly open. "You can't be serious about this. This morning, you said I'd be doing photocopying and inventory stuff." This has to be some joke, some ploy he's using to get a reaction from me. Because this is ridiculous.

More ridiculous than all the other stuff that's going on?

My wrists where the strange marks tingle. What the hell is happening?

"Change of plan." Mr. Wilson's eyes fall on Percy, and the little animal actually nods. "I'm sure you can understand how quickly things change, how we need to adapt when unexpected things happen." His voice is loaded—is he referring to the man who threw the knife? The Greylake—hell, it could've even been Elliot himself. But I can't work out what exactly Mr. Wilson is getting at.

"Together," he says, "we can make huge new discoveries."

My mouth is dry. "Rats are riddled with diseases."

"I'm sure Percy isn't."

"What about Hantavirus Pulmonary Syndrome?" I raise my eyebrows, glad I listened last year in Biology. How I remembered the name of the disease, I don't know. "That can be deadly."

"Well, I'm sure you won't be eating any of his droppings, so there's nothing to worry about there." His face is hard, and his voice is stern. He looks me dead in the eye.

I stand up. "And what about the other diseases?" I ask. "If it scratches me, I could get rat-bite fever—"

"If *he* scratches you—"

"You don't even know that rat's gender!" I raise my voice. "I bet *you* haven't even picked it up. Trying to get me to do this is just wrong. This would never pass health and safety standards."

"What health and safety don't know about won't hurt them."

"Oh, so you admit it then? That this *is* disgusting. You can't make me do this!" Confidence fills me, and for once I actually feel like I deserve to be Jack's twin, like I'm as strong as him. "No, I am not picking up a wild rat that could be carrying God knows what disease just to do some stupid research for you."

Mr. Wilson crosses his arms. Percy squeaks. "We'll see what Mr. Jamelson has to say about this when he finds that you refused to do my detention. He did, after all, announce that all detentions today are to go ahead—which means, Miss Taylor, that you should be doing as you're told."

I snort, that strange confidence still filling me. "And we'll find out what he has to say when he hears that you try to force a student—a student who is under *your* care—into unethical experiments that could cause great harm, both psychologically and physically, and that are against the said student's will." I glare at him. "Goodbye."

I make it to the door before he realizes what my intention is. As soon as I am outside, I run. And I keep running, heading for the study room. I throw open the door. Jack, Nika, and Macey are the only people in there, and I am glad.

"You'll never guess what just happened," I pant, trying to catch my breath, and update them as quickly as I can.

"You go, girl!" Nika knocks one of Macey's textbooks onto the floor. He frowns at her.

Jack looks ready to explode. "He made you hold a wild rat—"

"I didn't actually hold it," I point out.

"Nah, because you walked out." Nika high-fives me.

Jack looks across at Macey. "Isn't there some sort of organization we can go to about this? It just ain't right—"

"Isn't," I correct—then wince. I'm more like my mother than I care to admit. "Sorry."

Macey's books are spread out between us, so if any teachers come we can claim we are doing work.

Macey frowns. "There should be some sort of student body we could contact. And the ethical guidelines department…" He looks across at me. "But it would be your word against his."

"Not unless we go and capture Percy," I mutter.

"Percy? He's named it Percy?" Nika shrieks with laughter, then quietens down as Jack gives her a very, very stern look.

"I am going to get into so much trouble," I say. I look across at my friends. "He's probably going to Jamelson now."

"Well, then you'll tell Jamelson what really happened." Jack clasps his hands together on the table so tightly his knuckles whiten and look like milky drops.

I bite my lip. "That's what I threatened to do when he mentioned Jamelson, and—" Tears come to my eyes, and I wipe them away, angry. It is stupid to cry. Jack never cries. I take a deep breath as Nika puts her arm around me.

"It'll be fine," she says. "We're here."

"And you're not going to any more detentions without me," Jack says. "They can't stop me from volunteering for detentions."

Macey looks horrified. He's never had a detention— voluntary or otherwise—in his life.

"And if Jamelson does summon you to his office about this, I'll go with you too." Jack pats my arm. "It'll be okay. We always stick together."

"I don't think Mr. Wilson's going to report it though," Macey says. "He's not going to want Mr. Jamelson finding out about the rat."

"Yeah, you've got a point. That would just be trouble. And the teachers don't want that," I add, thinking of Mr. Wilson's reaction to the knife-throwing. I lean forward. "Have any of you heard any teachers discussing the knife that was thrown at me and Lily? Like, Jamelson deemed the school safe, and yet no one's talking about it."

Nika and Jack both frown.

Macey leans in closer. "But isn't that because it was the Greylakes behind it? School's not going to get involved in gang disputes."

My shoulders tighten. "Still, it's not safe."

They all nod, but a strange kind of atmosphere settles between us for a few moments, until Nika stretches.

"Anyway, let's get to the canteen," she says. "It should be lasagna today, and I actually want to get some this time. Year 7s scoffed the lot last week."

We gather our bags and head for the door.

"We can film later too," Macey says, holding the door open for me. He glances at me, makes direct eye contact. "If you're up for it? We can shoot the scenes out in the field."

Macey's making this film for extra credit, something to supplement his UCAS application. Although he's applying for a science-based degree, his tutor advised him that it would be good to have a creative project too. To show he's versatile.

But filming it *today*? And on the school field? I turn over the idea in my mind. We'd be outside, away from teachers there—out in the open. And if there are Greylakes around, it would be so easy for one of them to get the knife in me properly this time. And in the dark, they could creep up on us, and—

"Jade?" Macey's giving me an odd look. In fact, all of them are. I've stopped in the doorway.

"Uh, yeah," I say, and I want to look at my brother and ask if he'll be there too. Because I feel safer around Jack. Only I can't say that—I don't want to appear weak. So I just nod. "That'll be fine."

ELEVEN
Elliot

I'M NOT STUPID ENOUGH TO WALK ONTO THE school grounds—too many teachers would recognize me. It's only been two years since I was expelled and the school has a surprisingly low turnover of staff. Lily's told me exactly who is still there. And I ain't risking it.

So I do what I always do when I wait for Lily in the evenings. There's an alleyway off a backroad that is fairly accessible from the western edge of campus. It's where Lily and I always used to meet.

I text her. *I'm here. You coming?*

It's biting cold out here and my breath fogs in the air as I scroll up through our conversation. Since the other day when I lost my temper with her, Lily's not replied. And I didn't mean to lose my temper—of course I didn't. But she cost me money, and Robbie doesn't make allowances.

I breathe out hard. Maybe I should never trusted Lily to be a runner, not when she's not actually one of us. but I had to get rid of the gear fast. Spencer texted me about a cop tip-off, and Lily was there with me. We were in the garage, her on my lap, kissing, getting hot and heavy, when the text came through.

Ten minutes, it said. That was how far away Spencer thought the cops were. And we'd only just stocked up again. Annabel had met our guy yesterday, so the garage was full of it. What else was I supposed to do? Lily was there—looking innocent in her school uniform, with that big rucksack. She hadn't taken much persuading to take the gear, not when I told her I loved her. And I do. I'm not using her.

But then she lost the gear. She was only supposed to have it overnight.

But she came back, scared, the next day. And as soon as I saw her, I knew something had happened.

"What do you mean it's gone?" I roared, grabbing her arm. "It's just grown legs and walked off, has it?"

"I think they knew," she whispered. "Dan Roveman's brother's in my class and he—"

"The Devils?" I wiped the back of my hand across my mouth. "That's all Robbie fucking needs."

For years, the Devils weren't any serious competition to us, because this town was Greylake territory. It always has been. But then the Devils got new leaders, including Dan Roveman—a former Greylake. Damn. I should've shot him when I had the chance.

"And he's got our gear?" I demanded, shaking Lily.

"I don't know!" Tears appeared in her eyes. "But I only left the bag in my room for two seconds—I was hungry and I—"

"You left three-grand worth of drugs unattended?"

"I'm sorry!" she'd cried and cried.

But *sorry* didn't get the drugs back. So yeah, of course I was angry.

I breathe out hard, staring at the message thread between me and Lily. She's not even opening my messages now. I try another one: *I'm sorry.* Even typing the words makes me feel wrong. The Pollizzis don't apologize. Not ever. That's what Dad taught me, before he went inside. Antonio Pollizzi was one of the biggest Greylakes ever. Respected, feared. Of course I'd follow in his footsteps.

I phone Lily. It clicks onto voicemail. I wait for the tone.

"I'm sorry, okay? Babe, let's just forget that happened, all right? I love you, and I'm not going to let this ruin what we have."

No. She's mine. From the moment I first saw Lily Taylor, I knew that girl was mine.

TWELVE
Ariel

"COME ON, SON, YOU'VE GOT TO DO BETTER than this," Wes says, towering over me.

I blink and rub the back of my head. The crash mat is soft beneath me.

We're at the gym in the warehouse, and this was supposed to be a quick practice. My trial's next week—the day that will decide if I can graduate as a dispatcher and work alongside my brothers and sisters. Each of them passed their trial the first time, so there's a lot of pressure on me. And, right now, that pressure's getting to me.

Wes holds out his hand, and I grasp it. He pulls me up and shakes his head.

"Yeah, I know." I breathe hard and shake my arms out.

"Just don't think about it too much," he says. "I know you're skilled. Yeah? Just believe in yourself, but don't get too inside your head."

But that's the problem—I am too *inside my head* right now. The trial is a big deal. It'll be where I prove to my father that I've got worth. Upon passing my trial, I'll join the other dispatchers. I'll be going out with them, searching for our people. Getting them out.

Before the treaty, dispatchers' jobs were very different. They got their name because they'd literally 'dispatch' individuals they found—namely, the Xphenorie, or as some of us call them, the Fenners, because 'Xphenorie' is a mouthful. But that was back when the war was ongoing, before we had come to an agreement. Then, the Xphenorie fed freely on humans, and we were the humans' protectors. We'd each guard different families, and we'd work together, killing the Fenners.

Now, we don't kill. We rescue our people—the Calerians that the humans are holding captive, because the human police think we're dangerous, and they can't see the Fenners, the real danger. We may have the treaty with the Fenners, and that may be keeping the humans safe now, but we still have to learn to fight though. How to disarm someone.

"Let's try again," Wes says. He tucks the gun into his waistband. "Scenario two."

Scenario two—Wes will walk past me 'innocently,' and then pull the gun on me. My job is to disarm him before he can pull the trigger. The gun's only loaded with paint.

I nod. "Right."

"YOU'LL PASS IT, NO PROBLEM," LUCY SAYS between large mouthfuls of spaghetti bolognaise. "I know you will."

I rub at the bruises on my arms. Paint hurts. "I've only got four days. And it was a good job Wes was doing that session and not my father." Not that my father does a lot of the practice sessions—but I know he'll be there for my trial. If he's not the instructor, he'll be one of the judges. And all my siblings will be there too. All six of them.

"You'll be fine," Lucy says.

I watch as she just eats faster and faster. Annoyance rises in me—that's happening more and more around her now. My brother said it means I'm not in love with her anymore. But I'm not sure that I ever was. Only, now everything about her annoys me. And it's not just the noisy way she eats. The fires—they're becoming a bigger problem. Much bigger.

She's still doing them. On a smaller scale than the last one, but I followed her last night.

She crept out and up to Bambry Woods. She crouched in the woods and summoned fire to her hands, then scattered the flames around her in a circle. She let the circle grow taller, walls around her, and her eyes were alive with it.

I let the fire get as tall as I dared before I revealed myself, using my own command over our special type of fire to bring it down a bit. I'd expected her to be angry or something. To be annoyed that I'd followed her out there. But she'd just smiled—smiled like she'd known I was there the whole time. Like I'd clean up her mess.

Like I always do.

I stir my own dinner with my fork. The bolognaise sauce is really runny and little droplets of grease float in it. I don't like it, but you don't tell Kash that you don't like his food. Not unless you want a slap. So I eat it, feeling the contents of my stomach slip and slide about.

A couple of the other dispatchers arrive, including my brother Ricardo. He slides into the seat next to me, and then Lucy's making way for her friend Rose to sit.

"There's more Fenners in this area," Ricardo says. He's two years older than me and my father's clear favorite.

"More?" I ask.

He nods. "We're not sure why. But we've got Xphenorie gathering. Tav says they're watching the school."

"The school?" I frown.

Ricardo nods. "They're not doing anything there—just watching. But we don't like it. We've got one dispatcher undercover in there, but Dad's getting edgy."

My frown deepens. "There's no reason for them to be watching the school—unless they're planning an attack. But that would break the treaty." That would mean all-out war between the Xphenorie and us. It would be like centuries ago, before we had the treaty, when the Fenners fed and killed on humans, and when we protected them as best as we could.

But protecting the whole school?

"How many Xphenorie are there?" I gulp, and then I'm imagining going there, finding their bodies. Just like I found the two dead Calerians two years ago.

No. That was different. That was gangs. This is…

"Tav's seen close to a hundred," Ricardo says. "And Kara and Johnny have both corroborated that."

"A *hundred*?" I exclaim. "What's attracting them to the school?"

"Young teenagers are always sweeter for them," he says. "We know that—but they're only flocking around this one school. And, that, we don't know why. But if the Xphenorie are going to break the treaty and start feeding again, we need to be ready. So, let's just hope that if it does happen, if the Fenners break the treaty, that we've already broken out some of our captives. Else we've got no chance, and the humans can't protect themselves. Not against a species they can't see and don't know exists. We need all the dispatchers we can get." He gives me a look. "You better not mess up your trial."

THIRTEEN
Jade

THREE HOURS LATER, THE SKY HAS TURNED A deep purple as night heads in, and a strong wind has picked up.

I hug myself, trying to keep warm. My eyes travel back to the shadows on the edge of the field, where the trees start. Is anyone lurking there? I don't think there is anyone there— but it's hard to see through the eye-holes of this mask, the one Macey insists I wear when I'm playing Lady Kavorna. Still, I don't even know who this Lady Kavorna character is— Macey said something about her being based on a historical figure, but I couldn't find any info on her when I did a quick Google search a few weeks ago.

"Look, are we nearly done yet?" Nika asks for the umpteenth time. Near her, Jack is looking equally bored and fed up. He's holding Macey's state-of-the-art camera—but not in the careful, precise way Macey holds it. He's not even looking at it now; no, my brother's focused on Nika.

Macey peers over Jack's shoulder at the camera's screen. "No," he says, shaking his head. "This scene still isn't right. Nika, as the audience person, you're supposed to say when the light's not right. Look, you can't even see Jade here—she's just a shadowy figure, and we need to be able to see her mask so the audience know it's her."

"Well, maybe the bloody light isn't right because it's getting dark," Nika mutters. "And I'm freezing."

Well, she wasn't the one who had to take her hoody off to be filmed. I lift the mask from my face. It is heavy, adorned with many colored beads. As are the sticks which Macey insisted I carry 'for authenticity' as that's what Lady Kavorna would've worn. My hands are sore, and I'm not quite sure why. The skin just aches, kind of similar to how the old woman's fingerprints on my arms hurt. At least they're not visible though, under the long sleeves of the black jumper Macey gave me. I'd wanted to keep my hoody on but he insisted that Lady Kavorna would never wear a hoody.

"Nika," Macey says, folding his arms. "This whole film takes place at dusk or night. It wouldn't be authentic if we filmed it in the day under bright sunlight. And Jack, can you angle the camera up a little more next time?"

"But how do you expect the lighting to be right if it's dark?" Nika asks, just as Jack nods.

Macey grunts. "Moonlight," he says, rolling his eyes.

I fold my arms and shudder with the cold—and something else. The darkening sky looks… I don't know how to describe it. Hell, even the darkness is *different* now. It's…heavier? I mean, the air does feel thicker, grittier. And suddenly, just as I'm thinking about the air, an image flashes into my mind—a woman in her thirties, lying on a hard, paneled floor. A woman…dead.

I jolt. The woman from that article? The dead fire-woman?

I breathe deeply—no, it can't be her. That article had no photo with it. This can't be her. It's just my mind playing tricks on me. Because I'm scared out here now, scared of the night. I shake myself. I'm just being silly. The night isn't dangerous. It's not like anything bad is going to happen. Not like that old woman's going to reappear and grab me. Or any Greylakes—not with four of us out here. And we've been out here ages and no one has come over to hurt us. We've been safe here, so far. Safer than we were in the school.

"Just five more minutes, then we can go in," Macey says.

"We better not miss the last call for hot chocolate tonight," Jack says. "I actually wanted some today. Miss Lazear's making it and she always brings in that Belgian chocolate. And I've still got some Baileys left in my room to add in."

"We've got plenty of time until then," I say, looking at my phone for the time. As much as I wish my brother wouldn't constantly find excuses to add alcohol to things, I know it's pointless arguing against him. If anything, that just makes him more determined to drink more.

Predictably, five minutes turns into ten, which then becomes into twenty, and it is definitely dark by the time we get back into the school's buildings.

"Jade, do you mind doing another session with me another time?" Macey asks. "It should be the last one, but we still need to get Lady Kavorna's soliloquy."

"Of course she doesn't *mind*," Nika says, her eyes on me. Her voice is lighter now—and I know that look on her face.

Don't, I mouth at her.

"Don't what?" Jack asks.

"Jade?" Macey's looking at me expectantly.

"Yeah," I say quickly. "That's fine."

"Jade *lurrrrves* you!" Nika says in a stage whisper to Macey.

"That is so childish," I say. "What are you, twelve?"

Nika laughs, and I glance quickly at Macey. He's blushing. I look away quickly. I only like him as a friend—that's all it is anyway. He's just one of my best friends. And that's all there is—because I've never really had a crush on anyone. When Nika talks about which guys she fancies, it just all seems foreign to me. Something that I've never experienced. And I can't even imagine myself going on a date or doing anything sexual.

And maybe that makes me strange—because am I the only one like this? I mean, Lily's clearly slept with Elliot. Nika never actually told me she had sex with Dom, but there were a lot of rumors about how they slept with each other pretty quickly after they got together—and each time someone mentioned it, Nika went very red. She didn't correct the person, just looked flustered, so I guess that means it's true. My brother, I don't know about, but last year he was caught kissing a girl in the year below. Caught by her brother and punched for it. And Macey? I look at him, trying to remember if he's done anything...like that. But Macey's quiet. I can't remember him ever going out with anyone. Can't remember him ever having a crush.

"Come on, it's past your bedtime," Jack says to Nika, putting his arm around her shoulders.

Nika laughs and whispers something to him, and then they're walking ahead of me and Macey. Suddenly, I don't know what to say to Macey. Do we speak at all? Or would that just make it awkward? He hasn't actually said anything since Nika said that very childish thing. He's just gone red.

Macey glances at me, but when he sees me looking at him, he jolts and focuses his eyes straight ahead again. Oh God. This is awkward. So awkward and—

"Oh no." Nika stops in front of us, and I nearly walk smack into her.

It's Dom, standing in the corridor ahead. Nika turns to me, and her eyes are frantic. She starts to go back, but Jack catches her arm.

"Just walk straight past him," he says. "Don't change your route because of him."

But I can tell that's exactly what Nika wants to do. Change her route.

Dom shows no indication that seeing Nika is bothering him in the slightest, just keeps standing where he is. He's not blocking the corridor this time, and he looks a whole lot more *with it* than he did this morning.

"All right?" Macey nods at Dom.

"Yes." Dom's voice is flat. "You lot just been outside?" Once again, he aims a frown at me.

Macey nods. "Just a bit of filming."

"Might be best to stay indoors at night." Dom's eyes bore into me.

"Hey," Jack says. "You can't tell my sister what to do. You can't tell anyone."

Dom shrugs. "Just safer. That's all. Gangs and that."

I don't speak. My mouth is suddenly too dry.

As we sidle past Dom, I can't help but notice how he gives *me* a strange look, his eyes resting on me for a long time. And not in a nice way either—more in a scrutinizing way, like the one Mr. Wilson used. A prickly feeling wraps around my neck, and it only gets stronger once I've passed him.

I throw a glance over my shoulder at him—and his eyes meet mine. I jolt and glance at the snake tattoo on his shaven head. It doesn't move. Of course not.

But he's still staring at me.

Dom is creepy as hell.

I walk faster away, almost as fast as the pace Nika has set.

"What a dick," Jack mutters.

BY THE TIME WE GET TO THE BASEMENT IT'S just gone ten, and, predictably, it is packed. The curfew for being in your room is only half an hour away, and everyone is making the most of their last few minutes. The sound of computer games is loud. Unlike our common room, which only has one console and wide-screen, the basement has four, as well as several other games, computers, a snooker table, and various other devices. The TV in the corner is on faintly, but most people are watching the *Call of Duty* battle on one of the wide-screens. There's a small gaggle of girls in the corner listening to Kelley-Anne. It takes me a moment or two to realize she's talking about her new boyfriend—apparently he's older and got his own car, and that instantly gives Kelley-Anne more popularity points.

"Hey, Taylors! Look at this!" Craig shouts from a sofa.

He beckons the four of us over—he often greets us that way when there are more than one of us, even saying once that Macey and Nika are honorary Taylors. Nika hadn't liked that though, saying, "I'm a Takada, thank you very much," while Macey had just shrugged and gone along with it.

Craig holds a newspaper out to me, his eyes wide. "This is madness." He laughs. "What some people will do for thirty seconds of fame, right?"

I take one look at the headline—*The Discovery of Secret People*—and then scan the article. It appears to be a write-up on it all from some top scientists and part of the post-mortem for Shelley's body. I turn to Macey. His eyes are narrowed.

"I knew it." Macey grabs the paper from Craig.

Craig holds up his hands. "What? Hold on a minute. You actually believe in this stuff?"

"It's perfectly plausible," Macey says.

"Huh." Craig looks at me. "And do you believe in this?"

I shrug. The problem is, I don't know whether I believe all this talk or not. I mean, Macey clearly does and he's usually right about everything. And these people are being called 'fire-people' and Jack and I did see that super strange fire. It wasn't an ordinary fire. And I think of that image I saw earlier—the woman, Shelley, on the paneled floor. Something inside me just tells me that it was her I saw, even if I can't explain it.

So it is real? I do believe in it? I press my lips together.

Craig takes my silence for disagreement. "Thank God at least one of you is sensible. All a load of nonsense, right, Jade? And what about you two?" He looks at Jack and Nika, who both laugh and shake their heads.

"Pretending doesn't make something go away," Macey mutters. "And mark my words, this is real. There'll be official announcements soon. God, can you imagine just walking past one of these fire-people? Like, passing someone in the street and not knowing what they can do, who they are."

Craig's eyes darken. "If it's true, they need locking up. It's disgusting. I bet they've been watching us loads, studying us. Spies—that's what they are." He wrinkles his nose. "At least we now know how dangerous they are."

"What?" I ask. "They?" I ask, just as Macey says, "Being fire-resistant isn't dangerous."

"They're not just fire-resistant," Craig says. "Didn't you read the whole article—the second page? They've found *live* ones…apparently. And they can control fire. From their fingertips. They can just make it erupt. They're the *masters of fire*. That's what they're being called. Anyone who can get fire to erupt from their fingers is dangerous. That's a given. So, if any of this is real, we need to hunt them down. Kill them before they dowse us in flames."

FOURTEEN
Jade

FIRE.

I can hardly breathe. My mind's spinning, and Macey and Craig are arguing but I can't process their words. All I can think about is that strange fire and the old woman who grabbed me—was she one of them? Suddenly, my head's pounding and I just have to know. I need to know. Everything inside me burns with the need to know.

I leave the basement, ignoring the shouts of the others, and head back to my room, examining my arms as I go. The marks around my wrists are key—I know that. They're proof that the old woman grabbed me. And they *could* look like burns. I squint and frown. Did she use her fiery fingertips on me? Use her fire to burn me…because these people are dangerous?

But my skin doesn't *feel* burnt. It just feels odd. Strange. Maybe it's a bit thinner than usual, in those places?

I reach my bedroom door, type in the passcode on the lock-unit, and—

"Hey, wait up."

I turn to find Nika behind me. She's panting.

I hold the door open for her and she breezes through. My head spins even more. I need to write this all down—everything that I've realized has to be connected. Inside my room, I scan my stuff for the notes I made before, on the back of that essay plan.

Only they're not here. I can't find them.

I frown. Okay, I can write it all again. And I have to, because I've already forgotten the fire once, so I could wake up tomorrow and all of it could be gone. And this is important.

I make some quick notes, and then Nika gets ready for bed and falls asleep almost instantly, leaving me to my worries for the night.

I end up texting Lily. With everything that's gone on since her pregnancy reveal, I've hardly actually thought about what it means. That my sister is having a baby.

Are you sure about what you said? I press send on the message. I'm trying to be cryptic so if anyone else reads our texts, she wouldn't get into trouble. Because the school would punish her, wouldn't they? Well, I don't actually know, but I'm sure our parents would go ballistic. Either that or disown all three of us.

Lily replies instantly*: I think so.*

You haven't taken a test?

How would I get one?

I swallow hard. How indeed. *I'll get you one.*

And until we know the result of it—if she really is pregnant or not—we can't make any plans. Though what kind of plans we'd be making, I don't know. Part of me still can't believe that this could be real. That this is going on alongside all this other strange stuff. I trace my fingers over the marks on my right wrist, then try to match up my own fingers with the prints, as if I made them. But the prints are bigger and wider apart than I can make my fingers go.

I take a deep breath.

Our parents are going to kill Lily.

Then they'll kill me and Jack for letting this happen.

FIFTEEN
Jade

THE WOMAN BEHIND THE DESK AT THE pharmacy looks me up and down as I place the pregnancy test on the counter the next morning.

She tuts under her breath. "Kids having kids, eh?"

"It's not for me," I say—then wince. Although I don't recognize her, what's to say that she doesn't know who I am? And it wouldn't take much digging for anyone to find out which other girls I'm close to.

"Sure, honey," she says. She scans the pregnancy test.

It's more expensive than I'd anticipated, and for a moment I think my debit card is going to get declined. Thankfully, it doesn't.

I shove the test into my bag, and as I do so, my sleeve catches on the top of my bag, exposing some of my right wrist—and, under the artificial light in this shop, the marks look even worse. It's like patches of my skin are just...dead. Like there's no blood supply. I hear the woman's sharp intake of breath and I look up at her. Her eyes seem to have grown to about three times their size.

I wait for her to say something. She doesn't. She's just staring. The hairs on the back of my neck lift up, and I pull my sleeve back down. Her breathing gets heavier and louder and faster, like she's hyperventilating.

"Um, are you okay?" I ask—because I'm not sure if I should just leave. It's a strange reaction, but what if she's having a heart attack or something?

The woman's eyes lock onto me. Her mouth opens, but then she stops. And she leaves—exiting through a doorway behind the till.

I stare after her. Is she unwell? I call out again, asking if she's all right. But there's no response.

Weird, I think. I frown. Do I just go? I've already paid for the test and—

Footsteps. Coming toward me. The woman coming back?

But it's not her. It's a man. Early twenties. Spiky white-blond hair. His skin is so pale it almost appears to be translucent, and I can see the bluish hue of a vein running close to the outer edge of his right eye. He gives me a wide grin. His name badge says he's called Ariel. "You okay there?" He has a smooth voice.

"Uh. Yeah. Is she?" I gesture toward the door.

"She's fine." His grin gets wider. His eyes are a brilliant, pure blue, full of mystery, and twinkle under the fluorescent light of the shop. He looks strangely familiar—only I haven't seen him before, so this doesn't make sense.

I frown.

"Anyway, you want some more light bulbs?" Ariel holds up a box of incandescent light bulbs.

"What?" I laugh. Light bulbs? "Why would I want light bulbs?"

For the briefest of seconds, he looks surprised, but then he hides it well. "Well, most old ladies come in here for them."

"You're calling *me* old?" My eyebrows shoot up. And what kind of comeback even is that? "If anything, you look older. You've even got white hair."

"Well, that hurts." He slicks back said hair. "But you got me. I knew I should've dyed this again. And what about you? Ever dyed yours? I bet dark red would look great on you. And I've got just the packet of it I can sell you."

"No," I say. "I don't dye my hair." I've wanted to—but I'm not explaining about MCAS to a complete stranger though.

He's still smiling at me. Why is he smiling at me like this? Is he…flirting? I frown. "Well, uh, your customer skills are terrible. Shocking." I don't know whether to laugh or not. This is all…weird. I reposition my bag on my shoulder and start to turn.

"Oh, you're going already?"

"Yes," I say. "I have to get back to school."

"School." Ariel's voice is loaded, like there's some sort of hidden meaning in the word and the way he says it—only I haven't got a clue what he's meaning. I look up into his face. His eyes are intense, and something about them makes me think that he is analyzing me. He looks so much older now—twenty-five or something—but also worried. And then just like that, the worry is gone, and he's smiling again. "I can always walk you back to your school."

Walk me back? I stare at him. The hairs on the back of my neck stand on end. "Uh, what?"

"You did say my customer service is bad." He gives a smile that I think is supposed to be sly and mischievous. "Anyway, I thought your school didn't let students walk around alone? Especially with all the gangs out there."

"Uh, how do you know which school I go to?" I take a small step back.

He snorts. "There's only one in Northwood."

"I could just be visiting here," I say.

"*Could*." He smiles. "That means you're not. Anyway, my break's about to start. I can walk you back."

"Nope! You've only just started," shouts a deep voice from the back. "No break for you yet!"

I shift my weight from foot to foot. "Uh, I'm okay. Definitely. Thanks."

"Well," he says. "This is awkward."

"Is it?" I say, even though he's definitely right. I just want to get out of here. This is too weird, and I don't understand what's going on.

Ariel's still holding the box of bulbs. Did he really think I'd want them?

"Just, see you around then, I guess?" he says.

"Uh, yeah," I say, even though I have no intention of 'seeing him around.' God, is he actually hitting on me? Or is something else going on? I wish Nika was here—she'd know in an instant what was happening. And she'd know what to do—because if this Ariel guy is flirting with me, then I haven't the foggiest idea of how to flirt back. That's if I want to flirt back—and I haven't got a clue about that either. It all just seems…weird.

I leave as quickly as I can. As I exit under the bell in the doorway, I glance back at Ariel. He's smiling, still holding the box of lightbulbs.

I GET BACK TO THE SCHOOL IN GOOD TIME. I've got two free periods this morning, and it's almost the end of the second one now. Lily's still in her geography lesson though, so I wait at the foyer of the geography block as I can't remember which classroom she's in, and some of the geography teachers get weird about people hanging about outside their doors. I send Lily a message, telling her where to find me. She always checks her phone. Sure enough, the double tick shows she's read it a few seconds later. A few minutes later, the bell rings and she appears by my side.

"Did you get it?" she asks.

Before I can reply, Stacey and Anna, two of her friends, call after her, asking if she's going to the canteen with them.

"They're doing omelets at break again," Anna says.

Lily's face goes positively green, and she shakes her head. "Not hungry."

I shepherd Lily away. The first bathroom we go into is occupied by a gaggle of Year 9s, so we go on to the science block, using the glass bridge between the two buildings. The toilets there are pretty grimy and the least favorable among students. And they are empty.

I put my bag down on the counter next to the sink and fish out the test. I hand Lily the box. Her face goes even more green as she stares at the words on the box.

"Just do it," I say, trying to give a reassuring smile. "Then you'll know."

She nods and hands me her bag, then wedges the oblong box between her knees as she ties her hair up into a high bun. "Don't want it falling into everything and getting my own piss on it," she says, before disappearing behind the nearest stall door.

I turn to the mirror and examine my reflection. I think I just look tired. Nothing out of the ordinary.

Something clatters in the stall.

"Oh, shit," Lily says.

"What?" I spin around. "You okay?" Surely the test can't have worked that quickly?

"Just dropped the test." She makes a frustrated sound. "And it's hard trying to pee with you listening."

"I'm not listening."

"Sure you're not," she says. I can almost hear the roll of her eyes, and I wait. And wait.

A few minutes later, Lily emerges with the test in her hands. I don't need to ask her to know the result. Her ashen face says it all, and she glances at me with brimming eyes.

"It'll be okay," I say. "There are options. We've got options."

"We. Huh." She throws the test in the bin by the sink. I hurriedly grab some loo roll from one of the cubicles and put in in the bin, on top of the test, covering it up. Calmly, Lily walks to the sink and washes her hands, and then undoes her bun, not bothering to dry her hands first. Her silky hair falls like a curtain. "Don't tell Jack," she says, turning to me. "I mean it, Jade. You told him about the…bruises…" She has difficulty saying the words. "And I asked you not to with him—and look what's happened."

"Well, what has happened?" I say. "Elliot's not been in contact with you, right?"

"He's been texting," she says, tight-lipped. "He's not happy. He said he was waiting for me this morning—"

"What?"

She rolls her eyes. "He says it all the time. But…"

"You saw him?" My eyes widen.

She shakes her head. "Well, yes and no."

"What do you mean?"

Lily sighs. "I started to go down there, to where I meet him, but there was some sort of thing going on."

"Thing?"

"Some men grabbed him, yanked him away and into a van."

My eyes widen. "What?" My chest tightens—and I don't know why I'm feeling worried about Elliot of all people. I hate the man. I hate what he did to Lily, to me, to Jack.

"Must've been Devils," Lily says. "I'm…I'm going to text him later, to see if he's all right."

"No, you're not," I say, shaking my head. "Lily, you've got to cut him off completely."

Her eyes flash. "I need to know he's all right."

"If you text he's going to think you're coming back to him."

"Coming back?" She snorts. "I don't think we ever properly broke up. He's worried about me, J. And I'm worried about him now."

I sigh. "Look, I wouldn't put it past him to stage that abduction or whatever, if he thought you'd see. He'll do anything to make himself the victim and get you back on his side."

"You didn't see it," she says. "He was scared."

"I highly doubt Elliot Pollizzi is scared of anyone. He's the one who does the scaring, makes other people scared. Like you," I say. "Look, just the other day you were crying, Lily."

"About nothing." She shrugs. "Hormones."

"Bruises aren't nothing," I say.

"Neither is a stabbing," she says. "You and Jack have to just leave this, okay? I can sort it out myself."

"Lily," I try, "Jack and I… We can help you."

"Really?" She raises her eyebrows. "Because the two of you seem to think he's going to jump out at you on any corner—you two obviously did something to him. And we all know that Greylakes always get revenge."

"But he hasn't," I say, swallowing hard. Apart from the knife—the knife that missed me and Lily.

She snorts. "Yet. So just leave it. I'll sort it. It's my mess. My life. I don't need you two."

I shift my weight to the other foot. "I'm just worried. You can understand that, right? This…this is big news here. And…" I wince. "Lil, you're…fifteen, and Elliot's nineteen. This…"

"It was consensual," she says, very quickly. She turns to inspect herself in the mirror and begins finger-combing her hair.

I shake my head. "It can't be—not when you're underage, and he's—"

"I wanted to." Her voice is small, fierce. Her reflection glances at me. "Don't turn this into something it isn't."

Frustration builds in me. "I'm not. But he's hurt you. No," I say before she can interject. "Your arms are proof of that. And now this… Coercing you to do stuff isn't right. That's not, uh, consent if you were scared to say no."

"There was no coercion. I wasn't scared. I wanted to do it. And I love him." With every sentence, her voice gets louder. Her eyes flash. "And I'm *not* having this conversation with you. Not now."

"But Lily—"

"I have to go. Anna and Stacey will be wondering where I am. Thanks for getting the test. But I'll handle it from here." She sniffs and wipes her hands on her jogging bottoms.

Handle it? What does that mean? But I don't ask. I just watch her leave. I can't push her. She'll come to me, won't she?

SIXTEEN
Jade

"GOOD. YOU'RE HERE," JACK SAYS THE MOMENT I reach my locker—he's leaning against the lockers on the other side. It's late—I'm about to go to my next detention with Mr. Wilson, and I'm already running late. Just came here to drop my bag and folders off.

After Lily left me in the bathroom, I was late to my next lesson, and that apparently set a precedent for me being late to everything else. Domino effect. Figures.

"I've got to go," I say. "Detention." Part of me hopes that when I get there, Mr. Wilson won't be there. I mean, nothing has happened about me walking out of my last one. No one's said anything.

Still, if this detention is going ahead, Percy better not be there.

"Yeah, and I'm coming with you," Jack says.

I stare at him for a few seconds, trying to work out if he is still serious. It appears he is. I frown, shake my head.

Haven't even got the energy to say anything. I just nod, weary.

To say Mr. Wilson looks surprised when my brother volunteers to do my detention with me would be an understatement. He opens and shuts his mouth for a few seconds, then nods.

"Well, you'd better take a seat. Both of you."

We're in Mr. Wilson's usual office. There's no smell of chemicals in here this time—nor any sight of them—but the door to the next room is open, and I can hear something bubbling. I glance at Jack and he nods and heads over there, then looks into the next room.

"What's that?" he asks, then he pokes his head back. "Jade, don't go in there. There's some sort of chemistry experiment." He closes the door. "This needs to be shut—for Jade's health. And you shouldn't be running anything when you know she's coming here."

Mr. Wilson snorts. "There is a sufficient ventilation system in there, so Jade is fine. She's not even in that room."

"We'll let my sister be the decider on whether that's fine," Jack says. He glances at me and I give a cautious nod. I think I'm okay. "But what is it anyway, in there?" he asks. "The liquid was changing from orange to a bluey-black—changing like that in the few seconds I saw it."

"An experiment far too advanced for you to understand."

Jack raises his left eyebrow. "Try me."

Mr. Wilson sighs. He sits opposite us. "I'm looking at the displacement reactions of halogens."

"Oh, so which chemicals are you using? Potassium bromine? And I suppose you've got iodine water. And chlorine water?"

Chemistry is Jack's thing, just as P.E. is Lily's. Or rather it was—because won't that change, if she's pregnant? My head spins. She'll have to tell teachers. Unless she goes for an abortion? But even then, teachers are going to have to know.

Mr. Wilson nods. "Yes, well, it's bromine water and potassium iodide." He looks suspiciously at Jack.

"But," Jack says. "I take chemistry. I know all the displacement reaction. I know what they look like. And I know that when bromine water and potassium iodide are added, no color change results. But that"—he flicks his eyes toward the now-closed door—"changed color. Why lie to us?"

"Why are you so keen to find out?"

"Why are you trying to hide something from us? What are you planning?" Jack's voice gets a little louder.

Mr. Wilson stands up. "I will not tolerate this kind of behavior from a student."

Jack stands too, and hesitantly, I join him. My brother growls, "And I will not just stand there and do nothing when a teacher tries to force my sister to hold a wild rat. They have diseases. And now this chemical stuff? You're looking a little shifty, *sir*. Are you sure you haven't got anything to hide?" He steps around the desk, his eyes level with Mr. Wilson's. "So, go on, share the secret. What is it? What were you gonna do? Make my sister drink it?"

"Jack—" I intervene.

"Answer my question."

Mr. Wilson looks mortified. "No, of course not."

"You tried to get her to hold a rat."

"That is her word against mine." The middle-aged man glances at me uneasily, before looking back at Jack.

Jack folds his arms. "Yes," he says. "Yes, it is her word against yours. But seeing as I told Mr. Jamelson about it this morning"—I shoot Jack a look—"and he knew nothing about it, it suggests that you didn't report her walking out of her last detention early, as then you'd have to say *why*." He laughs. "And besides, sir, everyone can read you just like a book. I know what you're up to."

Well, I am glad that my brother knows what it was, because I haven't a clue. Not with this, not with any of it.

"You know what your sister's like," Mr. Wilson says. "I realize she's had a hard time, and of course over-exaggeration will be prone to such a broken individual—"

"Excuse me?" My voice is louder and more full of venom than I'd thought possible. "My illness doesn't make me exaggerate—despite what people think. So, I've no idea what you're actually talking about."

It looks as if smoke is going to come billowing out of Mr. Wilson's huge ears and beaky nose at any moment. "I will *not* tolerate this kind of behavior from any students." He looks at me, fuming, as he barks, "How *dare* you bring your brother to gang up on me. I am not scared of either of you. You are pathetic children. And you are vile." He jabbed his finger at me. "Bringing your brother with you just because you didn't like having to hold that wild rat. I'd washed it first."

"I thought you were too scared to hold it?"

He levels a grim look at me. "Don't try to be clever with me, Jade. You know, you don't deserve a place at this school. It just shows what money can do. Neither of you, or that sister of yours, should even be here. Pathetic wretches."

"Verbal abuse," Jack mutters, his fists clenched. He steps closer to the shaking teacher. "And you just admitted to forcing Jade to hold the rat. Now, I have proof."

I freeze and look at Jack carefully. And then I see it. His phone in the top pocket of his shirt, the camera just peeping out. Only, I am sure that his phone doesn't do video any more. Not after he broke the camera on it. I mean, Jack's always breaking stuff. He's just clumsy and ham-fisted

Mr. Wilson swears. I can't tell if he's seen the phone or not. "Get out. Both of you. You scheming rats! You sly snakes!"

"Gladly." Jack grabs hold of my arm and pulls me free of Mr. Wilson's stony stare. Oh, if looks could kill.

My brother propels me through the door. I wince as his fingers close tightly around my wrist.

Jack, unable to resist one more comment, turns back slightly, looking through the doorway as he speaks: "Of course, I was only bluffing when I said I'd been to Jamelson. But, well, that's going to be straight where I'm going now." I watch him take his phone out of his pocket and glance at the screen. He presses a button. "Brilliant."

I grab his hand and we run.

"I can't believe you just did that," I pant as we round the corner.

He trips slightly, and I pull him upright, jerking his arm. "You'll thank me. He's not going to be causing you any problems now."

"Is that real though? I thought the video function didn't work."

He winks. "It doesn't. But Wilson don't need to know that, does he? But, he's gonna have to be nice to you from now on. And if he doesn't behave, we could always threaten him with taking the 'video' to Jamelson. Now, I think we should celebrate our little victory. I've got some drink in my room."

"Hmmm... I'm not convinced. He *is* going to have it in for me now, Jack."

"He wouldn't dare."

"And what about my other detentions? And my tutorials with him?"

Jack pants. "We still hold the advantage."

"Don't bank on it," I say. "He can worm his way out of anything, I'm sure. And anyway." We slow slightly. "Aren't Jamelson and he, like, best friends, anyway?"

"Two messed-up men. So, how about it? Drink?"

I shake my head. "Well, you can. That knock-off stuff you've got, I don't like it." And anyway, I need to keep a clear head. I need to message Lily and sort all this stuff out.

Jack rolls his eyes. "Oh well. More for me."

SEVENTEEN
Ariel

"GOOD LUCK." RICARDO'S VOICE IS ECHOING and distant, despite him standing right next to me. He gives me a reassuring pat on the shoulder. "You can do this."

Before today, I wouldn't say that I was a nervous person. I've always been confident, and when people said they felt sick with nerves, I never really got it. Thought it was just some exaggeration. Only, now, as I walk through the doors of the warehouse's gym, leaving my brother behind, I do get it. My legs feel weak, and I'm sweating—sweating buckets.

"Presenting Ariel Razoa for his first Trial," Tav says. She's a short woman, petite, and she looks fragile—but I know she's the strongest dispatcher we have. She is lethal—not just toward the Xphenorie, but also to humans and us.

A few years ago, there was a spot of trouble among one of our camps in Dorset. Mutiny was happening, and a civil war was brewing. Some Calerians wanted to kill the Xphenorie altogether—because it was the natural culling time for the

Fenners—and many of our people wanted to eradicate the threat altogether. The high council had refused to back it— we'd never be able to eradicate all the Fenners, and given they have a collective mind, the next time their numbers swelled, we'd be faced with millions of Xphenorie, all of whom would be angry and out to get us. We could've been wiped out.

When the Calerians advocating for killing all Fenners had refused to back down, Tav headed a team of dispatchers. They sorted out the problem.

Now, I look around the gym. It's been cleared out. Nothing in here, apart from two rows of benches where our camp's council sits. My father's in the center of the front row. There are two doors. One is the entrance Ricardo and I came through, the other leads to a store cupboard.

"In this room, there are three sources of danger," my father says, projecting his voice.

Immediately, I start looking around—even though I know that the time for the trial won't officially start until he rings the bell. It's sitting on a small coffee table in front of the seated council, inches away from my father's left knee.

"Once your trial has begun, you are to locate these sources of danger, decide the order in which you will eliminate these threats, and then carry out your plan to neutralize them. You will do so in as timely a manner as possible, and before death strikes."

Before death strikes? My gaze jolts up. What? Who's going to be at risk in this? Usually, with the trials, some of our people will pretend to be Fenners—the Xphenorie. They'll lurk in the background, dressed in black, and we have to disarm them. But now, I can't see anyone else in here. And there's never been any mention of death striking in any previous trial. Or at least no one's told me of that anyway.

I drag in more air, breathing quickly.

"Your trial begins now," my father says, and he rings the bell.

The door opens, and I get ready to see whichever Calerians are going to be playing the Xphenorie this time. Because of course it's going to be the same. It can't not be. My father must just be being dramatic and theatrical, saying that death may strike.

But the people who push through the doors are not Calerians.

My eyes widen as two humans stumble in. Both are young adults. The girl has bright purple hair and looks slightly younger than the man, who's tall and muscular and looking very pissed off.

"What the fuck?" the man yells. He's got tattoos that mark him as a Greylake.

Shit. Gangs. The council have brought gang members in here?

Gangs.

I stare at her. The woman. Blood-soaked hair. Pink and purple flesh, pulled out in handfuls. Stare at it, how it splatters the pavement. Terror on her face. But at least you can see she was a person. The…the other one, the man… He's just mangled flesh and congealed blood and muscles and bone…

Did the gang members know what these people are? Or, rather, were? Was this a hate-crime based on our species, or just a coincidence?

I jolt.

No. Can't flashback now. Can't—

The door shuts behind them, and the lightbulb flickers over their heads. Their eyes fix on me, thunder on their faces.

"Who the fuck do you think you are?" the man shouts, looking around at us. He turns to the council, sitting in the row. "What the hell is this?"

"You better let us go," the girl snarls. She pats her pockets, but her hands remain empty.

Both of them glare at me.

I take a deep breath. Do they know what we are? I risk a glance at my father, but he just taps his watch while keeping stern eyes on me.

Right—gang members. They're the threat. They're dangerous for each other—and in all other instances when our existence has been discovered, we've been hunted down by gangs like this. We've been knifed, drowned, shot. In New York, during the last 'discovery' of us, the gangs turned on us, running the witch hunts. It's people like this that come after us first—before the well-mannered citizens also form their own groups and join the witch hunts.

"Hey, I'm talking to you!" the man shouts, looking at my father and—

And then there's a gun. The Greylakes man has got a gun. He whips it out of nowhere and I spring into action.

I run at him, calling fire to my fingers. I brandish my flames toward him, managing to get between him and the council. My hands are my weapons in front of me, but he still holds the gun. Is it loaded? Would my father really allow a loaded gun in the hands of a gangster for my trial?

"Fucking freak." The man's eyes are wide, and I see his finger move toward the trigger.

I throw my fire at him, lunging with my whole body a split second later. I hit him, and the gun goes off. My breaths burst from me as I tackle the man, all the while listening for screams, the sounds of gasps and injuries—or worse.

But I can't hear anything other than the Greylake man yelling. I call up stronger fire, and I burn him.

He screams—a roar that dives under my skin. Guilt flashes through me. But the humans have to be in on it, on my trial, right? And we'll give them DC-10 after. It not only puts out cold-fire but also soothes burns on humans. We can't get burnt by our special powers—but they can.

My head jerks up just as the girl flies at me. I send fire at her too, hear her scream. The man's still struggling, and I think quickly before I punch his right temple. He slumps, unconscious, and I turn, ready for the girl's attack.

But she's running—for the door. The lightbulb flickers again as she gets there, yanks it open, her purple hair flying everywhere. And then she's gone, the door closing behind her.

My head spins. I look at the unconscious man. The threat he poses has been neutralized—at least temporarily. The girl has gone, so she's not a threat to me right now. And I know that there'll be dispatchers to catch her outside of this room. Can't have her bringing back more of the gang. And our people will stop her remembering. Some of us have those abilities—like Tris and Wes, and a few of the elderly people in our camp. They said it works a bit like hypnosis, and Calerians like them are in high demand among us. They can make humans forget about us—but it takes a lot out of them. That's why we can keep our existence a secret pretty easily if it's just one or two humans who find out, but once you've got a whole police force in-the-know, it's harder. Tris, Wes, and the others can only remove memories from one human at a time, and it takes them weeks to recover from exerting that amount of force.

I frown. Three dangers—that's what my father said. Yet I've only seen two.

The light dims.

The bulb.

I jolt and look up. The bulb is the third danger.

The store cupboard is to my left. I run, praying there are bulbs in there. My legs burn, and my hands suddenly seem too big as I yank the door open and search through all the tiny boxes.

There. Spare bulbs.

I grab a pack, nearly drop it with the amount of adrenaline racing through my body.

I pull out a bulb and sprint back. How long has it been? I can't think? Dispatchers are required to eliminate threats quickly. Have I already taken too long? And the gangster isn't dead, and the girl ran. Do those count as elimination? But I don't want to kill and I can't leave to find the girl, can I?

The light flickers again as I stand under it, reaching up. My fingers shake and I pull the bulb out—plunging us into darkness.

Immediately, I feel pressure on my skin. So much pressure—and it tries to distract me, this pressure. I drop the old bulb, faintly hear the tingle of glass as it breaks, and screw the new bulb in. It gets stuck at an angle. Shit.

I jimmy it around a bit, my skin burning. I haven't absorbed yet today—God, why didn't I do that?

"Come on," I mutter, moving the bulb more aggressively now, and—

Click.

Light—bright light, fluorescent—blares out.

I exhale, looking back at where the gangster man lies. He's still there, not moving, unconscious.

"Good." My father's voice rings, echoes in the room.

I turn and look at the council. None of them show any signs of discomfort from the momentary darkness. They were prepared for it—unlike me.

"An adequate time," my father says. "Slow, but nonetheless adequate. Points have been deducted though for letting the girl escape and for not killing the man."

"Not *killing* him?" I stare at him. "I wasn't going to murder a human for nothing. Even a…even gang members."

My father frowns. Does he think I'm weak for that? Should I want to kill them? Get revenge for what other gangs have done to our people? For what this gang could do to us in the future?

Tav, next to him, clears her throat. "Despite the penalty for one threat escaping and one not being dealt with in a more permanent manner, your quick thinking and action in replacing the bulb was good. This is a pass."

A pass.

My shoulders lighten, feel softer.

I passed?

"You'll start work immediately as a dispatcher," Tav says. "You will comb the streets, on the lookout for the Xphenorie and for any humans who pose a threat to us. You will do all you can to protect us and guard our existence."

I start to smile—then stop. We are killing humans now?

I start to speak, but my father cuts me off.

"Don't get arrogant about it, Ariel," he says. That's what he thinks I was going to say? Something showing arrogance and not repulsion at the idea of being used to kill humans? "This isn't a victory worthy of celebrating. We are desperate for numbers."

EIGHTEEN
Elliot

I OPEN MY EYES, SQUINTING INTO THE LIGHT of a streetlight and—

"What the fuck?"

I jolt up, disgust rippling through me as I realize there is a rat in front of me. The rat is eating a kebab. A kebab that looks very much like my favorite type of kebab. Or at least what was my favorite, because there's no way in hell now that I'll be eating that again.

The rat pulls the kebab away from me. Shudders run through me, and I rub my head. What the fuck has happened? I look left and then right. I'm on a road, but where? I take a few steps forward. Pain thrums through me. What the hell?

Was I jumped? I can't remember a fucking thing.

I brush my clothes down, then pat my pockets. My knife's there and my wallet. The wad of cash, separate. And my phone. But the gun's gone.

"Fuck," I mutter. Robbie's gonna kill me. I look around. It's dark, save for that streetlight—and the next ones farther down the road. My vision's blurry and my head feels strange, a little too light. Not like I'm high though.

But I can't remember anything.

I flex my arms—pain at the top of them. My biceps and—

Pain. It's like it's been unleashed over me, a rush of it as soon as I think of the word. It sears up across my face, my hands. My stomach. I stare at my hands, bring them closer to my face. Blisters. Burns. What the fuck? How didn't I notice them before now?

There's a metallic taste in my mouth. A dull throbbing in the base of my skull. Who would attack me—burn me—and take my gun but not the cash? Not my phone? It doesn't make sense.

I turn and start walking. Need to get home.

"MATE, YOU LOOK LIKE YOU NEED TO GET TO A hospital," Robbie says when I pound on the door, even though I've got my keys. But my fingers are hurting now. Bleeding too, because of the burns.

I shoulder my way inside and collapse on the sofa. My heart pounds, and I catch a glimpse of myself in the mirror on the far wall. My face looks...mangled. Red fleshy bits, with whiter bits of flesh too. And shiny bits.

"What happened?" Robbie asks. We've shared a flat ever since I became his second. Perks of the job.

"I don't fucking know." I breathe hard and lean forward, tilt my face to the right a bit so I can see in the mirror better. But it's not sinking in. "I got jumped, maybe? Can't remember. Woke up on a road. Back of town. No one else there."

"You lost the gear?"

I shake my head, pulling the bags out. And the cash. The phone. "Haven't got the gun though. That's gone." I stand up. "Man, I need a slash."

"What the fuck do you mean you've lost the gun?" Robbie steps right up to me, breathing hot breath all over me. He always does that when he's angry. Intimidation tactic. He taught me to do that too—one of the first things I learned when I was old enough to officially be a Greylake.

"Mate, I don't know. I must've been jumped—like I said."

"By Devils?" Robbie shakes his head. "Man, they're gonna pay for this. But you, El, you're gonna get that gun back. That's my gun—*my* numbers are on it. I ain't havin' that end up in the wrong hands. You got me?"

I nod. "Of course. Now move. I really need to piss."

Robbie steps to the side, and I move past him, get to the small bathroom. Smells damp and moldy in here as usual. The whole flat's not great. But it's ours. No more living with Ma in the cramped flat with that pig of a landlord. When Dad went inside, we lost the really nice apartment we had. Couldn't afford the rent. And then even when I started making good money, Ma didn't want to move again. Just stays in that shitty flat with the shitty landlord. I, on the other hand, got out as soon as I could.

When I've finished in the bathroom, Robbie's on the phone. He speaks louder and louder, more animated, cursing.

I slump down in the chair by the TV and turn it on with the remote. Flick through the channels, but nothing's grabbing me and I find myself looking in the mirror again. Are these real burns? Shouldn't they be hurting more?

I reach up and touch my face. Wince as fresh pain dives into me. Fucking proper weird this. I mean, I can't actually have been burnt or had acid thrown at me—that would be *intense* pain. I'd be screaming and screaming, right? Robbie's right—I would need a hospital in that case.

But this… A painful rash? Fuck, who knows?

"I'll call you back," Robbie says, his voice infiltrating my brain. He doesn't sound happy.

I look up at him.

"It was Annabelle," he says, then he turns to me. "She says Kelley-Anne's just got back to the school, not remembering a thing, and has been burnt on her face."

"Kelley-Anne?"

"You two together again?" He looks me up and down. "Thought you liked the other girl."

I wave his question away. "Kelley-Anne's got burns too?"

Kelley-Anne's nothing to me. She was only a bit of fun last year. That's all. Hadn't known that Annabelle had such a hot sister. What was I supposed to do? Ignore her? Kelley-Anne was the one seducing me. And it's all biological need, innit?

Robbie shrugs. "Apparently. And she's lost some of her knives, too. You know the expensive ones she had made, with all the detail?"

"With the gem stones in the handle?" I ask. We all use silver knives—trademark for the Greylakes, really—but a lot of us get ours personalized. Usually just little engravings.

Nothing fancy. But try telling that to Kelley-Anne. That girl's extravagant. I should know.

Robbie nods. "Look more like a theater prop than anything else. Well, she said she had two on her, and they'd both gone. But we ain't havin' any of this, right? Nah, you need to remember, mate. This is them fire-people. Like what those rumors said—only they ain't rumors if they're goin' after us. Mate, you need to remember which person did this to you, and then we're going after them. All of us. No one hurts the Greylakes and gets away with it."

NINETEEN
Jade

THE NEXT MORNING FINDS NIKA AND I wandering the outskirts of the park field—the one where Jack and I saw the column fire. I begged her to come out here after I read over my notes on the fire and the fire-people this morning. My notes hadn't disappeared this time. And I just felt like I needed to be here, like maybe it could jog my memory a bit.

Wrapping my coat tighter around my body, I look into the center, expecting to see the magnificent flames. But it has all gone completely. The only signs of the fire are the slightly charred grass and the tire-marks of the vans.

"I still don't get why they'd ask you *not* to talk about it," Nika says. "It makes no sense. Because surely if you tell someone not to do something, they do it?"

"Well, yeah," I mutter. "Something's going on. Has to be."

I scan the field for anything I might've missed. But my first observation seems to have been thorough, and I don't spot anything else. Disappointment wallows big inside me. I was so certain when I woke up this morning, thinking about the notes I'd made and what I could remember, that I'd find something out here. Something concrete. Or maybe the marks on my wrist would sting more, or reveal something. But they don't. There's nothing. Nothing at all.

Maybe I'm just putting too much thought into this? Using it as a distraction?

Lily's not speaking to me. She ignored me all last night in the basement and again this morning at breakfast, before she then accused me—very publicly, in the canteen—of spying on her. I wasn't, but she insisted I was, and her friends turned sour gazes on me.

"Anyway," Nika says. "I still don't get why we're even out here. Not that I mind getting away to have a cigarette, but you're acting weird, Jade. You have been the last few days."

Since the fire.

"Everything's weird now," I say. I press my lips together for a moment. "You know these fire-people? I think they are real."

"Girl, if that was true, there'd be more publicity. Nah, it just sounds like something you'd read in one of those books."

"You and your vampire books," I mutter, giving her a mischievous smile.

"Oh, come on! You like them too."

I raise my eyebrows. "I'm not *obsessed* with them. And anyway, contemporary thrillers are more my thing."

Nika shrugs, and we both lapse into a soft kind of silence. I think about Lily. I can't stop worrying about her. As Nika and I were walking here, I sent her a message. I apologized. I look at the message now. No reply, but she's left me on read. And we need to talk. I need to know what she's doing, whether she's keeping the baby or not. I need to be there for her.

"You could do some research about that fire," Nika says a little while later, as we sign back into school. "Like, you and Jack both saw that so we can say that's real. And you could probably find stuff online. See if anyone else has thought it strange that they're being asked not to say stuff about it."

"If they were asked not to say stuff about it, then surely they wouldn't make a website about it?"

She shrugs again. "Well, *you* didn't exactly obey the rules."

"I only told you," I point out.

"But Mace knows."

"Jack told Macey."

"Oh, well, I won't tell anyone," Nika says. "I doubt he will either. Your secret's safe!" She fake-cackles. "Anyway, Mace'll probably want to help you research the fire." She gives me a side-eyed look. "You'd probably make his day if you said you wanted to do research with him."

IT TURNS OUT THAT MACEY *IS* VERY KEEN TO research the fire too, when I suggest it just after dinner, and even offers me his MacBook, while he is fixing the Wi-Fi problems that my laptop has been having lately. Jack comes along too, saying he'll 'help,' but really I think he's hoping Nika will be there as well. She's not though—she's got a late meeting with her tutor. Something about the personal statement she's writing for her university applications. Nika knows exactly what she wants to do. She wants to study chemistry, somewhere in London, and then be a science teacher. And I haven't got a clue what I want to do. I don't even know if I want to go to university. I can never decide.

I push that worry away though and concentrate on my research on the fire. But the results that Google offers aren't proving to be very fruitful.

"Yes, come on," I mutter as I click onto the twenty-third link in Google's search results. We're in the common room and the Internet signal is annoyingly weak. In the other tab, I've got Messenger open on my conversation thread with Lily. She's still not replied. She hasn't even been online since this morning. I sent her more messages when I noticed she was missing from dinner. When I asked Jack if he'd seen her earlier, he'd just shaken his head, hadn't seemed worried. But why would he be? He doesn't know she's pregnant, and I can't say anything without breaking my promise to Lily.

But if she's still not replied soon, well, maybe I'll have to say something. Because what if she's done something? Still, I guess she can't actually be missing. It must just me she's avoiding, because if she wasn't in lessons at all, the teachers would've put out an alert or something. Whereas sixth-formers are allowed to leave the campus on their free lessons and after school, the lower school still have strict attendance rules. Teachers are constantly taking registers for younger students. Less so for us.

"You found anything about the fire, then?" Jack asks lazily, sprawled across the sofa opposite.

Aisha is cross-legged on the floor, next to Macey and my laptop, leaning against the sofa and looking half asleep. On the other side of the room, Craig and a few others are playing what they call 'Strip Hangman.' I don't know how it works—except that all the girls seem to be losing. And possibly on purpose too.

I stare as Lauren takes off her blouse, revealing her cami top underneath—and a lot of cleavage. Craig and several of the guys are ogling her. I feel myself getting embarrassed for Lauren's sake, just looking—but Lauren doesn't seem to be embarrassed. She's smiling. It's like she wants to be looked at. And there it is again—the thing that makes me different. Because I never want to be looked at. I'm not comfortable around people unless I've got all my clothes on. Even sharing a room with Nika, I go into the bathroom to change. And I can't imagine ever wanting to undress in front of a guy. Or a girl, for that matter.

"Jade?" Macey looks at me.

They're all looking at me.

"You said you'd found something?" Jack asks.

My eyes take in the words on the screen. "Yeah, there's this girl, or woman, called Simone Crickette. And she doesn't seem to know how to use punctuation, or the difference between 'there' and 'their.'" I scowl. "Anyway, she says she's seen a fire and was asked not to say any more about it."

Jack snorts. "She's doing a brilliant job."

"Oh, she's from Texas, but she lives in Italy now. And it was five years ago."

Macey looks up. "So, it's been happening for ages, and not just in England either? Bit odd. Definitely something going on."

"Hmm…maybe…" Jack makes a sort-of shrugging motion. "But you're probably reading too much into it."

I read the next few paragraphs and then look back at my brother.

"What?" he asks.

"Hers was slightly different to ours," I say. I roll my eyes. "Oh, this is crazy. She says she saw *someone* controlling the fire, like creating it." I think of Craig's words: *Anyone who can get fire to erupt from their fingers is dangerous…*

"The fire-people." Macey sounds breathy. "A connection, at last! Yes!"

"It's not a connection," Jack mutters. "It's just some batty lady's words that you're getting excited about."

My attention returns to Simone Crickette's blog. I blink a few times. Wow, she could really do with spell-checking her entries before posting them.

so yesterday this really crazy thing happened there i was just walking my neighbors dogs and that little staffy one was barking its head off and i'd just crossed into the park, and the ground rumbled. like at first i thought it was an earthquack and then i thought no! it can't be. and the dogs was going mad. i'd let them off there leads and they was running about yapping and snapping. And i'd just got meself a little fag out and as i was lightin it this huge fire came up from the ground!!!!! like it just appeared. pretty magical it was. and them little peeps controlling the fire appeared next to it runnin about they all were screaming and shouting. and the police and them nickety pickery peeps ran everywhere like. and the police people had this like potion and it made

*the fire go out and all the fire peeps was screaming. and
then they was escorted to this little car and they all got in.
and my dogs was going mad especially that staffy...*

"Seriously!" I grumble. "How hard is it just to use
commas and proper grammar? There's not even one capital
letter."

Jack laughs. "Yeah, well, you're a grammar nerd, so what
can you expect?"

"Well, certainly not 'nickety pickery peeps.'" I shake my
head and look back at the screen. My head hurts just from
reading the poor grammar and spelling. But then I focus on
a sentence.

And then they was escorted to this little car.

Does that mean the police really are kidnapping the fire-
people?

"Oh, just find another website, J, there's no point in
upsetting yourself over some person's grammar that you've
never met." Jack sounds annoyed. "Anyway, I'm hungry." He
looks down at Macey, who is still fiddling with my laptop.
He's taken the battery out as well as something else which I
have no idea what it is. "You hungry?"

Macey shakes his head, and Jack raises his eyebrow at me.

"No," I say. "Jack, you've only just had dinner."

"Yeah, and you didn't see the size of that bit of quiche she
gave me? It was tiny. How is a growing lad like me s'posed to
grow if we're fed the portions that petite girls eat? It just
doesn't make sense? Like, the same happened at lunch too—

it was that same woman serving, and she gave me barely two chips really. I mean, she even gave Lily a larger bit than me. I bet she didn't eat it all anyway. Waste of good food," he grumbles.

"Wait, you've seen Lily?" My breaths quicken. "How was she?"

"Moody and sullen as ever," he says. "But at least she's not sneaking out with Elliot now."

"That you know of," Macey mutters.

"What?" I look at him. "What do you know?"

He shrugs. "Hey, I'm just saying. It wouldn't surprise me if she was still seeing him."

"She has no reason to," Jack says. "She hates him."

But I love him. Lily's words echo through my mind.

"Not as simple as that," Macey says, looking at me. "Love never is. And we're teenagers. Everything's dramatic with us, right?"

I chew my bottom lip. Would Lily have gone to see Elliot, to see that he was okay after that supposed abduction? Sneaked out to tell him about the pregnancy? And how would one of the biggest gangsters of the Greylake Gang react to that? Would he hurt her?

My heart lurches. "Do you know where she is now?"

Jack shrugs. "Basement?"

I get up.

"Uh, I haven't finished your laptop yet," Macey says.

"It's okay. I won't be long."

Jack seems totally oblivious to how tense I am as we leave—he walks part of the way with me, on his way back to the canteen—and I'm glad. Don't want him asking questions. Not at the moment anyway.

I make my way to the basement. The atmosphere in there is wholly different to that of the last room; loud music is bursting out of the stereo, and some kids in the year below are having a fighting tournament in the part of the room out of view from the doorway. There are lots of excited shouts and cries.

"All right, Jade?"

Craig's voice behind me makes me jump. I hadn't realized he was behind me. He followed me from the common room? Still, it's not really following—a lot of people come here in the evening from the common room anyway. It's not like he's stalking me.

Stalking.

My eyes widen, and I think of the conversation I overheard the morning after Jack and I found the fire. A man was on the phone, talking about me. Was that Craig? Has he been following me, keeping an eye on me all that time?

"Uh, yeah," I say, turning. I try to look him up and down, as if that'll tell me what his intentions are—but of course he doesn't.

He smiles easily, and he's trying to talk to me, but I'm scanning the faces in here until I spot Lily. *There.* She's at the back of the room, laughing at something Anna's said to her. Relief fills me. She hasn't sneaked off to Elliot's then. At last, not now.

"And I swear Kas's nose has never been quite the same since," Craig says, laughing.

I turn back to him, absolutely no idea about what he's now talking about—other than Kas's nose.

He smiles, and he touches my arm lightly. I look down at his hand. What is he doing? He's still laughing. "Did you—"

"Who has taken it?" a voice suddenly screams.

I jump, turning, and see Kelley-Anne standing by the doorway. She is shaking, and her purple hair is lopsided. She swears loudly. One hand is covering one side of her face.

"Right, so who's got it?" Her tone is aggressive and accusing. "No one?" She pauses, and we all just stare at her. "Well, someone must fucking have it!"

"Um? Are you okay?" Rose—a tight-lipped girl from the year below—approaches her.

"Get away from me." Kelley-Anne throws herself down in the nearest seat and crosses her legs, flicking off her heels. They fly through the air and one of them hits me.

I grit my teeth, but I don't say anything. She still hasn't removed her hand from her face.

Someone turns the music off, and the room's suddenly too quiet.

Craig takes a step forward. "Kelley?"

"Have you got it?" She is up in a second, darting toward him. For a second, I think she's going to hit him.

"What the hell's up with you?" The words are out of my mouth before I can stop them.

Kelley-Anne turns to me, shaking. She brings an unsteady hand up to her bright hair, and pulls it free of the messy ponytail. "Shut up, Taylor." She laughs. "I know you wouldn't have it—not with your *condition*." She says the word like having MCAS is a joke.

"Hey," Craig says. "Watch it, Kelley." He looks back at me. "Jade's not done anything to you. So don't take whatever brawl you've had with Kyle out on her."

"My name is Kelley-*Anne*. Not Kelley. Kelley-*Anne*."

Rose shrinks back as Kelley-*Anne* stands and throws her arms out.

"And you know nothing about me. How dare you even say that. How—"

The main lights flicker on. I see a Year 10 student by the switches. I blink as light fills the room and—

I gasp as I see Kelley-Anne's face.

"Oh my God. Is that a burn?" I'm moving toward her, like I'm a magnet. "Kelley-Anne?"

Her hand is back up to her face in an instant, covering the mark. "Whoever has taken my fucking foundation is going to get it later. I *need* to cover this fucking thing up. It's not fucking funny."

"No one said it was," Rose says. She winces as Kelley-Anne glares at her. "But what is it? On your face."

"*Is* it a burn?" someone else asks.

"No—it's fine. I can cover it," she growls. "And if one of you hadn't taken my foundation, you'd all be none-the-wiser."

"Wait—how long's that been there?" I ask. Because now I realize it—it's the same type of marks that I've got on my wrist. Only hers are bigger and across her whole face.

"That looks bad," Craig says.

"Fine. Everyone, take a look." Kelley-Anne jabs her pointy nail at her skin and pulls it. "This is proof that those fucking fire-people exist. And they're fucking dangerous. All of them. They should be locked up." She looks me dead in the eye and nods, and then turns to Rose and another girl, still fuming as she makes eye contact with everyone.

"The fire-people," someone says, "like in that report?"

"But the police haven't confirmed that they exist yet—"

"They exist all right," Kelley-Anne says darkly. "And they deserve to die."

"Hey," I exclaim. "You can't say that. They're still people."

I think back to that thing that I'd read on Simone Crickette's. About how she said there were people controlling the fire and how they'd been escorted away. Could it be because they were dangerous? *Anyone who can get fire to erupt from their fingers is dangerous.* I glance across at Craig. His face is set hard, and he frowns.

Kelley-Anne turns on me. "Oh, so you're sucking up to them now, are you?" The burn on her face is ragged, but it looks old. "I should've guessed."

"How long have you had that burn?" Craig asks suddenly.

"Does it matter?" She snorts. "Those 'people' are still out there, running loose. They're still dangerous. They're still trying to hurt us."

"You need to calm down," Craig says. Two of his friends back him up.

"I am not calming down until I get my foundation back and all the fire-people are dead."

TWENTY
Ariel

"I CAN'T BELIEVE THEY'RE NOT TAKING ME," I mutter to Lucy. "All morning, I've sat in that briefing, and then I'm one of the few who aren't even chosen for it."

Lucy shrugs. "I wasn't chosen either."

"You're not the leader's son though." I shake my head. I'll never understand my father or the problem that he apparently has with me.

When I'd heard we were planning a break-out mission—to rescue my mother and the others who are imprisoned—I'd assumed I'd be involved. My body started buzzing with adrenaline.

Until my father closed the meeting—after I listened to all that meticulous planning—only to say that I would not be involved. Apparently, I'm needed to look after the camp. And, sure, while we do need some dispatchers here to guard the camp and protect the Calerians who aren't dispatchers, I'd really thought that I'd be going out there.

"My own mother's one of them, one of those imprisoned," I say. "It's personal for me—and that gives me the best motivation out of all of us to want to rescue them."

Lucy casts her gaze down. She shrugs. "Maybe that's why—it's too personal."

"But my father's going. No, he just didn't want me to graduate, that's obvious. He's never going to send me out on any missions."

"Maybe he's protecting you," she says, drawing me closer. Her touch is light but enticing. And the level of distracting where I really have to concentrate on what we're talking about.

"No, as if." I shake my head.

She stares up at me with her big eyes. She leans in closer, and then presses her lips against mine. "It'll be okay."

Okay? How can it be okay?

"And I'm glad you'll be safe," she says, before kissing me deeper.

I know what she's doing because she always does this—seduces me whenever I want to talk about something important. Something deep.

But, as usual, I'm helpless to it.

And, anyway, I think, maybe Lucy isn't the best person to be talking about this to. Not like she has any influence. No, I'll talk to Ricardo later. He could maybe have a word with our father. Yes, I'll talk to my brother. I've got to go over to that side of Camp anyway—it's my turn to feed the rats tonight.

FOUR HOURS LATER, AFTER A FRUITLESS conversation with Ricardo in which he says nothing could be done to change our father's mind, hundreds of beady eyes stare at me. Revulsion pulls through me as I stare back. I don't like rats—none of us do, really. But for some reason, they have masking properties. They can stop Xphenorie—if any are around—from detecting us easily. Hence why we breed them. Why we feed them. Why we look after them.

Only I think it's getting out of control.

The rats aren't scared of us anymore. That's the problem. They're getting bold, adventurous.

One clambers over my foot and I shudder, feeling its little feet on mine even though I've got Wellingtons on.

"Here you go," I mutter, scattering the food over them. Leftover scraps of vegetables and chicken bones with grease and sinewy pieces of meat still attached. Collected it from the kitchen on the way down here.

I empty out the two baskets, throwing the food away from me as much as possible. The rats go mad for it. They always do.

TWENTY-ONE
Elliot

"WANT SOME MORE?" ROBBIE OFFERS ME A baggie of weed, and I take it, pocket it deep in my jeans.

Spencer snorts—because Robbie always offers me freebies and never him—but Annabelle and Kelley-Anne just look annoyed.

"Are we not even going to talk any more about it?" Kelley-Anne asks. Her voice is a whine—she's a petulant whiner, always complaining about something. Even after we had sex that one time, she was complaining. All because I said that it didn't mean anything. But try telling a seventeen-year-old girl that.

Anyway, she should've known better. Everyone in Greylakes knows me and Lily are for real. We're going to be together no matter what. Kelley-Anne should've realized the hook-up for what it was and all it was ever going to be—just a one-off.

"Yeah," Annabelle says, her arm going around her sister. The two of them look alike, but thank God Annabelle ain't a whiner too. She's solid, that one. Good street sense too. Not like Kelley-Anne—who she now points at. "Something burned my sister's face. And yours." She nods at me.

My burns have healed massively in the last couple days, but I've still got some pretty bad-looking ones on my biceps. My hoody covers them though, and they only hurt a little when the fabric is against them. Not a big deal. Though I suppose Kelley-Anne's do look more severe. Her skin around her nose and mouth is red and rough, almost scaly-looking. I wonder if her face will scar. Robbie's pretty sure mine won't.

"And we all know it's them fucking fire-people, thinking they can get away with whatever," Kelley-Anne says. "Has to be."

"And we're sorting it," Robbie says. "We got the boys on it."

"Sorting it?" Annabelle raises an eyebrow. "Why aren't *we* sorting it? Hell, I want to kill the ones who did this to Kelley-Anne. No one touches my sister and gets away with it."

Robbie laughs. "Girl, you don't want to dirty your pretty hands with them. Anyway, that's what our boys are for. Do the work for us that we don't wanna do. If someone needs sorting, they do it."

"But this isn't just another gang," Kelley-Anne says. "How can you not see that? They're dangerous, these people. More so than any gang. We should all be out there, hunting them down, killing them *right now*. Not sitting here doing nothing!"

"We're getting a plan in place," Robbie says. "It's going to be big, so don't you worry. You'll see."

TWENTY-TWO
Jade

THAT NIGHT, SLEEP DOESN'T COME EASILY. FOR hours, I find myself staring at the whitewashed ceiling, counting invisible sheep, while Nika snores softly from across the room. But counting nonexistent sheep doesn't work—mainly because I keep thinking about the fire-people. My mind is just too active. I see generic figures running across mountains and volcanoes, spreading fires, see their shapes and shadows on my ceiling. I think of the old woman who grabbed me, and I realize I'm holding onto my wrist. I wonder if those gray patches are ever going to go. Tears pierce my eyes—what if they're permanent? And it sounds vain, worrying about that—but I feel self-conscious enough of myself already. I used to like wearing short-sleeved tops, but I need to hide these marks. And sure, it's not hot now so I can wear hoodies, no problem. But what will happen in the summer?

I roll onto my side and my tears spill. And I know it's stupid and selfish of me thinking about my marks when Kelley-Anne's are more severe. They're on her face and—

The door creaks open. There's a person, a person *there*.

I jolt, then relax. It'll just be Nika. But then my eyes fall on Nika's sleeping form in her bed next to me. She's not standing by the door. Someone else is.

I make some sort of incoherent noise as I scramble up into a sitting position, the covers wrapped round my legs. The person's still standing in the doorway—watching me. A dark figure. Can't see who it is.

"Who…who are you?" My voice wavers. My heart pounds.

The person doesn't answer.

"N-Nika," I hiss, reaching across the gap between our beds, to shake her awake.

But she doesn't stir.

I shout her name now, and my voice cracks even more. My heart pounds. Nika doesn't move. Oh God. Is she drugged or something? And who is this?

"It's okay," the person says. Soft, female voice. She steps closer and—

It's *her*.

The old woman from the fire. She looks at me. Her skin looks pale in the dim light, almost like it's creating its own light. Clouds of gray hair float effortlessly around her shoulders, but her clothes are dripping. Wet. I see the water soaking the carpet.

"Stay away from me." I shove the covers back, then I'm by Nika's bed, shaking her even harder, while my eyes are on the woman. "Nika, wake up!"

The old woman laughs, and then she steps closer.

"Stay back!" I yell.

She shuts the door.

Adrenaline fires through me and I look around. A weapon, I need a weapon. I grab the book from Nika's bedside table. It's not a thick one though, but I hold it as threateningly as I can as I scream—scream for help.

"I wouldn't do that," the old woman hisses. Suddenly, she's right in front of me.

I recoil back, swaying, and she grabs my arm but I yank it away from her. My blood pounds in my ears and I glance at my arm. More marks?

"Get out." I put as much venom in my words as possible.

"No, daughter," she says.

"I'm not your daughter! Just go."

"I am here to check on you, Jade," she says. "To see how you are doing."

I throw the book at her, and she ducks—ducks so quickly like she isn't actually old. The book lands on the carpet. A loud thud. My heart pounds. Someone's got to have heard that.

I make some sort of gulping noise. "Get out of my room."

But she doesn't, she just peers right into my eyes. I take a step back. My stomach twists.

"Go," I hiss.

The corners of her mouth lift up. "Yes, you're doing well. And soon you will have to join us, help us, save us… You were hand-picked for the purpose…just like my son."

"Get *out*."

She raises one hand toward me, palm flat. "I come with a warning—"

"No, just get out." And I scream and scream and scream.

"Jade! Stop it! You need to know this—it's important. The gangs are against us again." Her voice is a sudden shrill sound. "Join us, help us, save us."

I shove her back toward the door and—

Pain. My hands. No, my head. The light—it's getting darker, but it was already dark, and this doesn't... This isn't... My breaths make rasping sounds. I clap my hands to my neck, feel the scab from where Elliot cut me, and... And the woman's still speaking but I can't make out her words. It's just...

What's going on? What's...

My heart stutters, and I... I can't breathe. I can't—

And then there's nothing.

I WAKE, HEART POUNDING. MY BREATHS ARE too quick and I sit up, my head spinning and—

I'm on my bed, covers over me and—

The woman. Where's the woman?

But it's just me and Nika in here. And it's getting light. I look at the clock. The red numbers blink. 05.01. What? It wasn't... It...

"Nika," I hiss as I get out of bed.

She stirs and I hiss her name louder.

"What?" she mumbles, sitting up.

"There was a woman here," I say, and I'm searching the room, opening the wardrobes.

Nika grunts. "What?"

"An old woman—the same one I saw at the fire…who did this." I yank my pajama sleeve up and show her my right wrist. The marks seem to sting.

Nika squints at me, then rubs her eyes. "Jade… What time even is it?"

"Five," I say, "but look. Look at my wrist—that was her, at the fire. And she was back. She was standing right there, and wouldn't wake up, and—"

"For God's sake, Jade, it was just a dream." She lies back down, pulling the covers over her shoulder. "Go back to sleep."

"No," I start to say, but Nika growls at me. I blink several times. Was it a dream? I was thinking about the fire-people when I was trying to get to sleep… Maybe Nika's right.

I move back toward my bed, feeling silly. God, Nika may be annoyed with me now, but she'll be laughing about this in the morning—and telling everyone about it. I take several deep breaths and—

My bare foot touches something wet.

I look down. The carpet—the carpet's wet. My eyes widen. This is where she was standing.

I look toward the door. Footprints lead to the doorway, where there's a larger wet patch, the carpet discolored.

I suck in my next breath too quickly and nearly end up choking. She was real. She was here.

And she… I blink. *Join us, help us, save us…*

She wanted my help.

TWENTY-THREE
Jade

THE NEXT MORNING, I FEEL AWFUL. I RUB MY face and look at the carpet where the wet patches were—but of course it's dry now. I frown. Did I dream the whole thing? Not just the old woman but seeing the wet carpet later too? I mean, logically, I know a stranger could not have walked in here. The school is high on security, and Nika is never a light sleeper. Unless she had been drugged—though after the woman had gone, she'd woken. I breathe out hard, don't know what to think.

Now, I feel so unsettled. I'm jittery as I get ready, and my stomach feels like it's curdling as soon as I near the canteen and smell bacon. I turn and walk the opposite way, my head pounding.

Outside, I breathe in the cool, crisp air. I tell myself I'm okay, that this is all okay. And it is. It has to be.

My first two lessons pass in a daze, and soon I find myself making my way up to my room, a ton of coursework in my arms. I kick the door shut behind me, and then just sit on my bed. My body feels too heavy. Lack of sleep? Yeah, it has to be. My eyelids get heavier and heavier as I force myself to look at my coursework, to work out an order in which to do things. History and English have the closest deadlines. I groan and stare at the printed sheets. My vision blurs and the letters are dancing.

I shake my head and try to concentrate, but I don't feel right. I stare at my hands, then roll my sleeves up. The gray marks are exactly as they always are, but my arms feel different now—it's like my blood is too hot, like something's crawling and writhing under my skin.

The door flies open, and I shriek, looking up—

It's Nika. Not the woman.

"What's going on?" Nika asks, giving me an odd look. "You okay?"

My heart pounds and I nod.

"You free now?" she asks.

"Yeah." I try to calm my heart rate. "Until fifth period."

"Good," Nika says. "Because that practice exam this morning? I've flunked it *completely*." She rolls her eyes as she looks across at me, then tugs on her hair—she always does that when she's stressed. "It was just all stuff I didn't know, stuff we haven't even learned about yet."

"Really?" I frown. "So everyone will be in the same boat?"

"Well, that's just it—I mean, maybe I missed those lessons or something because Jack and Macey both seemed to know everything. I was just sitting there, pen in hand, and I couldn't think." She runs a hand through her thick hair. "And all around me, everyone else was just writing—and the sound of the pens scratching was just really annoying me. It was like the pens were all laughing. So, yeah, I need to go out."

"Out?"

"Yeah." She nods. "Distraction and all that. And you're coming with me."

IT DOESN'T TAKE LONG TO GET TO THE BLACK benches and the falling-down fence that mark the edge of school grounds. We step over the wire fence. It's an easy way to get out of school without signing out—not that I mind signing out, in fact I prefer it. But Nika and Jack always go this way, especially if they're going out to buy cigarettes. I didn't even suggest to Nika that we sign out and use the main entrance as I know she'd have just rolled her eyes and told me to live a little.

"Free at last!" she says in an unnecessarily loud voice once we've stepped a few feet away from the fence. She opens her arms wide and looks up at the blue sky.

I smile and hug my jacket closer to me. The sun is out, and my jacket is made of black leather—very soon, I'm going to be sweating, with it clinging to me. I dig my hands into the pockets and produce a lighter. It's Jack's. I frown, then remember a couple of months ago was the last time I wore this jacket and I confiscated it from him in attempt to help him quit smoking. The attempt did not work—the next day at breakfast, he had a new one in his hand.

As we walk, Nika continues complaining about the exam—until we get to the market, that is. It's one of Nika's favorite places. One of the cheapest too. Stallholders line each side of the road, their tables dressed in tartan cloths and various products piled high. With a soft "oh!" Nika wanders over to one that's selling angora wool scarfs. I turn to the other side of the road where the food stalls are, then spot a candle stall at the end of the row. I can't smell them yet, and there's a chance they're not scented candles, but I can't risk it. Even the smells of the hot food are making me nauseous.

"You want any lightbulbs?" a woman calls out.

I turn and realize she's looking at me. She's got a small stall—and apparently it only sells one thing.

"Lightbulbs?" I raise my eyebrows.

"These are just what you need, love."

My expression slackens into a sort of grimace. "I'm fine."

I turn and find Nika right behind me. She's got a new scarf draped over her shoulders—it's a bright green and it seems to both clash and go with her hair.

"What a weirdo," Nika mutters as we head off.

"I know, right." I snort. "What is it with people trying to sell me lightbulbs?"

"What?" Nika says.

I tell her about the guy at the pharmacy and then wince— is she going to ask what I was there for? But all Nika wants to know is whether the guy was hot.

I shrug. "I don't know really."

"You don't know? Jade, come on. You must know."

I think for a moment. "Well, I suppose he was attractive." I mean, I've heard many girls going on and on about how blue eyes and blond hair and killer cheekbones are hot. So, the guy—Ariel—must fall into that category of hotness.

"You should ask him out," Nika says. "It's ages since you've hooked up."

Hooked up. I cringe. I don't like that term—and I've never actually hooked up with anyone. But last year, Nika was getting on my case about how I never seemed to fancy anyone or do anything, so I made up some lie about 'hooking up' with a guy from a club. I mean, the going to the club part was true—Jack had got us fake IDs, and Nika, he, and I went. And I ended up uncomfortable in there—too many guys were trying to grind against me—so I stepped out into a little patio area for a breather. A guy followed me out. Not in a creepy way. He looked even younger than me and was just as anxious. We chatted for a bit—he was only there to prove to his mates he was 'cool,' much like me—and then we went back inside together. Nika saw me returning with him and had given me the thumbs-up, though she'd later said I needed to have better taste: "He looked like a right weed. You can do better than that, Jadie."

Now, Nika's eyes are sparkling at the thought of me going out with the lightbulb guy.

I shake my head. "I'm too busy with school." That seems like the safest excuse to go with—because I don't want to get into discussions with her about how there must be something wrong with me when I've never felt any of the instant attraction and love-at-first-sight feelings she—and the rest of the world—is always talking about. "Anyway, aren't we going this way?"

Nika has stopped, looking down an alleyway to the left, and I hold my arm out feebly in front of me, indicating the road ahead.

"But our house is down there," she says.

God, I haven't even thought about our house in ages—well, it's not actually *our* house. It's one that was empty a couple years ago, and we thought it would be cool to meet up in it. Me and Jack and Nika and Macey. We called it our den—until there was some notice put up about trespassers and squatters. Macey and I immediately stopped going, and Jack and Nika said there was no point in just them going. So 'our house' became very quickly 'not our house.'

"We haven't been in there for ages," Nika says. "Come on. It'll be fun."

I shrug. "Well, I guess we could walk past it."

We head down the alleyway, each of us stepping over frequent piles of dog shit. There are a lot more needles and syringes on the ground too than what I remember. In fact—I remember it as being exciting, a secret place. This road just looks like a tip, like the kind of place you should strive to avoid at all costs.

Nika wraps her new scarf tighter around her neck as we near the house. It's in a row with a few others, but all of them look derelict now. Paint is peeling off all the surfaces and several houses have boarded-up windows, including most of the windows of the house that was our den.

"Must still be empty," I say, wondering why the council even put up those notices about trespassers and squatters if nothing was even going to be done about it. Not like it's been developed or anything.

"Let's see if it's changed inside." Nika crosses the road.

"Hey," I call after her. "I… I'm not sure we should?" But she doesn't stop. I rush to catch her up. "Are you sure this is a good idea? What if—"

"Oh, quit worrying! God, you can be such a spoilsport, Jadie. Jack's right, you know."

"Right?" I frown.

"Yeah, he says you're scared of everything."

"I'm not," I say, but everything inside me tightens. They've been talking about me behind my back? And my own brother thinks I'm scared of everything? My throat squeezes a bit. Maybe I am boring... I blink quickly.

Nika's at the door of the house now, and I quickly follow her. The gravel crunches underfoot, and in the distance, I hear a couple of people shouting. Guys, by the sound of it. The hairs on the back of my neck rise as I look around, but there's no sign of them here.

I look up at our house. It definitely has seen better days. The walls are covered in grunge, and graffiti plasters the lower walls. Shards of glass litter the front garden. Oh, and the front door is wide open. It looks as though it has been kicked off its hinges.

Nika picks her way around the sharp implements on the ground and steps inside. I follow.

It absolutely stinks of piss in here, and the carpet is wet and squelches beneath my feet. Oh, God. I wrinkle my nose, trying not to breathe in anything, and follow Nika into the living room. All of the furniture has completely gone—there hadn't been much left when we were here before—and what I suspect are rat droppings cover quite a high area of the grimy carpet, which is ripped in several places. I swallow quickly, then feel like I've swallowed contaminated air and nearly choke.

"This is disgusting." I shudder. I look at my shoes. How much bad stuff is now on them?

"It's not that much worse than before," Nika says. "Shall we check the other rooms?"

"Okay," I say, even though checking other rooms is definitely not what I want to do. But I lead the way out, back into the hall, and open the door on the other side. Nika's words about what Jack thinks rings in my head. Got to prove that I'm not scared.

The door creaks as I open it a few inches. I peer in the small gap. It is gloomy inside and—

Something large and dark hurtles toward me.

I slam the door shut, my heart pounding, and brace my body against the door, trying to hold it shut, waiting for the impact of...whatever it was. The dark shape inside.

But nothing comes.

"What is it?" Nika's voice holds piqued curiosity.

I turn and widen my eyes at her. *Wait*, I mouth.

But even after a few seconds of waiting, nothing hits the door. No sounds from inside the room either. But *it*— whatever it was—had been going so fast...surely it couldn't have stopped itself that quickly?

"Jade? What's in there?"

"A...a thing," I say at last, frowning. *A thing*. How pathetic does that sound? But I don't know what it was.

Nika laughs, pushes past me, and throws the door open.

"No!" I shriek, trying to shove her out of the way. My left arm hits the wall, sending a jolt of pain to my wrist, as I try to pull her out of the room.

"What the hell are you doing?"

My heart pounds and I'm dizzy, can't see. "Just get out of the room," I hiss.

"Why? There's nothing here! Don't be a—"

"Nika, come on!"

She throws the door open wider still and goes right in. Oh, God. I hover on the threshold for a few seconds before I follow her. Sticking together is best, right?

I look around, expecting to see murderers and pirates and dangerous men. Or scary dark shapes. But my eyes just fall on Nika standing in the middle of the floor. There's a cobweb in her hair. And there's nothing else in here. But I know I saw something.

I swallow hard. The air is gritty. Still that rancid smell of urine.

"Well, this is boring," she says. "And the piano's gone. I told you we should've taken that back to the dorm."

"Yeah, because no one would've noticed us hauling a grand piano up there," I mutter as I look around again, searching every nook and cranny for something bad. It is cold and clammy in this room—well, it is in the whole house—and it doesn't feel right at all. It doesn't even feel like the same house we visited so many times before. Even though it was empty then, it had a cozy feeling. An exciting feeling, because it was our secret place. But this... This is just *cold*. And that dark shape I saw?

I breathe out slowly as I think of my nightmare... Maybe I had been awake then, and I was just seeing things. Like that woman, and this shape. Hallucinating.

"We should go, Nika." My voice cracks. "Now. I mean, we'll miss dinner if we're not back soon and—"

"Come on, Jadie. Let's check the kitchen. And upstairs."

Gingerly, I follow Nika as she explores the house with glee on her face as if it's her first time being here. Several times, I turn and look behind me, sure I've heard something. But each time, I see nothing. Only the dirty walls and the filthy carpet and—

"Oh my God. Is that blood?" I point to a particularly large stain on the wall.

Nika turns and looks. "Probably not. Let's hope not."

"I wish Jack were here." The words escape my lips before I realize I've even thought the thought, and immediately, I feel silly. They already think I'm scared of everything, so why am I just proving that point?

I shouldn't need my brother to make me feel safe—only I do. I know I do. I was terrified when we paid Elliot that visit. But Jack was calm. He had almost a kind of excitement in his eyes as we walked there. He *wanted* a fight. I didn't. There's no way I would've gone on my own.

But I am scared. I'm scared of a lot of things.

"Look, Nika," I say, trying to muster as much strength in my voice as possible. "We don't know what's here. There could be other squatters. This is stupid and dangerous. We should go. Come on. Let's leave."

I turn away, determined not to look at the bloodstain, but of course I see it out of the corner of my eye and shudder. And the blood just confirms my point—this feels wrong, feels dangerous.

"Wimp," she shouts after me.

"No, I'm just being sensible." I carry on walking, hating leaving her in there, but part of me is sure that if she thinks I'm leaving, she'll follow.

Instead, I hear the unmistakable sounds of her going up the stairs as I step outside. *Great.*

"Come on—Nika! I'm going." My voice cracks. "Goodbye!"

She doesn't reply, and I walk a little down the path, each step slow. Then I reach the end. I turn back, expecting to see her—but she's not in the doorway.

Why does she even want to come here anyway? It makes no sense. I roll my eyes again and wait. I shout—but nothing. Knowing her, she's probably watching me secretly from a gap in the boarded window to see if I am bluffing. Well, two can play at this game.

I leave the pathway and head back up the alleyway, toward the main road and—

The sound of Nika screaming fills my ears.

TWENTY-FOUR
Jade

FOR A SECOND, I FREEZE. THEN I RUN TOWARD
the house. My heart pounds.

Nausea grabs me as I race into the hallway. My fingers are
ice-cold but my core is burning. I look around, shouting
Nika's name. Nothing. The stairs—*right*.

My thighs burn with lactic acid. She's up here. "Nika? Are
you okay?"

I reach the landing—and step in a puddle of something.
My stomach curdles. Oh, God.

The floor creaks. I look about. The upstairs is even worse
than the downstairs. The wallpaper is peeling off in practically
every place and graffiti covers a lot of the bare wall space. There
is litter absolutely everywhere, and in the dim light, I can just
about make out several more ghastly stains on the ripped carpet.

"Nika?"

The landing isn't that big; there are four doors leading off
it, and I go for the nearest one, throwing it open, ready for

action. The room is completely empty inside, bar needles and syringes piled in one corner, and the atmosphere is thick and cloudy. There is no movement though, and—

"Get off me." *Nika*.

Adrenaline fills me, and I race out of the room, following her voice. I hear her shouting more, and other voices too, grunts and yells—but there's a rushing in my ears and everything is merging together. I plow into the next room, grabbing a pin from my hair and holding it out, like it's a weapon. Not a good one, but it's all I've got.

"Jade, get out," Nika shouts. "Get—"

"Jade?" a low male voice says. There's a laugh. "Oh no, Jade. Don't go. Come right in, darling!"

The sound of men laughing follows. Chills run through me. I hesitate, my weight creaking on the floorboards. No one at school knows we are here.

"Just go!" Nika shouts.

My heart pounds. I look back toward the exit—the stairwell. A lump forms in my throat. If I go, they're going to hurt her. Take her somewhere, and I won't be able to get help in time and—

"I'll get the other one," a deeper voice says.

Footsteps.

Shit. I stumble backward—acting purely on self-preservation—and retreat into the first room I went in earlier and—

No. It's a dead end.

I whirl around, heart pounding, head pounding, everything pounding, and lunge for the exit and the stairs—just as a huge hulk of a man emerges from the room at the end of the landing, the room where Nika is. I skid, my shoes slipping on the damp carpet, but I get to the stairs. My breaths make rushing sounds in my ears. I pull out my phone, nearly tripping on the stairs. My other hand grabs the banister just in time.

I have Jack on speed-dial. I press the 'call' button, and—

I scream as I trip, falling, air hurtling past me. I think I hear Nika's voice, but then my shin connects with something solid—steps. Pain erupts through my leg as I fall. Carpet burns my hands, and my head smacks against the wall.

At the bottom, I pull myself up, feeling dazed and—

Footsteps, right behind me. Feet away—but I can't turn my head.

A dull pain in my neck and—

My phone. Shit. Where is it? I blink.

"Jack!" I shout. Is my phone here? Did the call connect?

"Where'd you think you're going, babe?" a low voice says.

Life floods into my body, and I spin around. The man is at the bottom of the stairs, reaching for me.

I kick out, and—and the hairpin's still in my hand somehow. I jab him with it, but it barely makes a difference. He's so big, and his skin's all leathery and he just looks annoyed.

He grabs me by the hair and pulls.

I shriek. Twisting around, I try to get away. He grabs me by the waist and lifts me up, toward the stairs. I scream and scream, kicking out, trying to make it difficult for him to carry me up them—the space is narrow—but all that happens is pain searing through my foot and ankle as my kick connects with the wall.

"Cut it out," the man hisses at me.

"All right down there? Need any help?" Another voice.

Pain lassoes around me, and I shout something, and—

"That's enough," my captor growls. "One more sound from you and I'll—"

But I *am* still screaming. I can't stop screaming.

I see his fist coming at my face, but I can't do anything to stop it. Can't move my face, my body. Nothing. Everything's locking up, and his fist connects with my nose.

My head snaps back, hits something. Pain and darkness and warmth slipping down my face, my neck—

"What the fuck did you do that for?"

"She was fighting me!"

I blink through the haze and the pain… Numb—my face is numb. And my vision's washed out. But I see them. People. Several of them. Hands and faces, and they're lifting me. And then there's a crackling and hissing in my ears. too much of it. Like interference.

"Jade? Jade? Oh my God! What the fuck did you do to her?"

"Be quiet!"

"Jade? Jade, can you hear me?"

"Shut her up, will you?"

Pain grabs me—jolts of it through my body. I'm lying down—thrown? I blink hazily, trying to roll over. Trying to see. But everything's hazy red and dark, so dark, and I can't make sense of it. I'm lying on the carpet. The damp, moldy carpet. *No!*

Hot bile rises in my throat, and I expel it, coughing, choking. My eyes water.

I look up around me. I'm upstairs now. They carried me?

Three men stand by a boarded window—but one panel has fallen down a little, and light snakes in, pooling on the floor. But it is still dark in the room, and there is a horrible decaying smell. Two other men stand in between the door. That's five of them. Five. My head pounds, and my stomach twists again.

"Jade?"

I follow Nika's voice and see her on the floor, to my right. She crawls toward me, just as one of the men crosses to the doorway. Nika's speaking to me, and now her hands frantically press against my face and my arms, but something's happened to my head because none of this feels real. I turn my head. I need to know what the man's doing. The man by the door. The skinhead.

The door's shut now. He's in front of it now. Thick body, muscular.

We can't fight him. I know that. Oh, God. What have we got ourselves into?

"Jade?" Nika puts a hand on my shoulder and—

My stomach twists, and I throw up. Something dark and sticky that splashes onto my legs and feet. One of my shoes has gone. I stare at my socked foot with the dark liquid dripping from it, my head spinning.

"What the fuck have you done to her?" Nika shouts. "That's blood! She's throwing up blood—she needs an ambulance." Her voice is so high-pitched. "Call an ambulance now."

"She shouldn't have tried to fight us," one of the men says. "And girls shouldn't swear."

"I'll say whatever the fuck I want," Nika says. "And you need to let us go."

I try to look at her, but my vision is all swirly and foggy.

"Yeah, because that's just what we're gonna do, isn't it?" The men laugh. "And anyway, only one of you can walk. And you're not likely to leave her 'ere on her own, are you? Of course, it's fine by me, if you want to…"

"My…brother…knows we're…here." I think I say the words out loud, and I think they're true—aren't they? The call connected…didn't it? He'll know we're in trouble.

He won't know you're here *though.*

The men laugh. Throaty sounds. My vision is all in pieces. I'm only getting little glimpses and—

"Big deal. Like some schoolkid's going to be able to take on all of us."

They laugh, and then I see one of the men's tattoos. The devil on his arm. The devil… That's familiar… That's a gang. Elliot's gang? My heart pounds faster.

No… He's the other gang. The more powerful one. These are… What was it he called them?

"You don't know Jack!" Nika spits at them. "And you are so going to regret hurting my friend."

"Whatever, babe."

"And he'll bring his friends," I say. "He'll bring…Elliot Pollizzi and—"

"These are Greylake girls?" one man says. "Shit. We need to go."

"We're not just leaving them," another says. He advances toward me. "She's bluffing. These aren't Greylake. They're not marked. See?" He grabs my arm and wrenches me up, twisting me around.

I scream and—

And something snaps. Like scissors cutting a ribbon. Quick and easy, and there's energy inside me. So much energy.

"Get away from us." My voice is slow and threatening, and this isn't me and I don't know what's happening. But I turn and with a newly-found surge of energy kick one of the men—the skinhead—catching him between the legs. He doubles over, howling.

"Bitch!"

I get ready to kick again, but something makes me turn—the door. I see a padlock on it, fixed crudely and it's locked. But I kick the door—and I'm not in control. What the hell is happening?

The wood splinters.

"Nika, go now!" I push at one of the still-standing men. He flinches and swears, but he's melting away. He thinks I'm part of Elliot's gang, the Greylakes, after all? But I haven't got time to think.

We've got to get out.

Nika slides past me, her eyes wide. She's staring at me, her face pale and—

And then I see the men. See the huge blisters forming on their skin in the places where I touched them. Sort of like what Kelley-Anne had. What the hell?

I look down at my hands and—

"Come on!" Nika grabs me and pulls me out of the room.

We run down the stairs and out of the door, and my whole body's tingling. Everything. Oh, God. I feel sick and—

"Keep going," Nika pants.

We get to the end of the street, but we're going the wrong way. Shit. We turn left, into another alleyway. Every breath I take threatens to burst my lungs, and my vision is rapidly deteriorating again. I continue to run, each time focusing on the tree or house far away, determined I'll get to it, then finding a new goal.

We're on a more main road now.

"People," I gasp at Nika, pointing to a group of what looks like students from the school of the next town along. The one we have the rivalry with and—

And my breaths fall away. I try to take another gulp, but I can't. I can't. I panic, turning to Nika, and I'm falling, falling into nothingness. A nothingness made of colors. Streaks of red and blue and yellow in darkness, swirling towards me, engulfing me in their sticky cobweb. And whenever the magical colors touch me my skin tingles and a very strange sensation reverberates through my body.

Among the cobweb are beautifully gnarled faces. I try to recoil—but I'm not sure I still have a body.

A woman's face with burned patches of skin floats above me, murmuring something, bringing up a sense of dread in the pit of my stomach. Her eyes are an unusual color—not quite blue and not quite red—and her hair is wild.

No, her eyes have changed…they are dark now…

"Join us, help us, save us…" she whispers in her strong, beautiful voice. Oh my God. It is *her*. The old woman—but she's younger now. The fog dances maddeningly around her, and the colors become ribbons she is controlling. "You won't get caught…"

Caught for what? I try to whisper, but no sound comes out.

"Death." A new face appears in front of me, and I shriek as I stare at him: an old man, with a long twisty beard and a shriveled prune for a face. "Kill them and it won't be your fault. You'll be saving our people and your people from a life of impending doom…"

"Kill the Xphenorie!"

"Save us!"

"Save them!"

Stop it! Stop it! I try to get up to push them away, but I can't move. My body won't work. I look up at them all in terror, as more and more come, bringing more ribbons with them which wrap tighter and tighter…

"Don't panic, daughter. Be strong…"

Leave me alone! I cry.

What kind of nightmare is this? Because it can't be real… It can't be!

I squeeze my eyes shut. After a few moments, their eerie screams die down, drifting away.

TWENTY-FIVE
Jade

"JADE? CAN YOU HEAR ME?"

Carefully, I open one eye. Nika leans over me. She looks absolutely terrified as she strokes my hair. I wonder if I am dead. After all, I don't hurt anywhere way near as much as I should…

Not after the gang and—and those people!

"Have they gone?" I look about for the woman with the burned patches of skin, or the old man with the shriveled face…

"They didn't follow us from the house," Nika whispers. "They must really be scared of the Greylakes. That was such a good idea of yours, mentioning Elliot's name."

My head just spins. I nod somewhat woozily, still looking about the street. I can't see that man or woman.

"The cobweb…" I mutter.

"I think she's concussed." A blond young woman with tanned skin appears next to Nika. "I'm a nursing student," she says, and I smile at her—until I notice a blue snake on her neck.

The tattoo is eerily like Dom's. Frowning, I wait for it to move. It doesn't. But there is something odd about it, I am sure. Or maybe I am just going crazy? Again, I look at the snake. It is kind of compelling, urging me to touch it. I ignore the feeling. I mean, how weird would it be if I started touching a random stranger's neck?

I look at the woman. She has long blond hair tied back in a messy bun, and I am sure she is wearing contacts. No one's eyes are that blue. She looks worried, probably self-conscious about me staring at her.

"I'm fine," I say. "I haven't got a concussion." I turn to Nika and wince as my head spins. "I'm fine. Let's just go back to college, yeah?"

"Okay," Nika says, and she and the woman help me up.

"I really am fine," I say.

After a few seconds, the blond woman joins her friends who are standing farther off.

"Thank you," I call after her.

"You *do* look better," Nika says as she touches my arm.

She must've taken my leather jacket off; it is lying on the ground near my feet. The air is kind of refreshing against my skin. I wince and look at my hand. It is pink and there are lots of raw bits. Gross. Must be from where I fell down the stairs.

The journey back is slow, and I feel as though I am in a daze the whole way. Nika keeps giving me strange looks.

"They're not following us, are they, the men?"

She shakes her head. "But what happened back there? I've never seen you like that…in that house… You were so hurt.

Like, all that blood. And that thing you did with the lighter, that was clever. I mean, at first I thought it was actual fire coming from your hands." She laughs.

"What?" I inhale sharply.

"It was just the lighter. Another stroke of genius." She laughs. "Though I reckon you made them think you're one of the fire-people."

I feel my blood drain from my face. My head spins, filled with images: The old woman at the sight of the fire. How she grabbed me. My burned wrists. Kelley-Anne with the same burn-type on her face. The reports of fire-people. The burns on those men.

I take a deep breath. Did I do that or did I actually use the lighter? The jacket's over my arm now, and I pat its pockets. Haven't got the lighter now. Oh, God. I don't remember using the lighter. Did flames come from my own hands? I tuck the jacket between my side and my arm, and stare at my hands, lifting them up a little. They look normal.

I shake them, but no flames burst out now.

I snort. This is ridiculous. Right? I can't be one of those fire-people. I just…can't.

We walk the rest of the way in silence. Northwood College's official gates rise up ahead, and we enter through them. No sneaking back in.

No one asks us where we've been.

No one has even noticed we've been gone.

NIKA DOESN'T WANT TO TELL ANYONE WHAT'S happened, least of all our friends as she says she feels stupid about how she walked straight into that situation, but I still consider telling Jack and Macey. Yet every time an opportunity comes up, it just doesn't feel right—even when I ask Jack if I can borrow his old phone, I can't answer his question truthfully about what happened to mine. I just say I've lost it. And I'm trying to protect him, I am. I know he'd be angry. Not just that we'd gone without him, but that we'd been attacked. No, I decide at last. It is best not to tell him. Especially when I've got bigger worries—like whether flames actually did come out of my hands. Whether I am a fire-person.

I mean, it's not like I can discuss this with Nika. I'm still not sure what her views are on these fire-people. I know Kelley-Anne hates them, and Craig thinks they're dangerous. But does Nika even believe they're real?

There's a small TV in our room, and that evening, when Nika's still in the common room with everyone else, I turn it on, finding the news channel. I'm only half paying attention to it—mainly concentrating on texting my friends from Jack's old phone, letting them know that I'm using this number now—when words catch my attention.

'OFFICIAL CONFIRMATION' appears on the TV screen, along with a badly-drawn cartoon picture of a man with fire coming out of his hands. It looks a bit tacky really.

"Yes, finally, we have official confirmation from the governing body that the fire-people—those first discovered by Dr. Joe Sera—do in fact exist," a reporter says. I've never seen someone look so excited. She looks like she's practically going to explode. "These images—released from the police only minutes ago—confirm the existence of these people, whose scientific name has now been revealed as Homo Sirodacts."

I look at the images as they fill up the screen. The first shows a woman holding her hands out toward a tree, with a jet of fire connecting her palms to the trunk. It looks like it's been Photoshopped. The second is much the same, as is the third. It all looks a bit ridiculous really.

Ridiculous. That word I keep coming back to.

"Government officials in Wolverhampton have also captured a live specimen of this new species... The woman—who says her name's Nina Waters—can be seen in this photo... Now, a main concern that we face is just how dangerous these people really are. The world's top scientists are working directly with many different bodies, and are carrying out extensive tests on the specimens that we have—both alive and dead." The reporter smiles at the camera. "Although we don't know how many of these beings are out there, it is unlikely that any of the public will ever bump into them..."

I think of Kelley-Anne and shake my head. Then I think of my own encounters with that woman—how many of these encounters were real though? The one on the field had to be—I've got the marks on my wrists to prove it. But the woman in our room at night? And earlier today, when I...fainted? Nika didn't say anything about an old woman. Or an old man. It was just that young woman with the snake tattoo like Dom's. The one who said she's a nurse.

And I can't actually be a fire-person myself—I must've used Jack's lighter against those men. That woman can't have turned me into one.

"And, of course," the reporter continues, "if you should find one of these new people, please call the number on the screen now, or contact the police immediately. While we don't know how dangerous they are, it is imperative that, for the time being, they are locked up. I have been assured by the policing bodies that they are taking public safety concerns very strongly indeed."

I chew my pasta. Kelley-Anne will be pleased they are being locked up. But it doesn't seem right. Well, I can see where they were coming from. No one really knows anything about these people. And fire itself is pretty dangerous. These individuals could cause huge amounts of damage wherever they go. But it just seems to me like they aren't being given a chance.

I shrug. The whole world seems to have gone mad. How could another species of human—specifically one that can control fire—just be discovered like this? This is the twenty-first century, after all. It doesn't even sound possible. In fact, it sounds like the plot line of an action movie or something...

Rise of the mutants.

Mutants. Again, I look at my hands.

No. I'm not one of them. That's ridiculous.

And why am I worrying about them? They're not going to hurt me. It's the gangs who are the real problem. The Greylakes and the Devils. And if Lily does end up having Elliot's baby, isn't that going to make her and her child a target for the Devils and anyone who wants revenge on the Greylakes?

I swallow hard. I need to be able to protect her. Lily is who I should be concentrating on. Not any of this.

TWENTY-SIX
Elliot

"LILY!"

I catch her as she's leaving the school. Like clockwork, she goes to the local library on Wednesdays. There's a book club there that she loves. It starts at nine, and because it's an academic-type club in the school's eyes, she's got permission to get back just after the curfew.

It still amazes me how my girlfriend's into books and shit like that. Especially given what I'm like.

But Lily and I work. Opposites attract and all that.

Her face flushes as she sees me, then she's smoothing her hair down. "Elliot? What are you doing here? Wait—what's happened to your face? Did someone attack you too?"

"*Too?*" I stare at her. "What's happened to you? Someone hurt you?"

Her eyes widen a little. "Uh, no." She looks around quickly.

"What happened?"

"It was ages ago. A knife was thrown at me and Jade. But it didn't touch either of us."

"A knife?" I swear under my breath.

"It's fine," she says. "Teachers reckoned it was a prop anyway. Didn't even look like a proper one."

I breathe out deeply. A knife that doesn't look real. "Describe it," I bark at her.

"Elliot, it's nothing. I'm fine," she says and gives me a smile.

"Describe it." My voice is like steel.

She does. And it's Kelley-Anne. It's her knife. Has to be. Shit. My breathing gets heavier. Kelley-Anne's going to pay for this. She's not getting away with it. No one tries to hurt my girl.

"But, anyway," Lily says, her voice soft. "What's happened to you?"

"Nothing," I say. The gray marks on my face don't even look that bad now. Don't hurt or anything. "But are you all right?" I ask. "You ain't been answering my texts. And you need to, Lil. Especially if someone's throwing fucking knives at you."

She looks from side to side. A couple of other kids from the school are about. I see one of them—a boy with ridiculously preppy hair—giving me the side-eye.

"Don't worry," I say. "Your brother and sister won't find out you're seeing me—and really, it's none of their business. They're just being controlling, Lil. It was them, wasn't it? They're trying to stop us being together. Have they taken your phone?"

"No," she says.

I frown. "But you haven't answered my texts."

She takes a deep breath as she looks at me—I can almost hear her heart pounding. "Look, Elliot."

"It's not on," I say, "what they're doing. They can't stop us seeing each other. We're in love, right?"

She nods.

"I've missed you," I whisper, pulling her closer. The smell of her shampoo—coconut—washes over me. Reminds me of all the times we've lain in bed together, where that scent just wraps around me. "God, I've really missed you."

She smiles a little—but then her smile gets bigger, and I know she feels it. Our connection. "I've missed you too."

"I know it's your family keeping us apart," I say. "I know it's not you. It's them, and soon we'll be free of them, okay?"

Lily tilts her face up. "How? What do you mean?"

I smile as I cradle her. She feels so right in my arms. So small. I have to protect her. For too long, she's been living in the shadow of her siblings, letting them control her, boss her around. And they don't want her to have her own life. They've squashed her, held her back at all opportunities.

But I won't do that. Lily's my girl. And yeah, I was mad before about the gear she lost—but she's not one of us. I have to remember that. She's not used to this life.

But she will be.

"Let's go back to mine," I say.

"But it's my book club."

"You'd rather sit with a load of old women than be with me? Lil, we've barely seen each other recently. Anyway, you can tell me all about whatever book it is this week. And we can get takeaway. That one you like from Church Street."

Normally, Lily smiles at this. But now she doesn't. She doesn't do anything—her face doesn't even have an expression. It's just plain, a calm, smooth face. No emotion.

"Lil?" I squeeze her shoulders a little tightly. "What's wrong?"

"Nothing." Her voice is small, but then she smiles brightly, like she's trying to reassure me.

"Look, you don't need to worry," I say. "I'm not mad at you about the gear. I promise. I just want to spend more time with you. You're my girl. Now, come on."

I lead her to the Chinese takeaway, and I'm splashing the cash a bit, showing off, ordering all her favorite dishes.

"Why are you getting so much food?" She frowns a little.

"Because we're celebrating."

"Celebrating?" Lily's voice wobbles. "What?"

I just smile. "That's the surprise. You'll see when you get back to mine."

TWENTY MINUTES LATER, WE GET BACK TO THE flat, containers of warm food in a bag. Robbie's out for the night, said he was meeting Spencer and some of the others to discuss plans, and we've got the place to ourselves.

Normally, Lily sits on the sofa when she's here—or she tries to lure me upstairs, giving me sultry looks and suggestive glances—but today she doesn't. She hovers in the kitchen as I dish out the food.

"You all right?" I ask.

Her lips press together for a moment. "What's the surprise?"

I laugh. "I got you a present." I indicate for her to go in the living room with a jerk of my head. "It's in there. The box by the telly."

She moves into the room. There's something off about her. She seems different, flat, no emotion now. I can hear her steps in the living room, and I listen carefully. She'll be at the TV now—yes, she's picking up the box.

Her eyes are wide when she returns, the box in her hand. "The new iPhone?"

"I know you wanted it, babe."

She smiles. "But this is expensive, Elliot. I—you shouldn't have."

"Only the best for my girl," I say. "It's already got my number on it, too. Plus a few of my mates if you get in trouble or something and can't find me."

"Wow—I don't know what to say." Her eyes spark—and that's her, that's *Lily*. My Lily. Not this timid version that her family's trying to turn her into.

"Food's getting cold," I say.

We eat from opposite sides of the kitchen table, dipping forks into the containers.

"What are you doing?" I ask as she sets both phones side by side and scrolls to the contacts.

"Transferring numbers," she says. "I wonder if it'll sync them from the cloud." She frowns.

"Don't worry about that," I say. "You don't need your other numbers on this one."

"What?" She squints at me, a small ghost of a smile on her face.

"You'll have to use both phones," I say. "Keep them both in use. People are gonna wonder if they see you with this one—and your brother and sister will stick their noses in. I've already paid for the contract for your new one, anyway. Just make sure no one else knows about it. Don't want to give anyone reason to look closer. Jack would take it away, assuming it's from me. And then you won't be able to contact me—because he'll be looking at your texts on your regular phone, right? Which isn't on, Lil. You're an adult."

"Almost an adult," she says.

"Okay, *almost*." I smile. "And as soon as you are, you can leave your brother and sister. Live here with me. See, it doesn't matter how much they try and keep us apart, because we find a way. We always find a way and—"

My phone rings. It's the ringtone I only have for Robbie. Irritation rises in me. Surely, he's not coming back now? He knows I've got Lily here—I told him this morning of my plan. So, whatever the reason he's calling has got to be important because he knows how much this evening with Lily means to me.

"Sorry. I need to answer this," I tell her. Her eyes are wide, and I turn away as I accept the call. "Mate. You okay?"

"The girls were right," Robbie says. There's a lot of background noise where he is—road noise. And voices. Someone shouting? "We do need to sort out these fire-people ourselves. They're not heeding our warnings, and we ain't having that. Meet me at the garage in an hour."

TWENTY-SEVEN
Jade

"DID YOU HEAR?" CRAIG CLAPS ME ON THE BACK as he slides into the seat next to me at breakfast and I nearly spit out my mouthful of cereal. Jack gives him a stern look, before returning back to the conversation that he was having with Aisha. But Craig's still grinning. "They've caught more fire-people."

"Yeah," I say, my eyes on Nika. She's over by the hot-food counter, in a queue with Jen. She said she'd queue and get some bacon for me too. As much as I try to explain to her what I can and can't eat due to histamine content, she just doesn't get it. Still, Jack will eat anything she brings back for me that I can't. "I heard on the news yesterday that it's been made official—"

"No, not that," he said, his eyes on mine. "It was just on the radio about two minutes ago that Greylakes have been out looking for them last night—well, the early hours—but they've caught *four*. And these four that were caught, the gang killed them there and then."

Killed them? My heart skips a beat.

"Why'd the gang look for them at night? They nocturnal?" Jack laughs.

Craig snorts. "No, they stand out then. The fire-people. They're allergic to the dark. Stupid adaptation."

"That wasn't on the radio," Jack says, frowning. "They didn't mention anything about any allergies these people have."

"The fire-people?" Aisha looks up, her dark curls going everywhere.

"Uh-huh," Craig nods, grabbing a slice of bread from the plate in the middle of the table. He looks up at Jack and me quickly, then back to Aisha. "There was like four of them caught earlier this morning."

Oh God. What if the Devils gang think that I'm one of those fire-people now? Because if Greylakes are going after them, then the Devils will be soon, too. They'll make it into a competition of who can kill the most.

"That'll be why we've got the new rules," Aisha says.

"Rules?" I ask.

"Haven't you seen them??"

I shake my head.

"Ah, there's loads," Jack groans. "How I'm going to be able to get more booze in now, I do not know."

"Come and see." Aisha is up in a second, grabbing my arm.

I get up and take a bread roll with me.

Aisha leads me through to the main office. And, sure enough, on the wall is a new noticeboard. There are quite a few younger students milling about it, groaning as they read. I look over their heads.

"What?" I exclaim, having seen rule number four. "They're changing the curfew?"

"That's not the worst one either," Aisha says. "Look at this one." She neatly and elegantly elbows a Year 7 out of the way and points to rule number sixteen. It is the last one. "Everyone's going to ignore it, right?"

"'No sixth-form students will be allowed out of the college's campus during their free lessons,'" I read. I turn to her, stepping back and letting the flood of younger children back to the board. "That is so stupid. I bet more people are going to go out now, just 'cause we're not supposed to."

Aisha nods. "And," she says, "it kind of takes away our privileges as sixth-formers anyway. I bet the teachers are going to make us study in those periods. It'll be like being in the lower school again!"

When we get back to the breakfast table, Nika and Jen have joined the boys, drawing up more chairs. Aisha and I squeeze back in, and Nika slides a plate of bacon, sausages, and toast to me. The only person in our group who's not here is Macey.

"They're veggie sausages," she says. "Quorn. They're all right, right? And it's only a little bit of bacon. And I got you the wholemeal bread."

"Thanks." I butter the toast and take a bite. I can eat that, but I don't have the heart to tell her that I can't have the bacon or sausages. Red meat, in general, is higher histamine than white. But it also depends on other factors too—like any preservatives or seasonings in the meat and how fresh it is.

Nika smiles though, and I can tell that she's pleased that I am eating the toast. Jack spears one of the sausages and turns to her.

"You know, those questions in the chem test yesterday—did you not think it was a little strange?" He bites off the end of the sausage and then waves his fork—with the rest of it—in the air.

Nika shrugs as she spreads jam on her toast. "Didn't know the answers anyway. And my practical didn't work."

"That's my point," Jack says. "None of ours did. But they all turned out identical."

"Yeah, but not how they were supposed to."

Jack nods faster, then speaks with his mouth full. "I think the teachers got it wrong. In fact, I'm pretty sure they did. That acid they gave us—I'm positive that it wasn't hydrochloric acid."

"It didn't react like it to the Sulphur." Nika squashes an impressively large amount of bacon into her mouth.

"But that didn't look like Sulphur though."

"Maybe it was an old batch," Craig suggests.

Jack nods, but doesn't look convinced. He tucks into another slice of toast, then stops to spread Marmite on it. "I think the teachers were getting us to make something. I mean, Mr. Wilson collected it all after, didn't he? And wasn't it a strange color? Wilson's always struck me as dodgy. What's to say he's not got us all making something for the black market that he'll profit on?"

"Oh, that's ridiculous," Craig says. "The teachers wouldn't be getting you to make some chemical."

"Chemical?" Jack raises his eyebrows. He's devoured that slice of toast in record time and now reaches for an apple. "Who said it was a chemical?"

"But the lesson was chemistry?"

"Yeah, but you also learn about rocks and crystals and shit," I say, thinking of the crystals that Nika put on our windowsill a couple of weeks ago. A few days later, she'd forgotten they were there and knocked them all off. Mess, everywhere.

"But that was a strange test," Nika says. She looks at Jack. "What've you got now?"

"Drama," Jack says. "In like two minutes."

"Shame," Nika says. "I wanted to go *out* out. But if everyone's in lessons—"

"I'm free," Jen says. "But we're not supposed to leave the school grounds now."

Nika snorts.

"Hey, Jade." Jack gets my attention with a prodding of his apple core—seriously, how quickly does he eat? His grin is mischievous. "Look over there. Got an admirer." He winks.

"Jack," I say, exasperated, but all the same I turn to look.

Dom Levaney is not who I expect to see—and he's definitely not an admirer. Not by any stretch of the imagination. He is staring straight at me. His eyes are dark pools that bore into me. Inevitably, I find myself looking at his tattooed serpent. The artificial light makes it a shimmery blue color—a bright, almost royal, blue—and its eyes are just as dark and thoughtful as its owner's. The snake is perfectly still. Again, I wonder if it's a new gang. Greylakes have the anchor tattoo. Devils have the devil. And this new one has blue snakes, like Dom and that blond nursing student.

But the way Dom is looking at me now? It sends shivers down my spine. I gulp. He is definitely watching me...spying on me. I freeze. Was he the one who'd been talking on the phone about me? Just remembering the menacing tone makes me shiver, and paranoia rips through me. Is his gang after me? Thinking I'm a fire-person?

Has he been watching me?

Jerkily turning back toward my brother, I can still feel Dom's eyes on me. My voice is weak when I speak. "I thought you hated Dom," I say to Jack, keeping my gaze as steady as I can. "So, why's this so amusing? Because it's not Nika that he's staring at?"

"Nah, it's just funny that the guy thinks he's got a chance with any of us," Jack says. "He's such a freak."

We finish breakfast quickly, and I head toward the English department. But just as I get near there, my new phone—Jack's old one—rings. I pull it out, looking at the caller ID.

I frown as I accept the call. "Macey?"

"Jade." He does not sound happy. "Come up to my room now. It's urgent." He hangs up.

Uh, what? I am still frowning. Macey never tells me to go to his room. He doesn't even like it when Jack takes me there because my brother's so messy and Macey's really house-proud. But why would he want me up there? What could be urgent? And to ask me to skip English too. No—wait. My eyes widen. He should have economics now. What's so urgent that Macey of all people is skipping lessons? And where was he at breakfast?

It doesn't take me long to walk to the boys' dormitory building. It's on the western side of the school's campus—about as far away from the girls' dorms as possible—but is accessible by the enclosed bridge that runs from the math block to it.

I push the door open. Teachers frown upon you even if you are milling about in the entrance to the wrong dorm. And you get into even deeper trouble if you are found outside a guy's room, whatever time of day it is.

My steps are quick, and by the time I reach Jack and Macey's corridor, my heart pounds too heavily, too loudly. Macey is waiting for me by their door.

"Come in," he says. His dark eyes are somber, but his tone is a little too high. He's nervous.

I step in, and he shuts the door. I've been in their room before, and it looks no different to how it did last time…except for a crate of beers in the corner.

"They're Jack's," Macey says. He pushes it under Jack's bed with a bit of difficulty.

"How many of those has he got?" I ask. "And how do you get away with hiding it?"

He sighs. "It's not my idea. And I'm far from comfortable with it. Anyway." He walks to his desk. "There's something here you might want to see."

I follow him and look at the large monitor that's rigged up on his desk, alongside his laptop. He indicates the screens, then crosses his arms before uncrossing them and letting them dangle awkwardly at his side.

I sit at the desk, on the little stool, and look at the laptop. There are loads of numbers and blocks of color in some sort of spreadsheet. The big monitor's screen has place names listed down one side—*Venice, Madrid, London, Normandy, Leicester, Paris,* etc.—and a map fills the rest of the scene with different markers on it.

"What is this?" I ask.

Macey takes a deep breath and leans onto the hardwood desk as he peers at the screen. He glances at me sideways, his eyes all shifty behind his glasses. "I did some more research on those fires."

"Yeah?"

He runs a hand through his dark hair. "I found this website." He gestures at the laptop screen. "Only this page was password-protected. But I hacked it."

I raise my eyebrows. "And I thought you were the friend who does no wrong."

He looks away quickly, but I've already seen how pink he is going. "The police have been hiding fires for *years*." He brings his hand toward the screen in a flicking sort of gesture. "This is the government's official record of all the 'paranormal fires' that they've seen." He does air-quotes around the words *paranormal fires*. "All the ones they've hidden."

"Paranormal?" I swivel on the stool so I'm looking fully at him.

He blinks too fast. "That's what they're calling them. The government."

I frown. It doesn't seem right the government would use the word *paranormal*. Aren't they supposed to be all about facts and figures, and evidence and science?

I turn back to the screen, then move the trackpad, scrolling down the spreadsheet. "But there are hundreds of fires logged?"

"Thousands," Macey corrects. "This is only page one. The most recent ones. The fire you saw was logged as number 3,455—it's even got yours and Jack's names in the notes section. The newest one is number 9,821."

"Wait. There's been over nine thousand?" I say. "And six thousand of them have been since…since Jack and I saw that fire in the park?"

"Altogether, yes. But that's not all." Macey leans forward, clicking onto another tab. His eyes are shadowy. "Look at this."

I look. It is a page very much similar to the one he just showed me. I frown as I take in the information. The numbers blur together, becoming one dark mass on the screen. Slowly, I look back at Macey, feeling sick. The numbers seem to be burned on my retinas.

"Is…is this true?"

He nods—one curt movement. "It makes sense. There are always buildings in cities that have underground rooms."

Anger unfolds slowly inside me, and my core feels too hot, like I'm burning up. "But that's not right. They said on the news that that Nina woman was the only live one they had, didn't they? They certainly implied it." I let out a long breath. "They *can't* keep them in cellars—that's just immoral and… Wait, are they allergic to darkness?" I think of what Craig said. "Is that true? How would an allergy like that even work?"

Macey frowns and then shrugs.

"Does anyone else know this?" I look back at the screen, then quickly away again. My eyes focus on the tatty curtains hanging at an angle by Jack's bed. The window's on his side of the room, and everything on that side is awry.

"Password-protected too," Macey says.

I let out a long sigh. "So, there are approximately *six million* fire-people being contained in cells underground, all over Europe, and no one is doing anything to help?"

"All I can guess is that human rights groups don't know about it," he says. "Seems to be only some official people that do—the ones who are covering it up. But I guess most of the police aren't even in on it."

I think of the police at the scene of the fire that Jack and I stumbled across. They certainly seemed to know what they were doing.

"And whoever owns the buildings where they're being held must also know," Macey says. "But it's been hidden from the public all this time, only now it's getting out. Those journalists and reporters."

"So now, they're pretending it's only just started happening?" I bite my lip and look across at him. "What are we going to do about it?"

Macey shakes his head. "We can't do anything. If whoever it is finds out that I've hacked into their records, God, I don't even know what they'll do. I don't want to get in trouble—else I won't get into Oxford."

"But this is immoral," I say.

"The fire-people could be dangerous," he says, and I know what he's doing—trying to persuade himself that inaction is the right thing to do.

But it's not.

"They are *people*, Macey. People, just like you and me. They have rights too."

"But we can't do anything." His face is sad, and he gently touches my arm.

I stare up at him, tears in my eyes. "No, this is wrong. Imprisoning people just because they're a different species is not right. Something *needs* to be done." I nod, conviction filling me. "Something will be done. I'll do something."

TWENTY-EIGHT
Jade

"I DON'T BELIEVE THIS," NIKA SAYS WHEN MACEY and I finish updating her and Jack on his discovery. She folds her arms across her chest and leans back against Jack's bed. The four of us are in the boys' room, and it's finally breaktime. The last two hours in lessons were agonizing. Not only was I late to English, but then I couldn't concentrate on *Frankenstein* and got told off by Ms. Daniels for my lack of attention.

I glance at Jack. He shrugs. "It could be a joke."

"It looks official." Macey points at the screen. "And it was password-protected too. A joke wouldn't be."

Nika frowns. "But it can't be true."

"It's been confirmed that the fire-people exist." My wrists burn. I look at the three of them. Should I tell them what I suspect? My mouth dries.

"But," Nika says, "they've, what, got five bodies and a live one? They'd have said if they had six *million* live ones. It's hardly an admin mistake."

"Maybe they don't want everyone to know just how many there actually are out there. I mean, look how angry Kelley-Anne was—she wants them to die. And the Greylakes are hunting them down. Devils will be as well. And if everyone knows there are at least six million fire-people, then I'd bet at least half the population would share the gangs' views that they're dangerous."

And the Devils could very well be after me and Nika...

I swallow hard.

There is a long silence in which Macey gets up and crosses to Jack's side of the room. He opens the window and then straightens the curtain. "Stuffy in here," he says as he turns back.

"Look," Nika says. "I still don't think there are six million of them being imprisoned."

"It does seem a bit far-fetched," Jack says.

"I reckon it's true," I say. "Macey's right—there are buildings in every city that always appear to be empty. Like the old nightclub here. Didn't Tesco want to buy it last year or something? But they were turned down. It would make sense. There could be fire-people inside there."

"Or the building could actually *be* empty," Jack says. "You can't just say any building that's empty is being used for them. That's just stupid."

"Kelley-Anne's been burned by one," I remind them. My wrists burn stronger. "That means there's definitely a live one in Northwood." I swallow hard. My tongue feels scratchy against the roof of my mouth. I've *seen* the live one. "They could be everywhere. They've got to be good at hiding from us, especially if there are still some that haven't been caught.

And what about the fires?" I look back at Macey. He is silhouetted by the window. "The two things have *got* to be connected. They've both been hidden for years: the fires, and the *fire*-people."

Nika yawns.

"Sorry," I snap, my temper rising. "Am I boring you?"

"Jade, calm down," Jack says. "Look, I still don't get why they've been hidden for so long? And the fires too? Why only pretend it's just started happening now?" He glances back over at me and the desk. "Why not have said when it really did start happening? Why announce it all now? Why not then?"

"The illusion of control?" Macey crosses the room and sits on his bed. His left leg shakes and I see the effort on his face as he tries to still it.

I swivel on the stool. I don't even know what to say. I was sure that Nika and Jack would believe this—that they'd have to know that Macey's found evidence.

Only it's not evidence that they want to believe. But if I tell them about my wrists, about what I think the marks are... And Nika said I used the lighter on the Devils gang, only I can't remember doing that.

It's going to sound ridiculous. They'll think I've gone crazy.

"Oh, come on!" Nika stretches out her legs. "You're both reading far too much into this. It's probably nothing. That stuff in the database is probably all made up—"

"Mine and Jack's names are in it though," I say. "Only the police knew about the fire. They're not going to have told anyone."

"It could still be made up."

"What? By the police?"

She nods.

Macey raises one eyebrow as he turns to her. "I expected you to be a little more open-minded to all of this. Especially given the books you read."

Nika rolls her eyes. "Yeah, I read them because it's obvious that it's *not* going to happen in real life. I don't expect to walk down the corridor, get attacked by a vampire, kidnapped, and taken to a palace where a long-lost prince decides to rescue me. Only to find that he's a vampire too. I mean, that's obviously not going to happen."

"What kind of books do you *read*?" Jack snorts.

"We're straying away from the topic here," I say, my voice low and strained.

"Well, there's not much more that can be said." Nika examines her chipped nails. "We can't really work it all out by ourselves. If the numbers are true, then it is way out of our hands. I mean, what are we—four teens—supposed to do about it?"

"She's right," Macey says. His dark gaze falls on me. I see myself reflected in his glasses.

"But we can't do nothing," I say.

"Then we have to work out who we can trust with this," Macey says. "There must be others out there who want to help."

Jack and Nika both roll their eyes.

My shoulders tighten. "Like that's going to be easy."

IT'S TIMES LIKE THESE THAT I WISH THERE WAS an adult I could trust. Because we have to do something.

Going to the media is an option—only Macey is worried his hacking will be exposed. And as much as I want to do something to help these imprisoned people, I don't want to do anything to get my friend in trouble. He's had his heart set on studying science at Oxford University for years.

Besides, what's to say if we did tell people that they wouldn't just cover it up? Or get us to stop talking about it? I gulp. People die all the time in Westbury. It's a notorious area for crime. The gangs and stuff.

I end up no further in my decision of what to do by the time I head to my last lesson of the day: psychology.

Recently in this class, we've been looking at paranormal experiences and extrasensory perception; before today, I didn't really believe it, but now? Now I start to listen, really listen. Well, except to the Sylvia Browne stuff—she just seems like a wannabe-psychic who used her 'powers' to get money. But the rest of it? Maybe it could be real—if it turns out it's not actually paranormal stuff and it can all be explained scientifically. Like the fires—there has to be science to explain it.

After the lesson finishes, I sit on my bed, kicking my leather ankle boots off. My textbook's next to me and it's fallen open on a page about precognitive dreams. I inhale sharply.

Quickly, I read, trying to push the image of the horrible old woman away. She's been in my nightmares/fainting-induced visions twice now. But both times were creepy. And they didn't feel like dreams, not entirely anyway. And anyway, I can remember them both. In fact, those are the only dreams that I *can* remember.

Surely, they aren't going to come true? I shudder. I definitely do not want to meet her again. But I was *hand-picked…hand-picked for the purpose.*

Whatever that is.

Only one thing is for sure: something is definitely going on.

And I'll find out what.

And then I'll know what I need to do.

TWENTY-NINE
Ariel

"SERIOUSLY?" I STARE AT LUCY. "YOU'RE REALLY being obtuse about this?"

"Oh, for God's sake, Ariel. You don't own me." Her eyes narrow, and she crosses her arms across her chest. Behind her, the trees whisper as the wind blows. The light's strange this morning. Still kind of dark for just gone nine.

I don't move, despite how piercing that gaze of hers is becoming. "I never said I did."

"But you're trying to stop me having fun." Her voice is sulky.

"No—I'm not stopping you having fun." I shift my weight from foot to foot. It's warm out this morning. Warmer than I was expecting. The heat is the sticky kind. "I'm trying to help."

"You just told me to go back home. Ariel, it's not even dark. It's daylight. There's no problem being out here."

I let out a long breath. God, why is she being so annoying? "I've just seen a Fenner around."

"But I can handle myself," she says. "And it's not like one of them is going to attack me. The treaty's there for a reason. You're being sexist and controlling." She glares at me. "Now, I want to walk by the canal, so I'm *going* to walk by the canal. Alone—because that's my right."

I breathe deeply, trying to calm down. "Lucy—it's dangerous. It's nothing to do with you being female. It's to do with numbers. That Fenner was not acting normally. They're all planning something, and I don't like it."

"Blah, blah, blah," she says. "Get lost, Ariel. You've become a right dick since you graduated. I'm a dispatcher too, you know. And I've got more experience than you, yet you think you need to protect me? Well, you don't. So you can get lost."

She turns on her heel and marches away.

I stare after her, my heart beating loudly. But I don't follow. Lucy's made it clear that she doesn't want me trailing her.

I take a deep breath. I'm on patrol round the town. And that Fenner I just saw, lurking out by the library, was acting suspiciously. I get out my phone, need to call it in.

Wes answers. "All right, son?"

I get straight to business and tell him about the Fenner.

"Amber just called in a similar sighting too," he says. "I've left a message for your dad, but he's in another meeting about the extraction."

The extraction—the plan to free the entrapped Calerians. The plan to rescue my mother. My heart squeezes. I try not to think of her too much because it makes me sad. Because it makes me realize just how big the raging hole in my heart is.

"Well, it's probably not anything Dad needs to worry about," I say. "He's got enough going on with that mission. I'll keep an eye out here."

"Okay, son," Wes says. "Let me know if there are any developments."

"Will do," I say, then I hang up. I take a deep breath and I see my mother's face in front of me. Pale blue eyes, alabaster skin, and soft blond hair. The kindest smile. And lavender— I remember the smell of it. She always wore lavender perfume.

I continue my patrol around the town. I don't see any more Fenners. I just think about my mother.

"Soon, Mum," I whisper. "I'll see you soon."

THIRTY
Jade

"HOW MANY WEEKS ARE YOU?" I KEEP MY VOICE low as I look at Lily. This was the one thing that I didn't ask the other day, and perhaps one of the most important things that I need to know.

She shrugs as we crossed the road, following Nika and Jack down the high-street. Macey is somewhere behind us. Despite the school's new rules, we've all gone out shopping in the nicer part of town, about as far away as we can get from the dodgy area with the dark alleyways and the abandoned house where the Devils attacked Nika and me. It was surprisingly easy to get out of the school grounds too. There weren't even any teachers there to stop us. Besides, it's the weekend now. Saturday morning. They can't actually stop us going out at weekends. Human rights and all that.

"About two months? Maybe two and a half?" Lily shrugs.

"What?" I exclaim. Loudly. Very loudly indeed.

In front of us, Jack and Nika turn around and look at us.

"Uh, nothing," I say quickly, as Lily gives me an alarmed look.

Macey catches us up and looks at each of us, a rather confused expression on his face. I wince as his tall figure blocks the sunlight from my eyes, sending shards of quick pain through my skin for the briefest of seconds. And then I frown—because that was better, surely, to have the blinding sun blocked from view?

Oh, shit.

But I push that thought away. No, it's not happening.

"What's going on?" Macey runs a hand through his already-messy dark hair. "Are you okay?" He peers down at me. "You look a bit—"

"I'm fine," I snap as I move to stand on Lily's other side, next to Nika.

The sun is now behind me, and it feels wonderful on the back of my neck. I've already tied my hair up into a quick ponytail as it had been making feel hot and sweaty, and the intensity of the beautiful heat is delicious. My skin laps it up.

I risk a quick glance at Macey. He doesn't look happy but is staring at Jack and then Lily and then Nika. At everyone but me. We still haven't worked out what we're going to do—what we *can* do—about the imprisoned fire-people.

"Lily?" Jack looks at her.

"What?"

"What's the matter?" His tone is blunt, and I know that look in his eye—that glint. He knows something is up.

"Nothing!"

Jack raises his eyebrows.

"What? Everyone's assuming there's something the matter with me all the time and I'm sick of it!" Lily huffs and then turns and rushes into the nearest shop before I can say anything.

I go to move after her, but Jack stops me, grabbing hold of my wrist. "Don't, Jade."

"Let me go. She needs me."

"Let *her* calm down. She's just in a mood."

"Let go of my wrist." Tears spring to my eyes, and he lets go abruptly, and I run.

I start to follow Lily into the same shop, but as I get closer to the doorway, a wave of nausea creeps up on me. I look into the shop. It is dark and gloomy. My stomach gurgles—oh God, no. I know that feeling.

I run, passing the shop that Lily disappeared into, heading straight for the supermarket at the bottom of the road. There are toilets there.

The pavement is rather busy, but most of the people move as I run towards them, tears threatening to spill. I don't even know why I'm so close to crying, either. I can't hear any sound of fast footsteps behind me—I don't think Jack, Nika, nor Macey are following me. At least they have some sense. I wipe my eyes with my sleeve.

A car hoots, and I speed up, realize I'm in the middle of the road. Disorientation pulls at me, and I force myself on.

There aren't many people in the supermarket, and I go straight to the toilets, no delay. After a few seconds of standing in the cubicle, my heart thumping like mad, the nausea begins to seep away. A few minutes later, in front of the mirror, I stare at my reflection.

I don't look *too* bad. In fact, I don't look like I've been so close to crying once I've wiped at my eyes. And I don't really look that ill either. My skin has an eerie pallor to it, not a vampire-glow or anything. No, my reflection looks like a badly Photoshopped image that shows the colors slightly more intensely than they really are. And I don't even have any foundation or powder on. My face had felt too hot for that this morning when I thought about applying makeup. Instead, I'd just watched Nika apply her eyeliner. She always does it so perfectly.

I mutter something unintelligible to myself as I run the tap. The trickle of water cascading down the marble basin is soothing. It snakes around on the stone surface in its own captivating dance, before plummeting fearlessly into the ring of darkness.

The door opens behind me, and I startle, expecting it to be Nika. It's not.

It's Kelley-Anne.

I stare at her. At her black eye. At her swollen lip. At the blood on her face.

"Oh my God. Are you okay?" My heart pounds. "What's happened?"

Kelley-Anne glares at me for a moment, then marches past me to the sink. She runs the tap and splashes water on her face, wincing. I stare at her profile. Her left eye looks terrible. And, well, her whole face does. Her purple hair also doesn't help—if anything, it seems to be drawing more attention to the purple bruising around that eye.

"Did someone do this to you?" I ask, then I feel stupid. *Of course* someone did this. She's been in a fight? Attacked?

She doesn't answer.

"Kelley-Anne?"

She turns to me, looks me dead in the eye. "Go into the shop and get me some foundation. I need to cover this fucking thing up."

I hurry out, my stomach churning. In the supermarket, I head to the small section that has makeup and grab a pot of foundation. I don't think it's the right shade for her skin—probably too dark as Kelley-Anne is very pale—but I pay for it and give it to her all the same.

She doesn't thank me, just sticks her finger right into the middle of the pot and scoops up a thick layer of the mousse. I watch as she smears it over her face, grimacing as she spreads it around her left eye.

I want to ask if she'll pay me back for the foundation—but I'm not brave enough. So I just stand here, watching, feeling awkward.

Then my phone rings, and a picture of Nika flashes up on the screen. It's a pic of her in a bikini—I raise my eyebrows. Interesting choice from Jack. Still, I decline the call. I'll go and find them in a minute anyway.

"Just go," Kelley-Anne barks at me. "And don't say a word of this to anyone."

"Right, okay," I say, my voice wobbling.

My phone bleeps with a text. Also from Nika: *Where are you?*

I head out of the bathroom, very aware of Kelley-Anne glaring at me and text back a quick reply: *I'm coming. Meet outside Game in five mins?*

After about a minute, I take a deep breath and glare at my reflection. I nod slightly, then open the door, going back into the supermarket.

The shop I am meeting them outside isn't far away. Just a few blocks down and to the left. Nika, Jack, and Macey are already outside it when I get there. Lily isn't.

"Where the hell did you go?"

"Where's Lily?" I counter Jack's question with my own. "She not back out yet?"

He shrugs. "Must still be in Boots. Where did you go?"

"Toilets," I mumble. I look up and met Jack's suspicious eyes. "Felt sick. But, uh, something weird happened."

"Weird?" Jack narrows his eyes at me, raising one eyebrow. It's a thing I really wish I could do. In fact, everyone at the school seems to be able to do it, apart from me.

""Yeah," I say.

But just as I'm about to tell him about Kelley-Anne, Macey exclaims, "Look, standing out here is torturing me!" He claps his hands to his chest in a theatrical manner. "They have the new *Call Of Duty* game."

"Well they should do, given their name," Nika replies.

"Fine. We'll go in here." Jack looks at me sternly. "And no running off."

Macey is through the door in an instant. Nika follows him.

"I'll text Lily and tell her where we are," she says.

I follow them into the shop, about to seek out the CDs, but Jack stops me.

"You okay?" His eyes hold concern.

I nod.

"You can tell me if something's wrong, you know."

I smile. "It's fine. And I would tell you, I would." I swallow hard. "I'll go and wait outside for Lily, I think."

He gives a small nod.

Outside, the air is cool and golden, a beautiful contrast to the muggy atmosphere of the shop. I sigh and walk down the street in the direction of Boots—and then I spot Lily.

My heart lurches when I see the look of fear on her face—and how she's running. Straight for me.

"Jade! Oh my God!" Her face is paler than usual, and her eyes hold the depths of despair.

"What's happened?" I touch her shoulder. "Has something…?" I gesture to her stomach.

She shakes her head. "No, but…oh my God. By the canal. There's a girl. On the high side. You know. In the out-of-bounds bit by the tennis court."

"What?"

"Come on!" Lily pulls me with her, back the way she came.

We run down the street. It is almost deserted. The pavement is slippery here—the gutters infamously don't work—and it's always wet here, even on the hottest of days.

As we get nearer to the canal, I hear voices.

"She looked like she was going to jump," Lily says. "Oh, God. What if…"

A small gathering of people is assembled on this side of the canal. I overtake Lily and push my way through the crowd, trying to see what's going on.

On the opposite bank, on the concrete platform, stands a girl barely older than me. She has long pale hair that billows around her. She wears a simple dress made of a white, floaty material, making her look like an angel.

A man stands behind her, dressed completely in black, whispering in her ear. Little tendrils of dark, smoky-looking stuff linger in the air all around him, making his skin look a dark gray color. The tendrils are also wrapping themselves slowly around the girl. She shivers and grimaces as though his words cause her pain.

I turn to the people behind me. They're all just staring at the couple on the other side—they aren't doing a thing at all. Anger rises in my throat. She's being held hostage there.

"Has someone called the police?" I address a middle-aged woman with a sun hat on. "We have to get that man away from her."

She looks at me, confused, then returns her gaze to the girl and the man.

"Hello?" I take a few steps forward. "Has *anyone* called the police? An ambulance?"

A few people shake their head. A young boy of about five or six lifts his hand to his head, folding his fingers into the shape of a phone, and begins to speak into his palm.

"Lily, call the police," I instruct, handing her my phone.

Lily takes the mobile, rather hesitantly, and begins dialing the number. More people are joining the crowd of onlookers, but to my amazement, no one is doing a thing. Why? Is the man armed or something? I turn back to look at him. Can't see a gun. But he's got hold of the girl and is slowly pushing her toward the canal's edge.

The canal is at least twenty feet deep in parts and the banks are vertical and high. The man's face is hard, and mostly in shadow, but I can pick out his distinctive features—deeply-set dark eyes and a beaky nose—and the scar on the side of his face. He is tall and leans over the girl a little more, wrapping his body around hers.

She whimpers as she tries to fight him off. Her eyes meet mine, and she mouths something at me. I don't know what though.

"Let her go!" I shout. I turn to a man near me. "Can't any of you help, at least?"

"Telling that wee slip of a lass not to jump ain't gonna help this wee situation in the slightest, lass," a man says. "She ain't gonna listen to any of us wee folk."

"What? Jump? What the hell are you on about? She's being held *captive* up there. She's not planning to *jump*… There's a man… Can't you see he's hurting her? Bloody hell! Why has no one already called the police?" Even if they think she's going to jump, and apparently can't see her captor, they should've still phoned for help. "Are you all stupid or something?"

A few people murmur pathetic answers.

I glance at Lily. She's still on the phone, looking confused.

I turn to my left. Right. There's a bridge a good two hundred yards down that way, but I know it is much closer than the one on the other side. I set off, running down the path, still unsure of what exactly I am going to do, once I reach the other side and the girl and the man, but I know that I have to do *something*. Someone has to.

I reach the bridge quicker than expected and my earlier nausea returns as I cross it. My stomach twists, and I try to ignore it.

On the other side of the canal, I run along the path, my feet kicking up gravel. My heart pounds faster. The girl and the man are not far ahead. My eyes sting and I feel sicker. The sun's too hot on the back of my neck. And—

"No!" someone shouts, and someone else screams.

I look up through smarting eyes and see the man look at me for the briefest of seconds, before—before he throws himself and the girl into the water.

THIRTY-ONE
Jade

"NO!" I SCREAM AS THE MAN AND GIRL HIT THE water, and—

Bright light. Energy. It explodes from the water—a flash of it and…and the sound of sizzling. Thrashing arms. The girl's head bobs up for a second, but then he surfaces too. He sees her and grabs her head with both hands, shoving her back under the surface. She screams as she's submerged again, air bubbles rising to the surface.

I wait for her to rise again, to get away from him, but I can't see what's happening. All around me, the crowd are shouting, but I can't make out their words. I just stare at the water. Dark shapes verb? under the surface, but no one is coming back up.

I kick my shoes off, lunge forward, and jump in.

Ice-cold water grabs me as I hurtle downward, my legs and arms cramping. My stomach clenches violently, and I kick my legs, propel my arms. My head breaks the surface, and I cough, spluttering.

Lily's at the water's edge, screaming something, but there's a rushing sound in my ears and I can't make out her words. I turn, treading water, my heart getting faster and faster. Can't see the man or the girl. They must be underwater. I inhale fast, trying to take the deepest breath I can, before I plunge under the surface.

I've never been able to see well underwater, and now is no exception. All I can see are murky swirling colors of drab grays and gloomy greens. Can't even tell if there's movement, if they're here. My lungs burn and my eyes sting as I try to see. Is that them there, ahead? Is that the direction? Pain wraps around my body as I swim forward—pain from the cold, must be. I'm going numb.

Shit. I need to find the girl and—

There. Is that a hand?

As my lungs threaten to burst, I surge forward for it, the hand, the fingers. But I lose sight of it. A rushing sound fills my ears, as well as the sound of…screaming? And—

Get to the surface now!

Lightheadedness swarms over me, and my lungs feel heavier, more painful. Pain everywhere. Yes. Need more air, need—

Something grabs my shoulder, pushes me down.

No!

I kick at it. The man? I don't know. Can't tell. My throat's squeezing and I can taste something rancid. And—and the water. The water's getting darker. Darker and darker until it's just pitch black. And is he still holding onto me, trying to drag me down? I… I can't tell. Can't feel my body… Can't…

Everything is dark, everything is—

My head bursts above the water's surface, and I choke, eyes streaming. I splutter, turning, trying to see him, the man—or the girl—but it's just me. No hand on my shoulder and—

Something splashes at the edge of the canal, six feet from me. A head bobs above the surface. It's the middle-aged woman. Her sun hat floats next to her. She's shouting at me, and then there's another splash. A teenage boy. And more and more people are jumping in. Shouts and cries fill my ears, but I can't make them out. There are too many crackling sounds in my head.

My skin burns as I tread water, turning round. The girl—I can't see her. Or the man. He's still holding her down? Shit. How long has it been?

"Jade!" Lily's scream makes me turn. "Jade, please get out!" She's crouching by the water's edge, one hand reaching toward me.

"But the…girl," I wheeze and then end up coughing. More water in my eyes, stinging. I bring a hand up to try and get it out my eyes and—

My skin. It's all mottled and broken. Blisters *bleeding*. I stare at my arm and then my other—it's like it too. What the hell?

When I get MCAS reactions, I come up in hives: itchy raised patches of skin. But this is not that. This is neither itchy nor raised, it's just literally like hundreds of tiny, bleeding blisters. And my throat feels fine. And my head. I'm not having difficulty breathing, my throat isn't swelling, and I haven't got that heavy feeling in my head. This isn't my mast cells misbehaving. This is something else.

"Oh my God," Lily shrieks from the bank. "Where's your EpiPen?" She turns around, looking at the grass, as if it'll be lying there. "Can anyone see signs of the ambulance?"

"It's…it's not that." I pant as I stare at my arms.

"Come on," a voice says, and I look up. There's a burly man next to Lily now, but he's looking at me. "Swim over here, and I'll get you out."

"The girl, though," I say.

"They'll get her," he says. And there are a lot of people in the water now.

My head spins and I'm lassoed by pain as I move forward, toward Lily and the man. He pulls me out, and I collapse on the ground. Out of the water, my skin sears even more.

"Oh my God," Lily says. "Jade, your skin! This is… Where's your bag?" She turns to the man. "She's going into anaphylaxis."

"No, I'm not," I say. "It's not the MCAS. It's…something else."

The man's frowning, and his face is going in and out of focus. "Stay still." He turns. "Is there an ambulance coming? There's something in the water." He looks back at the canal, and I see four or five figures in there now. "Get out! Everyone, out!"

"Jack, over here!" Lily yells, and then suddenly my brother's at my side. He touches my hand and I nearly scream from the pain.

"What the fuck?" he mutters. "Is this—"

"No, it's not the MCAS." But of course that's the conclusion my siblings would jump to. Because I do break out in rashes and—

There's commotion in the water, and I look and—

The girl. I see her. She's being pulled out and *her* skin is bleeding and blistering, angry and raw. Just like mine. I stare at her, and her eyes meet mine. Her eyes widen, and she points to me, tries to say something to the person holding her upright—but then she's being hurried away. Toward shelter? Somewhere warm? I don't know.

I can't see any sign of the man. Is he still in the water? I try to look, but I need to stand up to do that, and I can't right now. My legs feel so weak and wobbly just when I'm on the ground.

"Is there an ambulance coming?" someone asks again.

"But she's gone—the girl's just gone that way with…"

"*This* girl's still here though," another says. "She needs her skin looked at. And the lady over there's swallowed a lot of water. I think it's in her lungs."

I look to where the middle-aged woman—minus her sun hat—is now spluttering and choking, eyes streaming. Two women have gathered around her, their hands on her back, trying to support her as she coughs and coughs. She sounds like she can hardly breathe.

Jack's talking in a low voice to Lily. By the sounds of it, they're discussing whether this is an MCAS reaction—as if they know my body better than me.

"Where's Nika and Macey?" I ask.

"Looking for your bag," Jack says. He's still staring at my broken skin—it's also different to the gray marks on my wrists. "They were here earlier. Didn't you see them?"

"No." I breathe out slowly. "But is the girl okay?"

"She went that way," Lily says. "An elderly woman took her away."

An elderly woman? The hairs on the back of my neck rise.

"Where's the ambulance?" Jack mutters. "Hell, I'm going to phone for one."

"I already have done though," Lily said.

"Can't hurt to phone again. More people need help now," he says and glances toward the choking sun-hat woman. He pulls his phone out of his pocket. "Damn. No signal. Hold on."

He hurries away, holding his phone up high to the sky, squinting.

"You're cold," Lily says, and I realize I'm shivering.

But I don't feel cold. Not like I should do, with sodden wet clothes clinging to me. I just feel pain. My skin still feels like it's burning. I shift my weight a little and wince as the movement pulls at the back of my thighs.

"Ah, there you are."

I look up to see a man approaching me. He's middle-aged and his eyes are deep, bore right into me. He nods at me, but then when he's near, the look on his face gets more severe.

"Don't go to the hospital. Not unless you want us all exposed."

"Uh, what?" Lily said.

He dismisses her with a wave of his hand. "There's too many of you young'uns thinking you can play with fire with this." There's a severe look in his eyes. "And I'm not having us all exposed because of your stupidity."

I stare at him. "But I'm *injured*. My skin—"

"Fenners did that. Not the water. If you go to A&E, they'll find out. You'll be risking us all."

"But—" I cut off. He's a fire-person. He has to be. And he thinks I am too.

I look down at my hands, as if expecting flames to leap from the broken skin of my palms. But they don't. He's wrong—he has to be wrong. Has to be.

"Hey." Jack's back and he elbows the man away from me. "Who the hell are you?"

The man looks him up and down, then grunts as he shakes his head. His eyes rest on me. "Do the right thing. It's not just about you," he says, before he turns away.

Jack and Lily mutter something to each other.

"I think I should go back to the school," I say.

"I've *just* called an ambulance."

"Well un-call them," I say. "I'm fine. I'd just be wasting their time."

"You're not fine," Lily says. "You look terrible. Something's burned you in the water."

I force myself to stand, grimacing with the pain. "Look, I'm not going to the hospital. Okay?"

"Because that man told you not to?" Lily asks.

"Because I'm *fine*."

"Fine," Jack says. "But any signs that you're ill or whatever, and you're going. Plus, I'm telling the teachers about this. We need to watch you carefully. No arguments on that."

I groan. "Like they're ever going to let anyone off campus again."

THIRTY-TWO
Jade

THE SCHOOL NURSE INSISTS ON LOOKING ME
over when I arrive back, because, as luck would have it, she
sees our group arriving back. She takes one look at me and
frowns, then I'm ushered into the sickroom.

She examines the blisters on my arm with a magnifying
glass. "Were there chemicals in the water?"

"I don't think so—not with my MCAS. I would've surely
reacted to that."

"It does look like one of your reactions," she says.

"No. It's different." What is it with everyone thinking
they know my reactions better than me? "These blisters are
different." And it is strange that whatever caused *this* reaction
didn't actually trigger my mast cells.

"How peculiar." The nurse reaches for a glass up on the
shelf to her right, and then presses it to my skin. I wince from
the pain, but a few minutes later, she nods. Seems satisfied
that it's nothing imminently life-threatening. And I don't

think it is, anyway. The blisters stopped bleeding shortly after we left the canal, and already they're looking better.

"It could be chicken pox though," she says.

"Really? Coming up spontaneously after contact with the water?"

"Are they itchy?" she asks, pushing her glasses back up her nose.

I shake my head.

"Well, I want you to check back in with me tonight at seven. We'll see how it is then." She sets the glass down by the sink and then washes her hands. "And if there are any problems before that, come to me, okay? Or one of the other first-aiders."

NIKA MEETS ME OUTSIDE THE NURSE'S OFFICE and attaches herself to my side for the rest of the day. Her constant checking of how I am gets annoying and by dinnertime, I want to scream at her to stop. Yet I can't do that. I know she's just concerned.

At dinner, I can't bring myself to eat anything. Because every time I do, my stomach just twists and flips. I get this sometimes from the MCAS—even the smell of food can make me nauseous—but this time it's different. I'm just not hungry and my stomach's churning.

Everyone's talking in the canteen about me trying to save the girl, and as Nika and Jack lead me away, several students in the years below try and stop me for a chat. Apparently, everyone wants to speak to me. Well, everyone except anyone official. This whole time, I was expecting paramedics or police or someone to turn up at the school to follow-up on this. Especially when Lily and Jack had both called ambulances, and neither me nor the girl who was being drowned stayed to see them.

Because we're both fire-people?

I don't even know what to think about that. I just… I'm numb to it. I mean, it can't actually be real. Can it?

"You'll feel better in the morning," Nika says sometime later as I head back downstairs for my check in with the nurse. "You'll see."

The rest of the evening flashes by. The nurse is satisfied that my strange blisters haven't got any worse—if anything, they're a little better—and I climb into bed, hearing her voice in loop: *It's very strange, Jade. I definitely think the council need to look into the water content of the canal.*

I still hear her voice when I'm trying to get to sleep. Aside from the echoed words, my head is pulsing, and I am starting to feel like I am coming down with something. Brilliant. Just what I need—I mean, I can't actually be getting ill from this. I can't go to the hospital. I think of what that man said. Because I'm a fire-person too and I'll expose them.

But I need to talk to someone. I need to find that man or the girl who was being drowned. They're fire-people, right? I need to talk to them. Find out exactly what is going on with me. I need answers.

I breathe deeply. Nika's asleep in her bed, snoring softly. It is dark; the only light comes from the small gap in the curtains and the fire alarm that flashes every now and again above the door to the bathroom.

I look over to my bedside table, where my where my digital clock is. It's nearly one o'clock. But then the numbers are blurring, moving. My stomach twists, and I feel sicker. The walls around me feel like they're moving.

Oh, God. It feels a bit like an MCAS reaction—but I don't know what it could be from. I didn't really eat anything. Maybe it's the extreme emotion I'm reacting to. Because that can happen. When I'm really stressed—or any other strong emotion—my body makes more histamine that I then react to.

I sit up and hold my head in my hands, trying to get rid of the spinning room.

Seconds later, I propel myself into the bathroom, getting there just in time as I throw up into the toilet. My breathing is heavy, and I gasp for breath. Once I've finished emptying the contents of my stomach, I kneel next to the toilet, sinking against the wall, and when I feel like I am not going to keel over if I stand again, I move and shut the door. Darkness. Complete darkness in here. My stomach tightens again, bordering on painful.

I feel around for the light-cord. *There*. I pull it.

It's bright, the light, and I'd have thought it would hurt my head or something—but it doesn't. It just feels…better.

My eyes widen. I felt worse in the *dark*. And fire-people are allergic to the dark? That's what Craig said.

I gulp and try to breathe slowly through my nose. Try to stay calm. My heart races. Tomorrow I will get answers—I have to. I will. But what do I do now? I don't want to go back into the dark bedroom—I just get a strong sense of revulsion, just thinking about it.

I take several deep breaths. I'll stay here then.

I sink back to the floor and rest my head against the cool white tiles under the sink.

I'll sort this all out in the morning, I tell myself. I'll get answers. I'll fix this.

THIRTY-THREE
Jade

"JADE? YOU IN THERE?" NIKA'S MUFFLED VOICE breaks through my sleep.

I stir and sit up—then groan. It turns out sleeping on the bathroom floor is terrible for your back.

"Jade?"

"Yeah, sorry," I mumble, trying to ease my back.

"I really need the toilet," she says. "I can't wait any longer."

I open the door and Nika does a sort of double take when she sees me.

"You look like shit." Her eyes are wide with concern. "Why didn't you wake me? Oh, Jade. Look, I'll take you to the nurse in just a second, okay?" She rushes past me into the bathroom, and I step out, shutting the door.

I get changed quickly and examine my skin. It actually looks better. Like the blisters are a week old or something now. I pull on a hoody, wincing as more of the blisters come into contact with fabric. But I'd rather endure the discomfort than give people another reason to stare at me.

"I'm fine," I tell Nika as she emerges. "Really. I don't need to see a nurse." I just need to see one of the fire-people. I need answers. But I can't say that to her, I know that. I'd sound crazy. I think about Macey, about whether he'd believe me.

But it's one thing for him to believe that fire-people exist. Quite another for him to believe that one of his best friends has been turned into one.

Nika's not convinced that I don't need to see the nurse if her expression is anything to go by, but she doesn't push it. We head down to breakfast, and still everyone is staring at me.

"You're in the paper," Craig says, giving me a thumbs up.

Someone else thrusts a newspaper at me. And I see my photo on the front page and—

"Oh my God." I stare at the headline: **LOCAL SCHOOLGIRL SAVES FRIEND WHO ATTEMPTED SUICIDE**. "How can they? That's not what happened!"

"Yeah, I know," Jack says, sliding into the seat next to me. "You're not friends with her. That Lucy girl. Don't know who she is."

My jaw drops. "I think the other thing they got wrong is more significant than thinking we're friends," I say drily.

"The other thing?"

I stare at him. "That girl was not trying to commit suicide."

"But she was going to jump?" Jack says, giving me an even odder look. "Have you lost your memory, or something? Lily told me that girl was on the *edge* of the canal. What else could that look like?"

"What?" I squint. "No, there was a man—he must've been in the water too by the time you arrived. He had her captive."

I grab the newspaper and scan it for details of the man, for any mention of him. Only there's nothing. It's all just about me and Lucy Donneley.

Lucy Donneley. The name seems to pop out from the rest of the text, like it's glowing or something. But I've got a name now. A name of a fire-person. I just have to track her down. Is she on social media?

I turn to Jack. "Did you see a man climbing out of the canal?" Because thinking back now, there was no sign of him when people pulled me out. And no sign after. Where did he go? Did he drown?

"There were quite a few people in the canal," he says. "They were trying to help you and the girl. Several of them were there by the time I got there."

"No—I'm talking about a specific man. The one who was trying to drown her. Uh, he had dark clothes. He was all in black." I grimace, can't remember anything else about him. "He had his arms around the girl—around Lucy—on the canalside. He was the one who pushed her in the water. No, he threw himself in and he was holding onto her." I blink. That's right, isn't it? But my head's pounding and my brain feels thick and foggy.

"Are you sure?" Jack's staring at me. In fact, everyone at the table is staring at me. Craig's eyes are wide.

"Yes!" I say. "Definitely." My head spins. If Lucy's captor climbed out of the canal, he could've just been mistaken for someone who'd been trying to help, like the rest of us.

Either that, or they need to dredge the canal for his body.

"Witnesses have been interviewed though," Craig says, sliding along the bench until he's right next to me. "And they're all talking about attempted suicide. This woman here, look—" He points at the bottom of the paper. "She says she was already there when Lucy Donneley walked up there. There's no mention of anyone trying to hurt her at any point."

"There was definitely a man," I say. I look around. "Where's Lily? She saw him."

My eyes fall on her at a table the other side of the room. I get up from the bench, my head feeling heavy, and rush over to her. Her back's to me and she's stirring a spoon round and round her bowl of cereal, staring at the soggy Bran Flakes as they emerge in the pool of milk, rippling around the spoon. The seat opposite her is free, and I slide into it, startling Lily and two of her friends.

"You saw the man right, yesterday?" My words tumble out so quickly, it's almost like they're crashing into one another. "The man who threw Lucy Donneley into the canal. Because the paper's completely left him out of their report on it and—"

"What man?" Lily stares at me, frowning. There are dark smudges under her eyes and her face looks pastier than normal. Puffier too. "What man?"

"The man at the canal. Dressed in black. With the tendrils." My voice wobbles. I know how ridiculous that sounds. "You know she wasn't trying to commit suicide, right? That man was hurting her."

"But she jumped in, Jade."

I let out an exasperated sigh. Why is everyone saying that? "He threw himself in there, pulling her with him. That was not a suicide attempt."

"But, Jade, there was no one else there." Lily's frowning. "Not on that side of the canal with her. It was just the girl."

Suddenly, I realize everyone is looking at me. Students and teachers. But I can't back down. "No, there was a man was there. He was trying to murder her!"

Jack shakes his head, pasting a sympathetic expression onto his face. He's followed me over to Lily's table.

"No," I say. "This happened, this is real."

"Jade, I think you need to calm down," Nika says, appearing next to Jack. She glances at him and mouths something.

"Hey." My voice is sharp. "I'm fine. I'm—"

"I think she's hallucinating," Jack says.

"I'm not hallucinating! And I'm right here, you know. That was real—that man was real. God, I can't be the only one who saw him. I can't—"

I break off as I catch sight of someone else watching me. Well, everyone else in the canteen is, but one person's gaze is drilling deeper into me. The hairs on the back of my neck rise, and suddenly I feel colder.

It's Dom. I inhale sharply. The blue snake tattoo seems to be watching me.

I take a deep breath. He's spying on me. And he's got a tattoo—it has to be a sign of a new gang. And the gangs are hunting fire-people. Does he suspect that I'm one now? Is he going to kill me?

Shudders run through me, and I'm so occupied with Dom that I don't notice Mr. Wilson approaching our table. It's only when he speaks that I realize he's there, and I flinch, feel like I'm being trapped from all sides.

"Jade, come with me," Mr. Wilson says. His voice betrays no emotion. It's just neutral.

"I'm coming too," Jack says.

"We're just going to the nurse's office," Mr. Wilson says, his voice clipped, and he escorts me away. I move as if I'm in a daze. Jack's behind me.

In the office, the nurse takes my blood pressure and heart rate and temperature while Mr. Wilson and Jack update her. "Maybe we should get a psych evaluation, just in case," she says.

"I'm fine," I say quickly.

"Sweetie, it's okay, there's nothing to be worried about."

"I'm not worried." Only I am. Because it's clear now what's happening. They're all pretending no man was there. And I don't know why. I think of all the strange things that have been happening in this town recently. Ever since that first fire on the field. Has everyone been brainwashed?

I let out a small laugh. "Look, I must just be tired. Really tired. That's all. I'm fine." I rub my eyes. "I think I had a bad dream about it last night. It was just that I must've been thinking about. The two things merging, you know. Really. I'm fine. I'm awake now." I force another laugh.

Neither the nurse nor Jack nor Mr. Wilson look like they're convinced, but eventually the nurse nods.

"You'd better rest then today," the nurse says. "Good job it's Sunday, eh? You won't miss any work. Have a nice, relaxing day."

Yes, I think. A nice relaxing day in which I will find out exactly what is happening.

IT'S NOT EASY TO SHAKE OFF JACK OR MY friends because they all want to watch me, as if they think I might suddenly 'go mad' again, but eventually I manage it. There's a film playing in the basement, and we all take seats at the back. I see Kelley-Anne nearby. Her face looks flawless now—makeup? But who attacked her?

I'd planned to leave it a few minutes after the room has darkened before I left, but the absence of light begins to affect me almost immediately, and I make my escape and try to push my worries about Kelley-Anne to the side. I can't think about that now.

No one notices as I slip out of the basement. No one stops me.

I walk quickly to my room and grab my bag. It contains my EpiPen, Symbicort inhaler, medical ID card, and extra antihistamines. Then I make my way out of the school grounds, glancing over my shoulder every so often, half expecting to see Nika or Jack running after me. But they're not there.

I google Lucy Donneley's name but all I find are articles about yesterday. No social media accounts for her.

I groan and try to work out what I'm going to do. Do I go to the police? Because they must be aware of the fire-people. They were trying to put that fire out, after all. And in any case, there was a man trying to murder Lucy. That's a crime. The police need to know about him.

But would the cops just agree with what he was doing? Do they want all fire-people dead?

I breathe hard. Everything's a mess, and I don't know who I can trust.

Still, I walk to the police station. It's like my legs are independent of my brain now. They just carry me there. I swallow hard. The roof of my mouth feels too dry. Is this a mistake?

I breathe deeply and open the door, then walk to the desk. To the left, there is a long corridor, and it's full of people queuing. So many people. Uniformed officers make up a good two-thirds of the crowd. Most of the policemen and women have clipboards.

"Yes?" a man at the counter says loudly, and I realize he's wanting my attention.

Of course, I've just walked in here and up to his desk. But what are all those people doing in here?

"Can I help you, miss?" He looks flustered and tired. Like a bad caricature.

"I—I…" My throat constricts a little. What if this does make things worse? I think of what the man who spoke to me after the canal incident said. He didn't want me going to the hospital, so he wouldn't want me here either. "Sorry, I…" I start to say, but a shout cuts me off.

"Number thirty-one A, please!"

I turn, jolt. It's a policeman at the front of the crowd. "Have we got a number thirty-one A?"

"Yes! Coming through. Make way!" a voice says.

A very familiar voice.

I pause and watch as a tall, thin man fights his way through the crowd. The roof of my mouth gets even drier. It's Mr. Wilson.

"Miss, can I help you?" the man at the desk shouts, sounding positively annoyed now.

"No, sorry." I step back, frowning, and watch Mr. Wilson instead.

It is unmistakably him—no one resembles a goblin and a dog *that* much. In one hand, he is carrying a huge canister. It is silver and has writing on it in a neon blue color. I strain my eyes, trying to read it: *DC* are the only letters I can make out.

"Nearly three liters," Mr. Wilson says, smiling.

The officer who was shouting for number thirty-one A takes the cannister from him, and then calls for the next person: "Thirty-one B!"

"Excuse me?" Mr. Wilson says, turning to another officer. "Where do I get paid?" He turns and his eyes meet mine. His body jolts. "One second," he says, and then he's heading toward me. Quickly.

I shrink back, a dank taste taking over my mouth. My heart pounds. I don't understand any of this.

"Did you see that?" Mr. Wilson demands. But, before I can answer, he's speaking again. "No, you didn't, did you? You didn't see anything." His voice is hard. "You saw nothing at all, Jade. *Nothing.*"

I nod.

"Good," he says. "You saw nothing, and it's seeing nothing that will keep you safe."

He fixes one last severe look at me before he turns away and melts back into the crowd.

My chest tightens and I feel sicker. My heart gets faster.

Get out of here.

I run.

THIRTY-FOUR
Jade

OUTSIDE THE POLICE STATION, IT'S EERILY quiet. Mr. Wilson's words ring through my head, echoing over and over. I saw nothing? But what was that stuff? I frown. DC something? I've heard that before…that name. When was it? I frown deeper, can't remember. And why doesn't Mr. Wilson want anyone knowing about it? It can't be illegal though, given he was giving the cannister to an actual copper?

Unless it's drugs he's confiscated? I mean, everyone knows that this town has a huge drugs problem—mainly thanks to the gangs.

I cross the road, trying to work out what I'm going to do. Because going to the police station has just left me even more confused than before. But, just as I reach the other side, nausea pulls through me, quick and sudden—just like when me and my friends were walking into town yesterday, when I thought I had to get to the supermarket toilets quickly.

I clap a hand to my mouth, feel my torso shudder. Something inside my stomach twists. But no bile comes up. A crawling sensation flits through me, and my shoulders tighten. My insides all feel jittery, shaky, and I don't feel right. The nausea rushes at me again.

I take several breaths, trying to calm myself. My head spins. Maybe I need to sit down. But not here—my heart's pounding and something just feels very wrong about this place now. Very wrong indeed.

I keep walking and glance down an alleyway on the opposite side of the road and—

I freeze. There is a man down there, crouching close to the ground, and he's surrounded by black mist. It's those tendrils again, just like the man had who tried to kill Lucy Donneley. I inhale sharply.

This man is looking at me. Straight at me.

My body jolts and every muscle in my body tightens.

Run! the voice in my head cries.

Only I don't. I can't. I can't move.

The man stands up slowly. The mist is like a floating cape around him. A smile stretches across his features, causing a scar to divide his face in one swift motion. The whirling dark mist around him swirls faster, tendrils escaping, traveling toward me.

And he's getting closer, closer, closer. His head tilts to one side, and there's something gormless about him, something—

"Yes," the man says. "They *were* right."

My breaths come in dizzying bursts. And he's getting closer…closer…closer. Any minute now, and he'll be reaching out to touch me.

Run!

But I can't. I can't do anything. My body won't work. It's all locking up. Oh, God. What is happening?

"Jade!"

The shout comes from behind me, and I jump and turn. My movement is awkward and I nearly fall. It's the man with the white-blond hair from the pharmacy. He's running toward me.

"Jade! Move!" He sounds worried. And he knows my name? I didn't tell him my name. What the hell? I can't even remember *his* name.

I glance back at the tendril-man. His smile gets wider, and he nods at the blond man, the shop worker. Am I near his shop? My head pounds. I can't think.

"You know what this means, don't you?" The man's tendrils fly out with each of his words.

My nausea intensifies. The tendrils are still reaching for me, getting closer and closer. They're going to touch me. They're—

The blond man shoves me to the side at the last possible moment, pushing away from the tendrils of darkness. He turns back towards the dim road where the other man still stands—he hasn't moved. It was just the dark mist, the tendrils.

The blond man raises his hand toward him, palm out, and a flash of orange light erupts from his fingertips. No, not light. Fire.

I let out a shriek, my eyes wide. I gasp. *He's* a fire-person too? The man from the shop? What the—

I recoil back, just as he shoots the fire at the mist-man. Flame after flame, and it's being channeled in a straight line. A beam of fire.

I take a step back, my heart pounding. What is going on? What is...

And then the fire stops, and the mist-man has gone. Just...there's just what looks like ash on the pavement. I'd expected to feel sicker, watching a man be incinerated, but I don't. If anything, the nausea is leaving.

The man from the shop turns to me.

"Shit, shit, shit," he says. He's breathing hard and he looks at me. His face is flushed. "They're all going to know about you for sure now... They communicate way too fast." He pulls his hand—the same one he just shot fire from—through his hair.

"What?" My word is barely audible. Everything's just... This is too much.

He points at me. "Don't say a word of that—or this—to anyone. About yesterday or today."

"Yesterday? You know about that?"

"Of course. And it was to do with you. The Fenners suspected you exist—so one grabbed Lucy, trying to force her to admit it. But she wouldn't—and then you showed up. And I am so glad you stepped in to save Lucy, when you didn't even know her—and you put your own life at risk—so, thank you—but the Fenners know of your existence then. And just now too. There's been no outright war starting yet, nothing—which doesn't make sense." He's breathing fast. "My father reckons it's possible the Fenners are going to send their top people over, get official confirmation of you, before they do anything. Like, that's all we can guess is going on. But, you've got to keep your mouth shut anyway, Jade, until we know what is happening."

I stare at him. "What?"

"Because of the gangs," he says. "It's a dead giveaway that you're one of us, when ordinaries can't see them."

"One of *you*?" I stare at him. I *am* a fire-person? My head spins. And I don't get it—because I'd suspected this anyway, but hearing him say it, after what I've just seen, feels different. It makes it more real. More concrete. Then I frown. "Wait—they can't see the...the men with the tendrils? What the hell is going on? Who are you?"

He takes a step toward me, but I recoil. I'm shaking. Every part of me is shaking. And not just because I can now detect the faint smell of aftershave on him. It carries toward me in the weak breeze.

"I'm sorry, Jade," he says. "I'm Ariel Razoa. We met before, remember?"

I just stare at him, wary, then take a step back. My head's starting to feel achy.

"We didn't want to bring you into our group like this. But it's too late." He shakes his head. "And it's not supposed to happen. Not like this. You're a Calerian—like me. But you're not organically one of us—you've been changed, altered to be one."

"Altered?"

"DNA alteration," he says. "It's how we used to breed, thousands of years ago, but the treaty put a stop to it to protect human life. But now the Xphenorie know about you—they all do, because they're one organism really. And they're all going to think we've broken the treaty—because you exist and you shouldn't."

I start to back away, shaking my head. A strange laugh creeps up my throat, but it doesn't sound like me. Hell, I don't even feel like me. This is all just…too much. I mean, I wanted answers, but not…not this. I swallow hard and look at him. "I don't know what's going on. This is…"

"Neither do we. That's the problem, like I said. We were all born like this, born Calerian. But someone's transformed you. Changed your DNA so you're one of us. And that breaks—"

My legs suddenly feel insubstantial. Soft. "Changed my DNA?" This is…this is permanent?

Ariel's eyes soften. "Whoever's done this to you broke the treaty. Our people realized what had happened when you started transforming, and we've been trying to keep you a secret. But now the Xphenorie know about you, that one of us broke the treaty, and so there's now there's nothing to keep the humans safe from *them*. They're going to feed from the humans—killing them—and the war's going to start back up. Us against them. Because you're proof that one of *us* has broken the deal and so war is inevitable. It's just a case of *when*."

Everything spins around me. That woman. The fire. I roll my sleeves up, stare at my discolored skin. My head's feeling heavier and heavier.

"Jade, I need to get you to the warehouse."

"The warehouse?" I stare at him, wary.

"Yes. It's our base. We've been watching you. My father's the leader of our camp, and he wants to run tests on you, see if he can determine from your DNA who your creator is. He's been trying to test you for a long time, but we didn't want to scare you off. And in any case, he said it was best that we kept a low profile on you, in case the Xphenorie were watching us. But now you know it all, and you can see the danger now—because the Xphenorie will feed on humans, but humans can't see them."

Can't see them? That man who attacked Lucy… Was he one of them…these Xphenorie people? I take several deep breaths, but my heart's still pounding too fast.

"We need to move quickly," Ariel says. He holds out his hand to me. The same one that fire erupted from moments earlier. "We need to learn everything we can from you, and see if we can find that woman. She's the one who started all this by transforming you. And maybe if we deal with her, and show the Fenners that we've sorted it, we could prevent some of the bloodshed that's going to start."

I do not take his hand. I just stare at him.

"Come on, Jade. We've not got a lot of time. We need to run the tests at the warehouse. We need all the info—"

"You're a stranger," I say. A strange laugh builds up inside me. "I'm not going with you."

"Then come with me," another voice says.

I turn and see the new figure. He's walking swiftly over to us, the blue tattooed snake watching me.

My eyes widen. "Dom?"

He nods. "I'm a Calerian too," he says. "And I promise everything Ariel's said is true."

"No—you've been stalking me," I say. And what the hell? He's a Calerian too? "I've been *watching* you," he corrects.

As he says the words, a cold realization breaks over me. I was right before, when I suspected it was him. "You were the one in the store cupboard, talking about me on the phone."

"Like I said, protecting you—as soon as we realized what was happening."

My eyes narrow. "No. This is…"

"Jade, you know we're right," Ariel says. "Dom's told me you've noticed changes."

"I heard you being sick last night," Dom says, and I don't know how the hell he heard that. Unless he was right outside my room. "It's because absence of light is toxic to us."

"You're still transforming though," Ariel says. "So, you're stronger in the dark than we are."

I let out a strangled laugh. "That doesn't mean I'm one of you."

"It does," Dom says. "You know we are right. And I wouldn't lie about this. You're a Calerian. I'm sorry, but you are. And now we need to stop a war."

THIRTY-FIVE
Ariel

IT TAKES TWENTY MINUTES TO CONVINCE JADE to come back with us. The whole walk back she's got her finger on the speed-dial button on her phone for Jack—as she kept telling us. Dom's already told me that Jack's her brother and said it's best that we avoid any conflict with him. Apparently, he gives a mean right hook.

Jade and Dom walk ahead of me. He instructed me to walk downwind of her, said she's allergic to scents. I don't know why he didn't tell us this before, but I promise to wash off the aftershave as soon as we get inside.

Once we get to the warehouse, Tav sees us straight away and says she'll get the rest of the council. Dom takes Jade through to the sitting room, and I head to the nearest bathroom and do my best to wash the scent off. When I get to the sitting room, I find Jade watching everything with wide eyes. Moments after I arrive, the council makes its entrance too. All six of them.

Jade edges a little closer to Dom.

"So, you're one of us?" My father looks her up and down. "Remarkable." He turns to me. "She hasn't fully completed the transformation yet. I don't know when that'll happen, but it's imperative we find our rogue who is behind this."

Huh. As if I need to be told that.

"Describe the person who did this," my father instructs her. "We can send a description out with dispatchers now, before we get the results from your DNA analysis."

"She was…old," Jade says.

"Be more specific, dear," Tav calls out.

"I don't know…sixty?"

"Sixty isn't old," my father mutters.

"Seventy? Eighty? I don't know. I… Look, my head's hurting and I can't think." Jade shifts her weight from foot to foot. "She was old. Gray hair. Quite skinny."

My father looks at me. "Are you making a note of this?"

I nod and grab my phone. My father doesn't trust any notes that are not written down. He says memory is not a reliable thing.

He asks Jade more questions, but she doesn't really give any more concrete details. Finally, he nods and looks at Tav. "Chances are she isn't the only human this rogue has claimed."

Jade inhales sharply. "I'm not the only one?"

"Most likely not," my father says.

Not the only one? I glance at Dom, then Tav, then the other council members. No one's revealing any emotion. Their faces are all just blank.

"She… I think she said something about her son too?" Jade says. "That old woman. She was calling me *daughter*."

"So, we can assume there is at least one more out. A male. Do we have any idea who this other individual is?" He looks at Dom. "No other students showing signs?"

He shakes his head. "I don't think so—but you know what our signatures are like."

My father grunts.

Jade turns a questioning look on me.

"We can only detect if we're present," I say quietly. "We can sense each other, but one of us gives off the same signature as a whole colony."

"There *could* be more at the school." My father rubs his hands together in slow motion. "Dominic, go back there now. See if you can detect a signature there when Jade's not there."

"Signatures linger for days though," Dom says.

"I know that," he says. "But we need to find this male individual. We left it too long to get Jade, and we can't have another confused human-turned-Calerian wandering around. Not when we've got gangs to contend with as well as the Xphenorie."

Dom glances at Jade. "I'd rather not leave her here though. She doesn't know any of you."

My father sighs exaggeratedly and turns his cold gaze on Jade. I almost shiver for her.

"Do you understand the danger we're in, young lady? Not just us, but all humans? I assume that my son has told you about the Xphenorie?"

Jade shrugs a little. "A bit…but I don't understand."

My father shoots me an even colder glare. "Right, quick history lesson to satisfy the confused girl here, and then we're moving on. Tav, go and arrange for the machines for the DNA tests to be started up now. Jade, I'll explain as we walk. Come on."

"It's all right," I say to her, and then Dom says it too.

"You two can walk with us," my father says. "But once we've got Jade's tests running, we're getting back out there."

I nod, as does Dom, though he doesn't look happy.

The moment Jade starts moving, my father launches into his spiel:

"We evolved alongside the Xphenorie, millions of years ago. We need light to survive—I assume you know that much? Good. So, we need light, and they need darkness. Just as we generate our own light via cold fire"—he pulls a ball of flames into his palm—"the Xphenorie create their own darkness. That's how they can exist in the daytime, because the tendrils create the darkness they need."

"Also called the Fenners, for short," I add in because I think I used that term earlier in front of her.

"Yes, by those who are lazy and don't want to use their full name," my father mutters. "But they're the same, and they create darkness around them."

"Like tendrils around them?" Jade glances at me briefly. Her face is still flushed.

We head down a new corridor. The labs are right at the back of the warehouse.

"Yes," my father says. "That is correct. But these similar adaptations between them and us are where the similarities end. The Xphenorie have collective consciousness. Each of their human forms is connected to all others. There's a telepathic network between them. They stay in these separate forms for up to a year, before the culling happens. This is where they merge again, reducing their body count by about seventy percent. They regenerate in that time, and a month or so later, they…reproduce. That's probably the best word for it."

Jade's eyes narrow, and mild disgust fills her face. She steps nearer to Dom and even her footsteps sound worried now.

"But that is not the worst—they feed on humans. Humans cannot see them. Only we can. And feeding on humans is how they get their life energy. In centuries past, they fed on whoever they liked. Humans were dying out too quickly—and we also needed humans to survive. You aided in the survival of our race. We struggle with natural conception, and thus we evolved to be able to imprint our DNA on humans, transforming them into us. But the human race was not sustainable when both us and the Xphenorie were killing you in order to live, and when we were transforming the ones we didn't kill. We realized the problem.

"We made it illegal for us to reproduce that way—because we can still conceive babies naturally, it's just not as easy. That solved *that* problem for us, but we were still highly allergic to the dark. Still are. But human auras provide us some sort of protection. We used to kill humans too, the ones we didn't convert, devouring their auras, for then we could walk in the dark."

Jade flinches.

"We don't kill humans now," my father continues. "But we still need to absorb in order to cope with darker light levels and nights."

"That's why we integrate," I say. "All the dispatchers do."

"I'm at the school because of that," Dom says. "Even though I'm now twenty."

"You're twenty…and you're pretending to be seventeen? That's…creepy. Wait, you slept with Nika," she says. "And you're *twenty*."

"Didn't sleep with her," he mutters. "Just let everyone think I did. A lot of guys do that. And Nika just went along with it. But I broke up with her anyway," he says.

"She broke up with you," Jade says. "Because of your drug problem."

He shrugs. "Had to do something to stop her getting too close. Especially when it started to get serious. Didn't want to tell her what I am."

"Anyway," I say, clearing my throat. "We have to integrate into human society. The others mostly work day-jobs that give them a lot of socialization. Teachers, supermarket staff, nurses, and doctors."

"And the rest of us take shifts in our shops to get our daily doses of aura," my father says. "We've got shops throughout the country. We need humans to survive—else we die at night. That is why we created the treaty with the Xphenorie, to ensure humans live on. Now, instead of the Xphenorie feeding on and killing humans with no structure, they have monitored feeds from humans—it doesn't kill them. It's done at specific centers. And it means the Xphenorie are weaker overall."

I shift my weight from foot to foot.

"In return," my father continues, "we do not consume the auras of humans to the point that would kill them, giving us full protection from the dark—we only absorb small amounts of aura energy and use artificial light as much as possible. We do not transform humans into us, either. And the final part of the treaty is that neither the Xphenorie nor the Calerians will kill each other. So, that's the history lesson. If you've any questions, find someone else to answer them at a later point. For now, we need to concentrate on the matter at hand. The treaty outlines the exact ways each of our species may interact with humans—the Xphenorie have monitored feedings, and we absorb small amounts of aura. We are not permitted to convert humans."

"But now we have you," I say, and we reach the lab with the DNA machine. I hold open the door for my father, Jade, and Dom. "And the Xphenorie know about you. They're going to think we've broken the treaty."

My father frowns at me. He doesn't like people taking over the talking. He has to be in charge. I roll my eyes.

Jade's looking around the room, her face a little pinched.

"Okay." My father looks at me. "We have to assume the Xphenorie are going to start feeding on humans at any point. They'll assume we've broken the treaty. So, we need to be ready the moment they do. It's going to be war. Ariel, circulate that description of our rogue and notify all dispatchers to be ready. Dominic, get back to the school. The history lesson is over. You need to see if there's another converted human there. If there is, bring them back here. We don't want a Xphenorie running into them—that would just anger them more, make a devastating war all the more likely."

Dom nods but makes no movement to leave.

"*Now*," my father says. "And if this converted male isn't at the school, let me know and we'll have to do a house-to-house search across the town. We need that converted human here."

Dom exits quickly. I can't help but notice how Jade seems more nervous now without him here.

A few others arrive—namely the scientists who know how to work the machine. My father barks instructions at them, and they spring into action, getting the machine set up. Then he tugs at his goatee before his gaze connects with mine. "We're going to have to attempt the break-out now."

"What?" I stare at him. "But we haven't finalized the plans."

"If there's going to be war, we need all the numbers we can get. We need as many dispatchers on standby, all round the country, to protect humans. But we also need to get our people out. What's the minimum number you think we can use to get our people out?"

My head spins. I've only seen the plans a couple of times. "Maybe half of what we'd planned?"

"Then we make it a quarter. A quarter of our dispatchers will go immediately to the cellars to break our people out of the prisons the humans are keeping them in. The rest of us will be ready for war—and we'll also be looking for our rogue and the other converted human, if Dom does not succeed there. I'll have these orders sent out to everyone now," he says. "I'll lead the war operation, which means you, Ariel, will have to lead the break-out."

"The break-out?" My eyes widen. "But what about my brothers and sisters?"

"They're stronger fighters. I need them for the war with the Xphenorie."

My shoulders tighten, and I try to pretend like it isn't a criticism.

"What do I do?" Jade asks. "After this DNA test is done?"

My father snorts. "What makes you think you're doing anything?"

"But I can help. If these Xphenorie people are going to attack humans, I can warn them. My brother and sister are at the school."

"Humans can't see the Xphenorie," I remind her. "You can't warn them about attackers they're never going to see. Even if they're prepared, they can't fight them. That's the problem."

"You'll stay here," my father says. "We can't have you out there, in case somehow the Xphenorie you saw didn't report it. We can't risk another seeing you and spreading the word. In any case, Marli will start the DNA analysis on you now."

Jade looks at me, her eyes worried.

"It'll be okay," I say.

My father laughs. "Son, I thought you knew better to make promises you have no control over."

THIRTY-SIX
Jade

THEY TAKE MY PHONE AND THEN A NEW woman appears and introduces herself as Marli. She's Black, very pretty, and I can't help but be a bit intimidated by her beauty. She directs me to lie down in a scanning machine at the back of this room. It's not the easiest of things to climb into, and I bump my head on its ceiling.

"Hurry up," Marli says. She and I are the only ones in here. She is tall and there's something about her voice that reminds me of my mother. I'm not sure whether that's a good thing or not. I haven't seen my mother for three years.

I wonder what she'd say now, now that I've been transformed into another species.

Another *species*.

A laugh bubbles up inside me. It sounds ridiculous.

"Lie very still," Marli tells me.

I can see her by my feet, if I lift my head up a fraction. She turns away, and I see a pattern shaven into her undercut on the right side of her head. A snake.

"What do the snakes mean?" I ask.

"It's just a ruse," she says. "Pretending we're in a gang—if one of the actual gangs attacks us. Then they might be scared of retaliation. It was Dominic's idea. Not all of us have them. Now, lie still."

I concentrate hard on not moving a muscle. The woman starts the machine. A soft humming sound follows—it gets louder, and I feel it drilling into my body. I flinch.

"Be still."

I try. I didn't even know they could scan DNA this way.

The humming gets stronger, changes frequency, I think. An annoying high-pitched whine fills my ears. I hear the woman's steps as she walks around the machine. Her high heels tap the floor. I think she's leaning more heavily on one leg than the other.

A few minutes later, the machine quietens, and Marli instructs me to climb out. I do—in a very awkward and cumbersome way, banging my head on the ceiling again.

She tries to hide a smile, then asks me for a list of symptoms I'm having. "There have been no transformations in modern times, and there could be variations now to what's in the history books."

I mention the nausea and the feelings of confusion and disorientation. "And I've… I think I've been hallucinating. Seeing that woman a lot of the time when she's not actually here."

"*The woman,* as in the one who's caused all this?"

I nod.

Marli makes a note of it, and then she examines the gray patches of skin around my wrists. "These are the start points," she says. "For the DNA alteration. It's done using small amounts of our fire. A different kind of fire to what we normally summon. But all types of our fire leave the same marks on human skin."

"Right," I say. There are different types of fire? And the DNA alteration was what that old woman did to me? I wait for Marli to explain more, but she doesn't. "So, has Ariel left the warehouse now?" I ask her. "His father said something about breaking some people out of somewhere?" I think of the database Macey hacked into and how we discovered that so many fire-people were being held captive. Is that the same thing that Ariel's now going to try and sort out?

She nods and then ushers me out into a larger, communal area.

Everyone who is still here is nervous, on edge—I can tell by how jumpy they are. How no one is sitting around. How they're passing knives out between them. With a shrug, a young man gives me a knife too.

"Thanks," I say.

No one speaks to me now though, but they're speaking to each other.

"It's the waiting. I don't like it," someone says. "The anticipation of war."

"Is it actually going to be a war?" I ask.

They all turn to look at me—probably surprised that I've spoken directly. But I need to speak. I'm nervous, and one thing that always makes me feel better is talking to others. Plus, don't these people owe me, given one of them illegally transformed me, pretty much changing my life forever?

"Most likely." A woman nods. I recognize her and it takes me a moment to place her—she was the one manning the pharmacy counter when I bought the pregnancy test for Lily. The one who reacted to the marks on my wrists. Did she know then that I was transforming? Or did she just react like that because she thought one of her people had burned me?

Yet she did go and get Ariel. Was that when they realized I was transforming? And is that why someone was always trying to sell me lightbulbs?

"But they haven't done anything yet?" I frown. "And Ariel's dad said the Xphenorie have a collective consciousness?"

"That's true. And it most likely means they're making plans now."

TWO HOURS LATER, AND THE DNA ANALYSIS results are in—surprisingly quick. Marli reads from a printed piece of paper, then starts typing numbers into a computer. After several moments, she shakes her head and sighs.

"It's not one of us," she says to the other Calerians. "And whoever it is isn't registered on here. We're none-the-wiser who is trying to start this war."

Several of them grumble.

"You're causing quite the stir around here, Jade," a voice says, and I turn to see an Asian girl about my age. Her dark hair has streaks of purple in it, and it looks pretty cool.

"That's certainly one way to get the guys to notice you. And, let me tell you, they've all noticed you. You could have your pick, that's for sure."

I give her a small smile, but she's still staring at me eagerly.

"So, who do you want?" Her eyes seem to get brighter. "I can definitely help set you up with *anyone* you want. I'm like Cupid 'round here."

My smile gets more uncertain. "Uh, no. I'm okay." I blink. This is weird.

"You're not interested?" she asks.

I shake my head.

"What about girls?"

"No." I frown.

"You're not interested in *anyone*?" She pouts, then her eyes widen. "Wait, are you ace too?"

"Ace?" I say, frowning.

The girl slings an arm around my shoulder. "On the asexual spectrum. My mother is too—Tris Osborne." And then the girl's chatting away to me like we're best friends, and this just feels weird.

Asexuality? I make a mental note to look it up later. I mean, I have heard of it before. Something about not experiencing sexual attraction—and that does sound like me... I'd just never really put two and two together. If that is what it is. If that is what *I* am.

"Anyway," another voice says. A sterner one, this time. "What are we going to tell Mr. Razoa about Jade?"

I try to follow the voice, see who's speaking, but I can't work out who. Can't...

My head doesn't feel right. Dark spots hang in front of my eyes. I blink several times, but I feel different, groggy. Can't... And that girl has gone. The one who was so chatty with me.

No, this isn't right.

I try to take a deep breath—but it's suddenly like there's no air in here. There's nothing to fill my lungs with.

My heart—I can feel it pounding. Too fast, too hard.

"Jade? Jade, are you okay?"

Lucy—it's Lucy Donneley. Her face swims in front of me. She's okay, not...not dead. She's here.

"You're all right," I say. "You're okay, after that man that..."

"Yeah," she says, frowning. "I'm okay."

"But why did he do that...the Xphen—" I break off. Can't think of the rest of the word. "Isn't there the treaty? Surely that's supposed to prevent violence between them and..."

"He'd thought we'd already broken it, thought that I had, but..." She's still speaking, her mouth is still moving, only I can't understand her now. It's like she's speaking a different language and—

I... I don't know what's... Something's...

I turn, and then Lucy's not there. She's gone, and other people are here, and they're shouting.

A hand on my skin.

"She's clammy."

"Jade? Jade, can you lie down?"

Lie down?

I... I can't feel anything...can't...but there's pain. Pain in my stomach and...and something's wheezing loudly, and it's not stopping and...

No—oh God. No! Not…not *here*.

"She's having a reaction." Lucy. Lucy's voice, and I see her, the blisters on her skin, I'm focusing on them, trying to ground myself to the here and now with them and… "Like to the darkness, but it's not dark in here…"

"Humans have allergies anyway," a deep voice shouts. "Could be she's still got that."

"But what's she allergic to?"

"What do we do?"

"We can't call an ambulance for her, not when she's one of us."

I try to lift my head, try to speak. EpiPen. I need my EpiPen…but I can't…can't.

"Call Dominic Levaney or Harold Wilson," a voice shouts. "They'll know what this is and what to do. They have to!"

THIRTY-SEVEN
Ariel

BEFORE WE'VE EVEN REACHED THE COMPOUND where our people are being held, there's trouble. Not with the humans—for we've just walked through the city, bold as brass, mingling with the humans who are buying gifts from the shopping center or meeting up with friends for coffees. But within my group, within *us*. They're not happy that I'm in charge, and I can't blame them. I'm freshly graduated, and yet my father's put me in charge of dispatchers who've been working for the Razoa group for years.

"Is this going to be a problem?" I ask, turning to the nearest dispatchers. They've been grumbling among each other for a while now, shooting me looks.

"No," Keiron says, but his tone is sulky. He's never liked me, and he's also one of the most volatile of our dispatchers, temper-wise. In the last year alone, he's got in so many fights that my father's issued him written warnings. No dispatcher wants to be demoted.

"Good." I ball my fists. "Because we can't waste energy with problems among ourselves." I nod at the building ahead. It's the one that my father and the rest of our camp's council identified last week. I've got the floorplans folded in my back pocket, the cellar marked by a red circle. All the other dispatchers with me were privy to the original briefings and have the floorplans memorized. I only saw the floorplan for the first time moments before we left—and I realize how me being the only one who doesn't know it all off by heart weakens my position. Especially as I'm now the leader. "Let's go."

The building is the city library. Ornate architecture makes it look more like a cathedral or something. Pale yellow blocks of stone, with intricate carvings. Gargoyles flag either side of the huge, impressive double doors. They're open, inviting the world in.

I bound up the steps.

My energy's good. I absorbed more of the humans' auras as I was walking through the town. Just as well, because chances are the humans don't keep the captives in well-lit conditions.

They probably just keep them under minimum light levels to keep them alive. So, our people are going to be weak. And getting them out is going to be a problem. We've got drivers waiting with our trucks, but we've not got a lot of space in there. And we're about a hundred miles away from our camp.

"Oh my goodness," a human says as we enter. All of us. There's only twelve of us, plus the two driving the trucks who are still outside, given the numbers for this mission got slashed, thanks to the developments and threat of impending war. The human looks flustered as she pats her chest. "Can I help you?"

"Here for a conference," I say, keeping my voice flat and even. Her aura is glowing brightly, but I try not to absorb any. That's what we decided for these ones—because we didn't know how many humans would be in the library at this time, and we need to keep some of the auras 'fully charged' in case we run into trouble—like pitch-black corridors under the library—and need to top up. While we can make our own fire from our palms, if the darkness is trying to eat us at the same time, we can't last all that long without needing to top up our energy from an aura.

The librarian looks even more flustered. "But I don't think there's anything running now." She's looking us up and down.

We don't look threatening, because we always dress in a way designed to blend in. We're in a combination of smart casual and business attire right now. Perfect for a conference. All our firearms and knives are hidden seamlessly.

"It's the one on renewable energy," one of the dispatchers to my right says. I think her name is Elizabeth. She's new. A recent transfer from one of the London groups. "It's downstairs. Don't worry. I've been here before. I can show you the way."

And without giving the librarian a chance to reply, Elizabeth strides ahead, leading us forward.

We all follow. I make mental notes of all the exits I see as well as counting the humans in here. There's a children's group being run in the far corner. Other than that, there's another librarian and what I think are three parents, waiting for their children, talking among themselves. Five adults and eleven children.

I wish there weren't children here. Their auras are always easier to absorb than adults'. Just as the Xphenorie find it sweeter to feed from children and teenagers, we prefer those age groups too because we expend less energy as we try to absorb. I grimace. I don't want to take from children though.

Elizabeth leads us down the stairs, ignoring the librarian's protests. I feel the impact of the dimmer light in the stairwell and the corridor below, like pressure squeezing around me. But I don't let it show—none of us do. That was trained out of us early on, trained out of every Calerian. We have to blend in. I think of Jade. There's so much she doesn't know.

We keep marching. No talking now, as that uses up more energy in dimmer light.

Still, it's not painful yet—that will come with either a longer duration down here or if the light levels decrease further.

My heart hammers. We descend two more levels, and then reach the end of where the public can go.

The door ahead is padlocked. I nod at Johnny, but he's already getting the bolt-cutters out of his bag, not having waited for my signal. I breathe out hard as we wait. It doesn't take Johnny long, and Kara disarms the security alarm, and we're through.

And—

I feel them. The Calerian signature wafts over me. It's the same feeling I get when I go back to the warehouse—only, only it's…different.

I hear the intake of Elizabeth's breath. The others stiffen, looking at each other.

My mouth dries. I've felt this before—this particular *tone* of the signature.

No.

My throat feels too thick.

We're running. All of us. Using more energy—it's more economic if we walk in dimmer conditions—but my heart's pounding, and I know we can all feel the danger. My steps get faster and faster. We're a stampede.

"There!" someone shouts, and they evoke their power, lighting up the corridor so we can all clearly see the door at the end. Darkness melts away, and the signature energy is stronger.

But it's not right. Not right at all. It's just like at the—

No, don't think of that.

But my heart's pounding, and my stomach's twisting, and my knees are weakening. I reach the door and yank the handle. Nothing.

Johnny shoves me to the side, and then he's cutting through another padlock—a padlock that I hadn't even seen. It drops to the floor, and I open the door.

Pitch-black. No light at all. And—

The stench is pungent, racing out, filling my nostrils.

No.

I evoke, calling fire to my palms, just as all the other dispatchers do. We rush in—

I trip on something, go sprawling. Hit my chin and—

The fire lights up enough for me to see.

We're too late.

They kept our people in complete darkness.

I breathe deeply, because I know what this means. This is going to ignite war. *Another* war. Us against the humans. Because they've killed our people.

They're dead. Every last one of them.

Including my mother.

THIRTY-EIGHT
Elliot

"ELLIOT, NO, I CAN'T." LILY'S FACE IS FLUSHED ON the screen. She's been crying. I can see the tracks on her cheeks. "I really can't."

"You can't come and see me?" I laugh, but then I stop when I realize my girl isn't laughing. "Lil, we're together. Of course you can."

"No—you don't understand." She wipes away fresh tears.

I sit up straighter. She's crying. "What's wrong? What's happened?"

"Look, it's everything…" She sniffs loudly. "It's all such a mess and everything's happening all together. But Jade's missing."

"Your sister?" My eyebrows shoot up.

"Can't you send anyone out looking for her?" she whispers. "Please, Elliot. We're all really worried. And she's not answering her phone. It's been hours."

"Hours? That all?" I snort. "Lil, that's nothing. She'll be fine."

"No—you don't understand. She...she's not well, and we're worried. Jack's out looking too, and Nika, and some of the teachers, but they're hopeless—the teachers, that is. And they only sent two out. Two to cover the whole of the town. So, can't you help? You and your friends?"

She's looking at me so hopefully that something inside me stirs. I shake my head. "We've got bigger problems," I say. "We're catching fire-people now."

"The fire-people?" Lily frowns. "But Elliot, this is real with Jade—she's missing."

"The fire-people are real too," I say. "And they're a threat." As much as I hate Lily's interfering sister, Jade isn't. Hell, if any of the Taylors are going to be a threat, it'd be the brother. Jack. He's a fighter at least. But Jade is weak. She hides behind her brother, yet still thinks she's strong. It's almost laughable how she paid me a visit before, thinking she was tough.

"Elliot, please," Lily whispers. "I need Jade."

"You don't," I say. "You've got me. You don't need any of your family."

"I do," she says. "You don't understand. I've only got Jade. And Jack. My parents..." She falters, and her face pinches inward.

"I understand," I tell her. "I ain't got my parents now."

"That's different—they're in prison," she says with a small hiccup. "They still wanted you. But mine don't. They never did. They said it was bad enough one accidental pregnancy gave them twins. And then I had to come along too."

Her tears flow faster, and I want to reach through the screen, hold her. Tell her it'll be okay. That I'll make everything okay. And I will. That's what I do for my girl.

"And they hated us. They really did—do. They never visit us, Elliot. It's been three years since I've seen them—and parents aren't supposed to be like that. They're supposed to *be* there for their children. They're supposed to help them, and I need their help more than ever now. But they won't give it, and they don't even know. And I'm just so scared, because Mum's supposed to be my role model—but what if I'm just the same? Because this wasn't planned either. And that's why I need Jade, because she's been like a mother to me, and I need her around for all of this because…" She trails off and her head jolts. Her mouth drops open, makes an O shape.

"Lily?" My tone is dark, and her words echo through my head on loop. *But what if I'm just the same? Because this wasn't planned either.* "What are you talking about?"

She's shaking. "N-n-nothing."

"Lily." My voice is even sharper and she flinches. I clench my phone tighter, feel like I want to smash it. "Tell me you're not pregnant."

My chest rises and falls rapidly as I wait for her answer. I can't be a father. Shit. I can't… And Lily's at school and—this house, this house is no place for a baby. But she'll have to move in here. They both will. And I'm so caught up in these thoughts that I nearly miss Lily's words.

"I am," she whispers, her voice so small.

Everything inside me tightens. Pregnant. A baby.

I let out a long breath. "You're telling me this by phone?" I stare at her. "Not even face-to-face? And hell, you weren't even going to tell me." Rage unfurls inside me. "How far gone are you?"

She looks down, and I see the parting of her hair. She doesn't look back up.

"Lily?" I shout. My voice makes her jump. Hell, it almost makes me jump.

"I'm sorry," she says. "Jade told me not to and—"

"So, you were never going to tell me?" Something inside me snaps. "Because of *Jade*? What were you going to do? Have an abortion and pretend my baby never existed?"

"No!" she cries. "Elliot, I—" She crumples, and she's a messy crier.

Anger builds inside me, stronger and stronger. I think of Jade. She needs to learn not to mess with me once and for all. I mean, I warned her and Jack what I could do to them. Greylake threats aren't empty threats.

"Elliot, I'm sorry," Lily cries, gulping.

"It's okay." It takes an extortionate amount of control to keep my voice calm. "I'm sure Jade just thought she was doing the right thing." I breathe in and out slowly. "Don't worry, I'll find her."

"No, you can't go after her to hurt her," she cries.

"I won't." Inside, I am laughing. "And I'll tell my mates not to hurt a hair on her head. Wouldn't want to hurt you, Lil, would I?"

"You promise?" Her voice is small.

I flex my hands. "I promise. I'll find your sister. I'll bring her back to you."

I end the call and a small smile twists its way onto my face. Lily's so gullible—it's what makes her endearing. Even if she is naive and doesn't know how the world works.

Because, yes, I'll get my mates to find Jade Taylor, all right. And then I'll make sure she pays for everything that bitch has done.

THIRTY-NINE
Jade

"ARE YOU SURE YOU'RE OKAY NOW?" LUCY Donneley asks. She's sitting in a chair next to my bed, and she gives me a weak smile.

In the doorway, there's another woman. She looks Asian, has beautiful tawny hair, and wears red-framed spectacles. She introduced herself as a medic, a little while ago.

I frown, trying to think. How much time has passed? But I don't know. I'm disorientated. I always am after anaphylaxis.

My throat burns, feels raw, but I nod. "I'm okay. I just... I need my meds though. The, uh, antihistamines." I blink slowly. Usually, I'd be at the hospital now and they'd give me steroids too, but the medic said the humans would realize what I am as soon as they started doing tests on me. They'd lock me away, in dim cellars.

"You'll need to rest for the next few days." The tawny-haired woman gives me a sympathetic smile. "You gave us quite the scare there."

"We need to make sure we've got these EpiPens in here," Lucy says.

"And we need to watch her for a biphasic response," the tawny-haired woman says.

"A what?" Lucy says.

"The symptoms can sometimes return a few hours later." She strides toward my bed and then holds her right hand out to me. "I'm Tris, by the way. I doubt you remember the introductions earlier." Her smile is easy.

I shake my head.

"You were very disorientated and only semi-conscious. Anyway, I'm Tris Osborne. Lucy tells me you've already met my daughter, Dinah. She can be annoying, that one. Watch her. But, yes, I'm a medic. I'm primarily stationed up at Barnstaple, but I visit Northwood a lot. My brother lives here. And, luckily, I was already on my way to Northwood following Mr. Razoa's summoning. I was able to get here quickly and Lucy had already administered an EpiPen."

I turn to Lucy. "You found it? My bag?" But I can't see my bag. It's not on my bed and doesn't appear to be in this room. And it's a strange room. Just one bed and a blood pressure machine. The cuff, I realize now, is around my arm. Doesn't seem to be taking a reading now though.

"No," Lucy says. "But luckily, at the corner shop they have an EpiPen. I remember speaking to a guy that worked there and he told me he was deathly allergic to peanuts. So, I hoped they'd carry one."

"And you really should carry one all the time," Tris says.

"I... I do," I say. My voice sounds weak—so weak. "I don't know what happened to my bag."

"Well, in any case, how are you feeling now?

"I'm... I'm just weak, nauseous."

"And what is your allergy, Jade?" She turns to Lucy. "We're going to have to be very careful."

"It's...MCAS. Mast Cell Activation Syndrome. It's, uh, a..." I can't think of the words. My head's still foggy.

"I'll Google it," Tris says. She pulls out a phone and taps the screen for several moments. Then she looks up at me. "How frequent do you get these episodes and what are the triggers?"

I shrug. "It's generally well-managed... I don't know. Last full episode like this was a few months ago. Usually...it's smaller reactions. Uh, headaches, nausea."

Tris nods. "Right. Okay, well, Lucy, I want you to make sure that everyone in this warehouse knows of Jade's condition. We're all going to need to know the signs to look out for. We need EpiPens and—"

Lucy's radio goes off and a voice rings through the room, muffled. I can't make it out, but Lucy and Tris both freeze. Then Tris runs out of the room.

"What?" I look at Lucy. "What's happened?"

But Lucy doesn't answer. Her eyes are wide. "I... I have to go. Uh, sorry. Call if you need anything."

I take the blood pressure cuff off and pull myself out of bed. My legs are shaky, weak, and my knees feel wobbly. But I stand, and I walk. I'm slow, and my head's hurting, and I'm still nauseous. But I make it out of the room, into a corridor.

There are people bustling at the end of it, all moving quickly. Grabbing things.

"What do we do?" someone asks.

"Yes, Ariel just said that," another voice snaps, and I can't keep up.

Ariel. Something's happened to him? The mission he was on?

I try to ask questions, but no one answers me. I just get sent angry looks and get told to move out of the way. But something's wrong.

I try again and again, but people push me aside, ignore me.

I breathe deeply. It's got to be the Xphenorie. They've attacked humans? Stopped the Calerians from getting more numbers? Because of the war—because they're going to feed from the school. It has to be.

I hobble forward and through an open double door and into another corridor. I have to get back to the school. I have to warn my family and friends, despite what the Calerians have all said about humans not seeing the Xphenorie. It's still better that they're prepared, even a bit. Right? I can't leave my friends utterly helpless and ignorant to a danger that they don't even know exists.

Maybe if I'm there, I can help them. I'll be able to see the Xphenorie. I can tell them where they are.

Yes. That's what I have to do.

I take a deep breath, and then I slip out of the room, looking around, ready to run if someone spots me.

But no one does. They're all talking among themselves. No one looks at me.

I move down the corridor.

My head's foggy, and I'm disorientated enough without being in a new space. So many corridors and rooms inside the warehouse. It takes me several minutes—that seem to stretch on and on—until I navigate my way outside. But then I'm out, free—breathing in the cool air.

Shit.

It's getting dark.

I stare at the disappearing sun, at the orange and peach hues streaked across the sky, and suddenly I'm aware of my skin prickling, burning, feeling irritated. Is that really because of the lower light levels or is just because I know for sure now what I am?

My nausea intensifies. I think of the other night, curled up on the floor of the bathroom. After I'd finally stopped vomiting, I'd slept in the bathroom, on the cold tiles, with the light on. Am I really so intolerant to the dark now? Or do I just feel worse because of the MCAS episode?

Mr. Razoa said that I can currently handle the dark better than the other fire-people at the moment, didn't he? That my transformation hasn't completed yet.

I force myself to speed up. The Calerians' warehouse is on the other side of the town, but I think I can get to the school in thirty if I run. Damn. I wish I had Lily's love for P.E. I can't remember the last time I ran for thirty minutes, flat out. But I have to.

I have to get to the school. I have to warn Jack and Lily, and Nika and Macey. Hell, I have to warn everyone.

They won't believe you.

I push away the voice. It's not helpful. And, anyway, I'll find a way to make them believe me. I will.

Something flies at me—

I scream, ducking down and—

A dark figure. The Xphenorie?

I open my mouth to scream, but then there's more. More figures. All closing around me.

I turn, heart pounding. The wind whips my hair around my face, and it's like snakes trying to coil around me, squeezing and suffocating.

"Well, well, well, don't run, darling," a male voice says. Unfamiliar—I think. Or is this the Xphenorie that saw me earlier?

I spin, trying to see which one spoke, trying to recognize any of them—but they haven't got much mist around them. No tendrils and—

Something thuds against the back of my head.

Sharp pain and—

—and then there is nothing.

FORTY
Jade

I OPEN MY EYES, SLOWLY. PAINFULLY. Something wet on my face and my vision's not right. it's grainy, blurry. And—I blink, trying to see. Walls around me. A gray, tin ceiling. I blink hard, try to sit up.

There's light in here—a dim lightbulb, hanging from the ceiling by a wire. Part of the rubber casing has gone, revealing wiring inside. The light is on, but it's dim. And my skin—it's reacting to the darkness already?

Or am I just too focused on what I am now and imagining things, working myself up into a state? Either way, I've got to get away. Have to get away.

"Ah, you're awake," a voice says.

A voice I know very well.

I turn slowly, and I see him. Elliot is sitting in an office chair by the desk. We're in his garage. Just me and him? My head pounds. Weren't there others? Is it him? Not the Xphenorie?

"What are you..." My voice sound weak, scratchy. Nausea rises, and I touch my face. My hands come away sticky.

Elliot laughs—and laughs and laughs. His chair creaks, and then he jumps up, springs toward me.

I recoil back, but my reactions are slower. So much slower than they should be.

"I told you," he snarls. "I warned you what would happen if you interfered. Thought you could stop me finding out, eh?"

I stare at him. There are marks on his face. Gray marks—like the ones on my wrists and on Kelley-Anne's face. He's come into contact with Calerians too? Hell, of course he has. He's in one of the gangs that's hunting them, killing them.

Like he's going to kill me...

My breaths come in short, sharp bursts, and I try to calm them, because I need to remain calm. I have to. And talking to him, that's the best thing to do, isn't it?

"Finding out?" I whisper. Even my whisper doesn't sound like my own.

"The baby," he says. "*My* baby. And you thought you could get Lily to abort my baby—"

"I never said that." The words rush out my mouth, and I feel sick.

Elliot laughs. "Stay exactly where you are, Jade." He spits my name like it's poison as he moves toward me. His figure blocks the light from me and his shadow falls on me, seems to hurt me.

I whimper. I'm weak—oh, God. I'm weaker than I thought. And my head hurts. Must be where he hit me on the street. Am I concussed?

"Aw, are you scared?" he mocks.

That's when I see the spanner in his hands. My eyes focus on it and I can't look away from it.

My hand goes to my pocket, for my phone. But of course it's not there. The woman took it before I went in the DNA machine. And then after my MCAS episode, I never even thought to ask for my phone. And I walked out into Northwood, not even thinking of it.

"Please," I whisper, looking up at him. "Please, Elliot."

He just smiles and opens his arms wide. "Come on in, boys," he says, projecting his voice.

The sound of metal scraping metal fills my ears as the large garage door slides back. And I see them.

The whole Greylakes gang is here.

FORTY-ONE
Jade

SO MANY OF THEM. I STARE AT THEM. THE Greylakes. Thuggish men. Women. All of them are heading toward me. They're holding knives and spanners and wrenches and—

I go cold when I see the gun.

"Make her suffer," Elliot says. "Make her suffer a lot, and then kill her." He focuses back on me. "You should've listened to that first warning I gave you. Because no one messes with us. No one."

Adrenaline pounds through me. The door—the sliding door is still open. They're all advancing on me, but can I somehow get past them and make a run for it?

I try to push myself to my feet and—

Oh, shit. Pain reverberates through me, and my head suddenly feels too heavy. I fall to the side, crashing back onto the cold, stone floor.

The gang reaches me.

I scream as a booted-foot connects with my stomach. Scream and scream and—

"Aw, Jade, don't faint. Don't be weak. You need to take notice of this," Elliot says. "Feel this pain, because this is what you deserve. Do you hear me?"

His face, up close, garish. Eyeballs so round and protruding. Sweat on his red face, mingling with the gray marks. Teeth gnashing.

Foot in my stomach.

Fingers crushed.

Pain and—

Laughter—evil laughter. "Go on then, boys. Don't hold back."

I scream and—

And something breaks. Snaps. I feel it inside me. Like something's been cut and—

Fire explodes from me. Flames. Everywhere.

I scream, feel the heat of it and—

"She's one of them!"

"Freak!"

"Kill her!"

Flames pulse around me, and I'm breathing too fast, too fast for my heart to beat properly as I stare at the fire.

Some of the gang are screaming, and I see burns on them.

Burns that I did?

My hands lift up—almost like someone else is controlling me—and I stare at them. At the flames that are still flickering from my palms, my fingers, my fingertips.

The moment I stand, the flames surge. Men, women, screaming.

"Get out! Get out!"

I trip over a body. Charred, burned flesh. The smell wraps around me, makes me gag and—

I've killed them?

They're...*dead*?

Something jolts inside me, and numbness spreads through me. This is... This can't be real. It can't. It can't. I can't be a *murderer*.

Something clatters, and my attention focuses on movement. Elliot and some of the others who are still alive are running. I see them disappear and—

And I'm alone. Alone in here with charred bodies and fire, flames climbing higher and higher.

Am I trapped? No, I can't be. The flames are mine—they're not burning my hands.

I barrel toward the door, through a wall of the fire. It doesn't hurt me at all, and I run, get outside, and—

Cold air washes over me.

In the distance, I can hear sirens. So many sirens. For this fire?

I gulp.

I have to move.

I have to go. I—

"Jade?"

I jolt. "Dom?" I stare at him. He's panting hard.

"Come on," he shouts, and then he's grabbing my hand. "We have to get away from here."

I KILLED MEN, WOMEN. I KILLED PEOPLE.

My heart pounds and pounds, and I stare around the warehouse room. I'm back here. I don't remember the walk. Don't remember anything. Just...just Dom. And he's here. He's talking to that woman who did my DNA tests.

"The Xphenorie will find the bodies of the gang," she is saying. She casts a glance over to me. "Her signature will be on them. A Calerian signature. Another instance of us breaking the treaty. Contact Mr. Razoa immediately and—"

A phone rings. Dom's phone. Not mine—I'm holding mine now. Dom retrieved it from the lab where I'd left it.

I watch him answer his phone, watch him nod and nod.

"What is it?" the woman asks him, her voice clipped. "Is there more danger?"

Dom shakes his head. "Another update from Ariel. They're on their way back. But this..." He gestures toward me. "We've got to get rid of these men Jade killed."

"Can we dispose of them and remove her signature?" she asks.

"I don't know," Dom says. "Dispatchers would have more luck, but Ariel's team's a good few hours away. And I don't want to call Mr. Razoa and take some of those that are on duty here tonight because..."

My phone rings, and I stop listening to them, just concentrate on pulling it out of my pocket.

I stare at the caller ID. "Jack?"

"Jade..." His voice is distant, echoing. "Where are you? Are—"

Screams. I can hear *screams*.

"Jade? Jade, are you there?"

"I'm here," I say, breathless.

"I don't know what's going on," Jack yells. "The school and… Craig's dead and—"

A scream. A scream that rips my insides into shreds.

"Jack?" I jolt. "Jack!"

But he doesn't answer.

I look at Dom. My vision wobbles. "It's the school. They're being attacked."

FORTY-TWO
Jade

EVERYTHING HAPPENS TOO QUICKLY—AND IT'S like I can't follow it all. All I can think is my brother, sister, and best friends are in danger. We cram into a truck, all of us from the warehouse, to get to the school, to help the other dispatchers who must be there.

"Drive faster!" I yell, panting, out of breath like I've just run a marathon. I lean forward, trying to see over the front seats. A woman's driving, but I don't know who she is.

"I'm going as fast as I can."

But it's not fast enough. Not fast enough. Not fast enough.

I feel sick, and I try to phone Jack again—but I can't get through. It just rings and rings. And I think about the scream that I heard right before everything cut off. No—he can't be dead. Or worse. He can't.

I try calling Lily. And Nika. And Macey. No one's answering.

Dom's squashed next to me—we're all crammed in here, way more than the truck's capacity—and he's trying to phone his friends.

Neither of us can get through. We share worried looks.

"It'll be okay," a man says, trying to give me a reassuring smile from by the window on the other side. "Mr. Razoa was expecting this. He'll be there with his team. They'll protect your friends."

But what if they don't? What if they can't? What if it's too late?

Bile rises in my throat. I swallow it down quick and—

And the school comes into sight.

"Oh my God." I stare at the dark mist surrounding the buildings. It's a fog wrapping tightly, tightly, tightly. The air around it shimmers.

The engine gets throatier as we drive as close as we can, then the sounds of brakes squealing. We're all thrown forward, but no one appears hurt by it.

Everyone jumps out of the truck, and then someone pulls me out too. I stumble, lean against the truck. My breaths seem to fall away as I stare. My throat constricts. Nausea again—so sudden. I gag and retch.

"It's because of the Fenners," one of them tells me. "They make us all nauseous. Ignore it if you can." He gives me a small pat on the back.

"Where the hell are Mr. Razoa and the dispatchers?" Dom yells. "Has anyone seen him?"

My mind fogs as I stare around. No people here—no Calerians fighting. No sign of humans.

No…*nothing*.

"Right. We're going in," someone says, and then we're all running.

"Knives will injure the Xphenorie," the woman who drove tells me. "But only our fire can kill them. Injure them first with the knife and then you'll use less energy. We need to keep our energy levels as high as possible, especially now it's almost dark."

I don't know how I didn't notice the near-darkness this time—not when earlier I thought my skin was reacting to dim light. But the woman's right. It is nearly full night.

I grab the knife from my belt and new energy surges through me.

"Save as many humans as possible," Dom shouts—as if he needs to!

We pour through the gates. Dom shouts directions for us—and we're splitting up. All of us. I stare after them for a second. Then I hear a scream. One of them or us? And I don't even know if I'm thinking of humans as *them* or not.

Adrenaline fills me, crushing into my lungs, and I run, heading for the basement. That's where Jack would've been at this time, isn't it?

I throw open a door to the math block—it clatters against the wall and—

Figures cloaked in dark mist race toward me.

I scream, jolting back, then lift my hand up. Just like I produced the fire in Elliot's garage, it happens now. It's instinct. I'm not consciously doing this. Flames erupt from my fingers—a bolt of fire going straight for the Xphenorie.

Shrieks and screams. Something fizzles. Dark shapes shrinking, falling, disintegrating.

Until they're gone. Too late, I remember the knife in my other hand and the woman's words.

Because I killed them with fire—just like the gang. And I try not to think about them, those humans whom I killed earlier. Because I've got to stay in control here. Have to help. Have to find my brother and sister, my friends.

Have to...

A choking, gurgling sound fills my ears.

I turn, heart pounding, and see a figure lying at the side of the corridor. "Mr. Wilson?" I rush toward him, breathing hard. Blood has pooled around his body.

He looks up at me.

"Hide, Jade," he whispers, his words croaky and low. "Hide." He pushes me away with weak movements. "Too late for me, but...you can get away. Tell the others not to come back for me. I'm not going to make it."

The others?

My eyes widen. He's a fire-person, a Calerian, too? But my head spins, and I can't concentrate on that.

"Where's Jack?" My voice cracks. "Do you know where my brother is? My sister?"

But he shakes his head, and then his eyes still. His whole body stills.

"Mr. Wilson?" My voice rings out, taut, like it's about to shatter. I shake him, but he doesn't respond. A crawling sensation fills me and my stomach tightens.

I look around—and I see them, the bodies. They're everywhere. Students. Teachers.

Dead.

The floor suddenly seems too insubstantial. I'm sinking. I'm—

Breathe.

I try to breathe, ignoring the smells of murder and death. I crawl from one body to another, checking each for faces I know. But these students are all younger. Year 7s or 8s.

I gulp.

Go.

Somehow, I pull myself up and I run, my heart threatening to give out. Twice, I slip on blood. I round a corner, my stomach threatening to expel its contents, and nearly crash into the Xphenorie. Female figures, this time.

I conjure my fire—just as someone on the far side of the Xphenorie does as well. Our fire meets, and the Xphenorie disintegrate. I see a Calerian for a few seconds, before he's turned away, running. Was he one of those I traveled with? Or are Mr. Razoa's teams already in here?

Screams cut through the air. High-pitched. Young-sounding.

I follow the screams, jumping over bodies. Pain shoots up my right leg as I land awkwardly. More Xphenorie are fighting ahead, but I catch glimpses of flames and sparks. Calerians are already here.

I duck through a side door, plow down a corridor. My lungs threaten to burst and the pain in my leg's getting stronger, but I refuse to stop. I have to keep going.

"Jack? Jack? Lily?' I scream their names as I go, and I pass more students—some alive, huddled together, eyes wide—

but I can't stop for them. I have to find my brother and sister. Have to.

"Jade!" A hand grabs me, pulls me into a doorway. I catch my arm on it, spin around, trying to fight whoever it is, and come face-to-face with Kelley-Anne.

Her eyes are wide, and then she turns her head and shouts, "She's here. Jack!"

My eyes adjust to the darkness—so dark in this room. But there are people. So many. My friends and—

"Jack!" I spot him, and I'm running.

I crash into him, and everyone is shouting, but I can't make out words. I pull back, looking around. I spot Lily and Nika together, with Macey and a couple of younger students. Relief pulls through me. Everyone else in here is in my year group.

"Shut the door!" someone yells. "We can't have them know we're in here."

"Did you see them?" someone else shouts, and I realize the question's directed at me. "We haven't seen them—how many gunmen?"

Gunmen. They think it's shooters here.

Because they can't see the Xphenorie.

"We've heard the screams," Nika says. "And teachers told us to get in here, but then they disappeared—"

"It's…monsters," I say. "They're invisible." Then I realize how ridiculous and stupid I sound. But everyone's looking at me. "There's a war going on. The fire-people against these men who are invisible. But there are loads of them."

"What? How do you know if they're invisible?" Lauren asks.

"Because I can see them."

"Yes, you can see them, can't you?" a low voice says.

I turn, my heart pounding, and I see Craig. What? He's not dead? I thought…

I take a step back, stand on someone's foot.

"Jade, what's going on?" Lily's voice is too high. I can hear her breathing, and it's too fast. Like she's going to panic.

"And do you all want to know why she can see them?" Craig asks, throwing his arms wide. He catches a few people in the face. "Because she's a fire-person too. An unnatural freak of nature."

There's an intake of breath. Several people whimper.

"But it's all right," he says. "Because we don't have your people stopping us anymore. And we're going to sort it out."

We? I stare at him—and as I stare, tendrils grow from him. Dark tendrils, weaving through the air. A manic smile crosses his face.

Someone swears. "Where did he go?"

But Craig hasn't gone anywhere. He's right here—he's part of the Xphenorie. And he's invisible now for non-Calerians—but he wasn't earlier. He's been visible the whole time. Always a Xphenorie? My head pounds.

Craig raises an arm. In his hand is a gun. A gun that he points directly at me

FORTY-THREE
Jade

NO ONE SCREAMS AS CRAIG WAVES THE GUN around. I glance at Jack and Nika, my breathing hard and fast, like Lily's. If they can't see Craig, does that mean they can't see the gun he's holding too? Does his invisibility mask it?

"Time's up, Jade." Craig smirks. No one reacts. Thy can't hear him. Mustn't be able to. But he was visible before—always has been!

He pulls the trigger.

I duck as the bullet flies, and, somehow, it misses me. My breaths pound in my ears and—

Several people scream, and then fire blasts toward Craig.

But it's not my fire.

I turn, heart pounding, and see Macey—Macey *evoking fire*.

Macey? My eyes widen. He's one of them—us—too? What the—

Another gunshot. Screaming, everywhere.

I spin and grab hold of Jack and Nika, drag them to the floor with me. Where's Lily? I look up and—

Can't see her.

Another gunshot.

"Jade! Help me!" Macey yells, still shooting fire at Craig.

I jolt as I stand, heart pounding. I summon my fire, sending it forward and—

More people scream. They're screaming at me. Me and Macey.

Craig's face contorts as more fire reaches him—a third person? What the hell? I see Kelley-Anne with her hands in front of her. She's shrieking the most high-pitched scream as flames pour from her palms. Her face holds terror.

Kelley-Anne's a Calerian too? That's three of us.

But I can't concentrate on this because Craig's moving forward, toward Aisha. He grabs her, and our flames are dimming—dimming so much. I try to yield more fire, but there's pain in my hands now. My skin's prickling and—

It's too dark.

I glance up at Macey, see his ashen face. He's still producing fire—but the current of it isn't as strong now. It's weakening, and Craig—Craig is...feeding. His hands are on either side of Aisha's face, and her body's gone limp. He's holding her up by her skull.

"What's happening to her?" Jack yells, and I realize it must look like she's floating.

"She's possessed!"

"It's them!" Lauren yells, pointing at me and Macey, and then Kelley-Anne. And suddenly faces are turning on us.

"Get more fire!" Macey yells at me, and Kelley-Anne is summoning more too.

I try—hold my hands out and summon it, but...nothing. Weakness fills me, and my head feels too light. I need energy. We all do. "Switch the light on!"

"No, they'll find us in here!" Lauren shouts.

"They'll have seen the flames through the windows," someone else shouts. "Oh God. We're done for. We're all going to die."

"You're not going to die," I hiss.

"You're the freak." Lauren shakes her head. She points at me. "Get her out. Get them all out. It's them. It's the fire-people doing—"

Kelley-Anne screams as she turns to Lauren, sparks flitting from her fingers. "We are trying to save you."

"Get them out!"

Hands shove me suddenly, and I stumble, fall. Whack my head on something hard. Dark spots in my vision.

I see Aisha's body on the floor. My heart jolts. Is she...

"Jade?" Jack's voice, frantic. I think I hear Lily, too. And Nika? I'm not sure.

My head spins. Craig—I can't see him. Where is he? Did Kelley-Anne's fire kill him?

I see Macey pushing past me, toward the door. Or is he being pushed that way?

"And get her out too."

Four guys from the football team shove me, push me, half carry me.

"No!" Jack shouts.

The door flies open, and I fall across the threshold, dry-retching. Through blurry vision, I see Macey in front of me. Someone else behind me. I turn. Kelley-Anne. Her face is red, and tears fall down her face.

"We're helping you—we're…" Kelley-Anne's voice trails off, and I see her eyes go glassy as she looks behind me.

Macey coughs and retches, spews vomit across our feet. I jump back, and the door behind me—the one into the room where are friends are—slams shut.

"Oh no," Kelley-Anne says.

I look ahead—down the corridor. And I see them. Dark masses, tendrils, figures laughing and shouting.

"You think you three babies can protect those humans?" a low, sly voice asks. The tone is strange, sort of projected so the words have an echoing quality.

They're going to kill everyone in the room. My heart lurches and my chest squeezes. Jack, Lily, Nika… *Everyone.*

"Yes," I shout, and I try to sound brave. "We're protecting our people."

"*Your* people?" There's a snigger from the Xphenorie. "You ain't human, love."

"You're not getting past us," Kelley-Anne shouts.

"We'll see about that," the Xphenorie say, and it's all these figures here speaking. All of them speaking as one. The effect is deafening.

I turn slightly, trying to shield my ears. I can feel blood thumping through my feet. The Xphenorie move closer. All of them slinking toward us.

My heart pounds. My stomach twists, growing heavier and heavier. I'm aware of my skin prickling, burning, and I look across at Kelley-Anne. Large blisters run down her face now, down her neck, disappearing under her collar.

Macey's faring slightly better but—

They rush at us, the Xphenorie.

"Now!" I yell, raising my hands. I get two flames out, flames that barely lick the outer tendrils of the mist.

The closer the Xphenorie get, the weaker I become. My body's shaking and I'm...I'm falling. I try to stop myself, grab onto Macey, but he screams as I touch his skin. I see blisters, huge blisters and—

"Give up, little babies. This isn't your fight. Just let us have our dinner, and we'll leave you alive. For now."

Laughter.

My head spins. Someone shouts something—Kelley-Anne? I'm not sure. I...

"You're not getting in here!" I press my back against the door, then twist my head. "Jack? Lock the door! The Xphenorie are—"

Something hits my forehead.

Hot, white pain. My eyes and—

I slump, breathing hard. Lungs burning. What the...

Mist. Dark mist. Over me. Tendrils on my skin, touching me. Sizzling. The smell of burned flesh wraps around me.

And this is it.

I'm going to die.

Going to—

I try to open my eyes, but I can't... Are they already open? Did I close them? I can't tell, can't...

"Keep the door locked," Macey yells, and his voice reaches me and I see, I see something.

Dark eyes over me. Soft tendrils and mist. A crooning voice and—

"Children—my children. It's okay. Mother's here."

Gray hair, draping over me. Wizened face. Paper skin, wrinkled. Soft hands.

"It's okay," she says. And it's her. The woman who started it all. She's back.

Mother's here.

"Jade!" a voice shouts. Dom's voice.

And everything explodes in a world of fire.

FORTY-FOUR
Jade

I OPEN MY EYES SLOWLY. EVERYTHING POUNDS, hurts. My head and—

"Careful," a voice says.

I blink through the haze. Everything is a swirl of color.

"Ariel?"

He's above me, his face sort of hovering. "It's all right. You're safe now. We got you out."

Out? I frown, but my head's foggy. Out from where?

I try to sit up, and he helps me. My hands and arms are burned, covered in blisters, and my leg—there's something wrong with my leg.

"You'll be all right," he says and—

It all comes back, hurling toward me. The memories. My friends. My family. The Xphenorie. Kelley-Anne. Macey.

"What?" My heart pounds. "What happened? Where are they? Jack and Lily? Nika? Macey?"

"Here," he says. "We're at the warehouse, Jade. We got all that we could save out of the school and the town. We're holed up here."

"Holed up?"

"It's *war*," he says. "Come on. My father's trying to address the Xphenorie now. He's trying to stop it going any further."

He helps me sit up more and then supports my weight. My leg isn't as useless as I thought, but it takes me a while to stumble onto my feet. "Where's Jack? And Lily?" I ask again.

"They're safe. Come on. They're in the meeting room. Nearly everyone's there."

"Okay." I take a wobbly step forward. My heart pounds. "I'm coming."

Ariel helps me a little, and I ask him about Craig. "How was he visible to non-Calerians for so long? I mean, I thought all the Xphenorie couldn't be seen by humans?"

"They can't," he says. "We don't know why Craig was like that. That's never happened before. An anomaly, a fluke—that's all we can guess. Dom couldn't even sense him as a Fenner—Craig didn't make any of us feel nauseous like they usually do. All we can hope is that he's a one-off."

By the time we get to a big room where a lot of people are, my heart's pounding. There are a lot of people in here, but only one person is speaking: Mr. Razoa. I see him at the front, on some sort of stage, addressing a large screen. On the screen are the Xphenorie. Just seeing their image makes my stomach want to flip and I take several steadying breaths. I study the humans again, recognize a few from the year below at school. Where are Jack and Lily and Nika? Are they here? And Macey? Kelley-Anne?

"Do you not see how this will end, if this spreads?" Mr. Razoa's voice is loud. "You will wipe out the very people that you need in order to survive. Killing humans like this is suicide for you." He takes a few steps, then starts pacing back and forth. "We have to be practical in this matter. We cannot let our feelings control us."

"He's trying to reach an agreement with them," Ariel says, but I'm barely listening to him or his father. I've got to find my brother and sister. "They've only decimated our town so far, so—"

"Jade!"

There's a blur of movement as Jack dives toward me, engulfs me in a hug.

Tears run down my face. Relief. Over his shoulder, I see Lily and Nika. Some other students. Kelley-Anne and Macey. And Aisha—she's still alive. Thank God. A few teachers are here too. Some Year 7s and 8s. One of the caretakers from the school and two cleaners. And some elderly humans whom I don't recognize. But there's no more than fifty of us.

Are we all that's left of Northwood?

I pull away from Jack and look at Ariel. "Is this…everyone?"

"The Xphenorie have taken this town. A massacre. But your quick thinking—you and Macey and Kelley-Anne—you saved so many of them. All these humans."

He gestures around and I notice now that there are Calerians by every little group of humans. They're explaining to them what's happening. I can hear Jack saying, "But I can't *see* anything on that screen." Hear him protesting, saying all of this is ridiculous.

"Jade!" a voice cries out.

I turn and see Macey. He's smiling at me, but then he stops. His expression just drops away, like his face has lost all tension, and he's looking behind me. I turn and see Dom.

"Hey." Macey calls out. "Dom! You're one of these people as well?"

"Calerians," Dom says. I turn slightly so I can see him—he's right behind me—and then Macey's with us. "And you're one too, Mace."

"What about your dad?" Macey asks. "Does my mum know? Does she know about any of this?"

My eyes widen as I realize what's going on—Macey's mother recently married Dom's father. That's how Macey and Dom became stepbrothers last year.

"Yes," Dom says. "She knows. Don't worry."

"But they're…they're *married*," Macey says, shaking his head. His glasses slip down his nose a little.

Dom shrugs. "Human-Calerian marriages used to be common," he says. "Not so much now when we're encouraged to live in our camps for our own safety. But not all of us live in the camps. You've got lone Calerians out there too, mainly in the countryside—because we've got to cover all areas, have our people protecting as many humans as possible, in case the Fenners attack. Our camps are in towns and cities, but the Calerians in the countryside often end up marrying humans. Not all of these humans are told about us, but I know your mother knows. So, don't worry. She'll accept what you are."

Macey blinks slowly. "I… I wasn't worried about that— God, I haven't even thought of…"

"Look, I can fill you in on a lot of stuff now," Dom says. "Like about me, for start. Because I'm stationed at the school. I'm also twenty, not seventeen. We have our people stationed at most schools, just in case. We keep an eye on things."

"Okay." Macey's eyes take on an unfocused look. "I need to phone my mother," he says. "I'll catch up with you on all this…later?"

I watch as Macey slips from the room. Dom gives me a shrug and then leaves too. Says he needs to smoke.

I wonder if what he's smoking will be illegal. Maybe his drugs problem is real, not just part of his cover at school to explain why he doesn't quite act like the other students and why he and Nika broke up.

I turn and stare at Ariel. My neck aches, and my shoulders feel stiff, like I've been carrying a rucksack that's way too heavy. I'm so close to feeling too overwhelmed by it all.

"Ariel," says a voice, and he turns.

The speaker is tall and looks like Ariel.

Ariel nods at me, then inclines his head toward the newcomer. "This is my brother, Ricardo."

Ricardo nods at me. "Who's that?" He points toward my friends and it takes me a few moments to realize he's pointing at Nika. She's on the edge of the group, talking to Lily.

"Nika," I say. "Nika Takada."

"Why?" Ariel asks Ricardo, then his eyes widen. "Oh."

"What?" I look at them both.

Ariel frowns, looking at his brother. "Can you get Marli to test her?"

"*Test* her?" I say, just as Ricardo nods and leaves. "What? Nika needs testing too?" I frown. "She's not one of us—is she?"

He shakes his head. "But she's not… She's not reading as humans normally do."

I frown. "What does that mean?"

"I don't know," he says. "But we'll do tests. See if there's anything in it. I mean, I didn't notice this earlier. And, sometimes, we can be wrong. It could just be me being tired."

"But your brother sensed something too?"

"Like I said, it could be nothing. Probably is nothing."

"But is she okay?" I ask. My voice wobbles.

Ariel gives a bright smile. "Yes. Like I said, we can do tests later to confirm. It'll be nothing. Don't say anything to her though. I'm sure she's fine. Don't want anyone panicking. Anyway, listen to this." He nods at his father. "He's still trying to appeal to the Fenners."

I turn and look at Mr. Razoa, up on the stage.

"These were acts by rogues," Mr. Razoa shouts into the microphone. "And that woman is dead…"

"She's dead?" I look at Ariel.

"She converted her last human," he says. "After the school, in the battle that raged across the town. We think she was already dying, so she just did the fourth conversion, knowing it would kill her. Four conversions always kills a Calerian."

"Four?" I stare at him, feel my stomach twist. There's one more of us then? "Is it Nika?" I ask, despite what Ariel's already said. Because he could be wrong. But, then again, what are the chances of the four new Calerians being me and Nika and Macey and Kelley-Anne? People I know. And, bar Kelley-Anne, people I'm friends with?

"No, it's not Nika," Ariel says.

"But you just said you're not sure what's going on with her. You want her scanned."

"I'm talking about four new Calerians who we know for certain have been transformed," he says. "But can we just listen to my dad, at the moment? This is important."

"...so we will reinstate the treaty," Mr. Razoa is saying. "And we will overlook the events of today. We will overlook the human deaths and carry on as we were."

Overlook the human deaths?

Horror pulls through me.

"We will accept this truce and—"

The Xphenorie laugh, and the sound is forceful enough to cut off Mr. Razoa.

"A truce where your side has four more people now?" the Xphenorie ask.

"No, we are equal," Mr. Razoa says. "We are. Look how powerful your people are now, having fed unrestricted for the first time in centuries. We are weak in comparison. But we will overlook that if the treaty can be reinstated."

"No," the Xphenorie says. "We've had our time hiding in the dark. You've proven yourselves untrustworthy. We're going to feed as we want, from now on."

"Then we have no choice but to go to war with you," Mr. Razoa says. "Is that what you want?"

"Call it war if you want." The Xphenorie shrug. "The time for treaties is over."

"You'll get used to it soon," a male voice says close by, and I turn, see a Calerian looking at me. I think he's trying to be reassuring. "You probably won't transform fully for another week or so. That's what your tests indicated. But your transformation seems to be slower than Kelley-Anne's and the latest guy's too, just going on your summoning ability."

"The latest guy?" I ask. "Macey?"

The man shakes his head. "No, the other one."

So, the fourth person transformed is a guy. Not Nika.

The Calerian points to the side. "There he is."

I jolt, look to the right, and see the figures. A Calerian girl and a human. Only… No!

Rushing sounds fill my ears.

No.

My stomach sinks. The anchor tattoo on his arm blurs as my vision swims.

"And we meet again, Jade," Elliot says with a dark grin. He moves closer to me.

"Yes," the Calerian girl says, apparently oblivious to the menace radiating from him. "Jade's been transforming for longer, at a slower rate though. But she is still better placed than we are to help you understand the changes you're going through."

Elliot leans over me, bending until his mouth is by my ear. "You better watch your back," he says. "You killed my gang. And I'm going to make sure you pay—not today. But one day soon. We may both be these freaks of nature now, but I don't forget. I never forget anything, Jade. This whole species and war stuff is going to be the least of your troubles. You'll see. Because you thought you could play me. But you can't, and I'm going to get revenge on you when you least expect it."

THE SPIRIT OF FIRE SERIES WILL
CONTINUE WITH
BLOOD OF THE PHOENIX
IN 2022…

ACKNOWLEDGEMENTS

Spirit of Fire was the first-ever manuscript I finished writing. I was seventeen and the book was a total mess then. It was almost 140,000 words long, had subplots that didn't make sense, and was a general disaster.

But it was a story that I'd absolutely fallen in love with, and I knew that one day, I'd go back to it. I'd sort it out, and hopefully it would get published.

I can't believe that the day has finally come. This book has gone through a lot of changes: almost every chapter has been extensively rewritten; the middle part of the story was replaced completely; I added in Elliot's and Ariel's points of view and then ripped apart the whole book again. By the time I was finished, it felt like it was both the same story and a different one. And I'm so proud of it now, because these characters mean a lot to me.

So many people have helped me with this book, and I owe all of them my thanks.

To my beta-readers, Maria Sinclair, James Parson, Imogen Grant, Chloe Osborne, Lucy Conley, Kadda Reely, Helen

Pierce, and Ehlana Pierce: thank you for your feedback on earlier drafts. Your enthusiasm was so motivating.

To my editor, Emily Colin: thank you so much. Your expertise and skill is second-to-none! Thank you for all the work you've done on this manuscript.

To Barbara at Broken Candle Book Designs: this cover is perfect! It captures this book exactly, and I fell in love with it the moment I saw it.

To Sarah Anderson: thank you for the gorgeous interior formatting for the paperback. It really is stunning.

To Michael: thank you for your support. I'm lucky to have you.

To Mum, Dad, and Sam: as always, thank you for everything.

ELIN DYER lives on a farm in Devon, England, where she hangs out with her Shetland ponies and writes YA fantasy novels with ace characters--sometimes, at the same time. She owns a frightening number of books and hopes that the floor in her house won't break due to the weight of her library. Elin holds a BA Honors degree in English from the University of Exeter and is currently pursuing her MA in Creative Writing from Kingston University.

She also writes YA dystopians and thrillers as Madeline Dyer and ace romance as Elin Annalise.